SOWERS OF DISCORD

Book Five

Salvaggio's Light

An Epic Contemporary Romance Serial
By C. L. Cattano

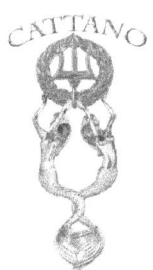

VAGARY PUBLISHING

Sowers of Discord
Book Five
Salvaggio's Light

A Vagary Publishing Book
Copyright © 2017 by C. L. Cattano

Cover Art, Title Page Art and Typesetting Copyright © 2017 by Chynsia Hinesley

Published by:

VAGARY PUBLISHING

www.vagarypublishing.com
inquiry@vagarypublishing.com

Rogena Mitchell-Jones, Independent Literary Editor
RMJ Manuscript Services LLC *www.rogenamitchell.com*

ISBN: 978-1-947852-01-3
First Edition

WARNING

It is suggested readers of this story be adults over the age of eighteen.

This dramatic romance series has many scenes describing sex as well as intense emotional scenes and acts of violence.

This is a serial story with themes that flow from one book into another with lots of twists and turns. Reading this series from the beginning is highly suggested, or the reader may not be able to follow all of the story lines.

Go to the Salvaggio's Light Facebook page to join other readers who are talking about the series.
www.facebook.com/SalvaggiosLight/

Join the C L Cattano mailing list and check out my website at www.clcattano.com.

Acknowledgments

WE MADE IT! We are now to the halfway point in the Salvaggio's Light serial! I could not have done it without the help of friends, family, and a freaking awesome editor!

Dedication

For Marie — Mia dolce.

Salvaggio's Light

An Epic Contemporary Romance Serial

Shattered Paradise
Blue Inferno
Secrets & Rivalry
Wildling's Claim
Sowers of Discord
Fire of Wrath*
Confronting Darkness*

Coming Soon

"Lost are we, and are only so far punished,
That without hope we live on in desire."
— Dante Alighieri, The Divine Comedy

1

The next day...

ROUSING THE GIRLS early Tuesday morning, Rafe Salvaggio got them out the door to start the day. They headed to The Kiki Bistro for breakfast before work. At their table, Rafe was helping Bronte with her meal while Eden was drinking her coffee and looking through the cohabitation agreement. She hadn't read the entire thing last night, and Rafe encouraged her to read it this morning in case she had questions, or there were things they needed to discuss.

Eden looked up at Rafe and grinned as she watched her try to keep Bronte clean while she ate. "Rafe, I think I've thought of something we might need to add," she said as she tapped the papers.

"Okay," she said absently as she wiped her hands on a napkin then looked up. "What is it?"

"You have to do what you did to me last night at least once a week!" She laughed and blushed as images from last night flashed through her mind.

"You liked it that much, did you?" Rafe chuckled and winked.

Abby appeared at the table and sat down next to Eden with her coffee. "What are you two lovebirds so happy about?" she asked bleary-eyed. She looked from one to the other. "Oh, you've had more sex, and on a Monday, no less," she droned and rolled her eyes.

Eden leaned in close to Abby. "More incredible sex," she whispered then laughed softly as she blushed.

Rafe wadded up her last napkin and shook her head. "I need to get more napkins. I'll be right back." She stood from the table and walked over to the counter.

Eden looked to make sure Rafe was far enough away so she couldn't hear. "Abby, you have to tell me some more things about Rafe from before I met her," she insisted as she clutched Abby's arm. "We were together for over four years, and it's like I didn't even know her. I may have to ask Julia, too. I know she doesn't like anyone talking about it but," she paused looking over at Rafe, "I have to know where she learned to do the things she is doing to me now."

"What'd she do?" demanded Abby, alarmed. "Did she hurt you? Are you bruised up again?"

"No, no, nothing like that," Eden whispered quickly. "Last night, she made me," she looked knowingly at Abby, "you know," she opened her eyes wide, "before she even really touched me." She grinned as Abby looked at her with squinted eyes.

"She makes half the women out there come just by walking into the room," said Abby and waved her off.

"No," said Eden putting her hand on Abby's arm again, "that happened, but Abby, I mean," she hesitated, "orgasm," she whispered, "really intense orgasm." She looked over to check where Rafe was standing. "We were, you know, doing things, and she was just breathing on me. The next thing I knew—" She shuddered, feeling the thrill run through her again and looked at Abby's doubtful face. "Yeah, that's all it took, and like I said," she nodded, "she wasn't really touching me. She was holding my hands so I couldn't move them and used her breath to..." she laughed, "to drive me crazy!"

"That's impossible," said Abby shaking her head doubtfully. "It was a fluke. You were just extra turned on or something."

"Or something is right," said Eden as she sat back and smiled. "But the rest of the night, I swear I was on the verge of passing out from the things she was doing. I'm trying to get her to put in this agreement that she'll do it again." She picked up the papers and waved them. "Just to be sure."

"What's this?" Abby took the papers from Eden. "Cohabitation?" Her face twisted into a frown as she looked at Eden. "So you're moving back in with her? Whose idea was it to have this agreement?"

"It's Rafe's idea," she said as she gave Bronte another piece of egg. "I asked her if I could move back in, and she thinks we need it." She looked up and saw Rafe returning, so she signaled Abby to stop the discussion.

Rafe walked back to the table with a load of napkins. "Sorry I took so long," she said with a frown as she put the napkins down. "I have to go. Clarice just called, and they're in crisis," she explained then leaned over and kissed Bronte. "Call me later and let me know what you want to do." She kissed Eden then headed off for work.

"Okay, bye," said Eden breathless from the kiss. She waved, watching as Rafe walked out, amazed and happy the beautiful dark-haired woman was hers again. She looked over at Abby who was still examining the papers. "I'm reading it over to see if I want to change or add anything. She wants us to take this very seriously."

"So, you're going to sign it?" asked Abby as she flipped through the agreement. "You're really going to move back in with her?"

Eden started cleaning up Bronte. "Yeah, I think I am."

"Are you doing it just for the sex? Because if you are, Eden, it's just not right," said Abby worried.

"Abby!" Eden couldn't hide that she felt insulted at Abby's insinuation. "No, I'm not doing it just for sex. I love her, and I want to be with her," she insisted.

"I hope so because," said Abby cynically, "between three to six months from now, things will start to change in the sex department. Then you'll start seeing her for who she really is again. Maybe you should wait a few months," she suggested wanting Eden to be practical and careful.

"I thought you wanted us to get back together," said Eden, perplexed.

"I do," said Abby then took a sip of her coffee, "but I want you to do it with your eyes open. Just look at this agreement," she said tapping the papers. "This is Rafe. She has just about every scenario covered and mapped out. You told me you didn't like her controlling ways, and her coming up with this agreement is pretty damn controlling."

"She said it was to protect both of us," said Eden hesitantly. "She said I could have it looked over by a lawyer if I wanted."

"Maybe you should," Abby recommended. "Do you just want to trust Rafe the agreement will really protect you? Think about it, most agreements are weighted to one side or the other, and if you're not careful, you can get screwed," she said disapprovingly.

"So, you don't think I can trust her?" asked Eden uneasy with the thought because of everything she was dealing with in therapy.

"Not what I said." Abby held her hands up in denial. "You just need to treat this the same way she's treating it. You should take her advice and have a lawyer look at it."

"She said she got it from Katheryn, so you know it's thorough," Eden revealed.

"Eden!" Abby laughed in disbelief. "Katheryn is Rafe's lawyer! She's paid to protect her interests. You need to have someone else look at it. You know how contracts are, and you can't treat this one lightly just because it's with Rafe and you're having great sex with her."

"I know," Eden said thoughtfully. "I'm not taking it lightly. I'll take it to Susan, one of the corporate lawyers at work today," she resolved. "If she thinks it's okay, I'm going to sign it. I want to move back in with her. I want us to become a family again," she said remembering their time together last night when they were under the table playing with Bronte.

"I don't mean to bring you down, but just because you move back in doesn't make you a family," said Abby with brutal honesty. "This agreement pretty much just makes you a roommate."

"I know." Eden sighed as she put the papers in her briefcase, hating how Abby had brought her mood down.

2

MASON ESSEX TURNED off the water in the shower and could hear the music from the sound system again as he held the dark-haired girl close to his body and kissed her. He looked down into her dark eyes, and he could see they were very clear and focused. It had been a struggle, but he had managed to get her to start eating decent food and keep her clean and drug-free since he had picked her up. Drugs were one thing he didn't like mixed with sex. He liked only natural chemicals the body made along with the stimulation of the senses, especially sound.

It was clear the dark exotic looking girl, called Trouble by her pimp, was a second-generation whore. The first time he saw her, a woman who looked just like her was sitting on the lap of the pimp he only knew as Tony. There was also an old lady the girl called Nan rolling tamales in a small kitchen in the back. Tony kept the dark-haired girl high to keep her compliant. When Mason first saw the girl, Tony hadn't drugged her again yet.

Mason could tell right away that Trouble didn't belong there. The reason Tony had to drug her was she was smarter than he was. Whoever got her mother pregnant must have passed on some brains. The only thing holding the girl back was the fact she was on drugs and being pimped. If she got out of prostitution and into even a semi-normal situation, who knew what she could do with her brains. Mason knew she was smart when he saw her folding paper into origami. Tony was calling her a 'retard' for doing it all the time, but he obviously didn't know how difficult it was to do some of the complex shapes the girl was creating, even while high.

Grabbing a towel, Mason draped it over Trouble. He rubbed her head and dark brown body, drying and warming her, and then wrapped it around her. He grabbed a second towel and wrapped it around himself then led her into the small locker room and sat her on the bench. He opened up a locker and handed her a hairbrush then watched as she brushed out her hair.

"Your hair looks really nice now," he said noting the improvement since having a better diet and being able to take care of it daily over the last month since she'd been with him. Her exotic look was even more alluring now that her hair shined and her body had a healthy glow.

Trouble didn't say anything. She rarely did. Mason figured it was probably because speaking usually led to a beating from her pimp. Mason knew she didn't trust him either, and it was okay. She only needed to trust him one time—later. Then she would never have to worry about him, Tony, or anyone else again. It was all part of his new plan, and he hoped she would use those brains and take the opportunity he was giving her.

"I'll bet your real name is Trudy or Tracy," said Mason with a smile, and Trouble frowned. "Don't tell me, it's Trever!" He laughed, and Trouble gave him a slight smile shaking her head.

"Well, that's a relief," he said laughing again along with Trouble's silent laugh. At least he thought it was a laugh.

Mason leaned back against the locker, and Trouble looked up at him warily. She reached out and grabbed his towel as she went down to her knees in front of him.

"Whoa," said Mason and lifted her back up to the bench. "No, Trouble." He sat down next to her. "We're not going to do those things anymore," he said tenderly. She looked at him and began to tremble as panic filled her eyes. "It's okay," Mason assured her and pulled her close. "It's okay." He knew she was terrified of going back to Tony and being beaten and drugged again. He hadn't meant to make her think she was going back there.

Pushing her back gently, Mason looked into her face amazed there were no tears. He hadn't seen her cry once. Most girls he had dealt with cried rivers at the drop of a hat for things a lot less traumatic. He kissed her nose. "I've taken care of Tony," he said firmly. "I'm not sending you back there." He looked at her for a moment to make sure she understood. "I have something for you," he said with a smile, excited about this part of his plan.

He got up and went back to the lockers, opening one as he spoke. "I wasn't sure what you preferred," he said candidly. "I was just going to buy you a dress because it's what women in our church are all supposed to wear. But I did some research, and I read some girls," he hesitated, "in some situations prefer, feel... better... safer out in the world," he turned and looked at Trouble with his face ruddy with embarrassment, "wearing pants instead."

He laid out a dress on the bench and then a pair of cargo pants, a t-shirt, and a hoodie along with undergarments. "You should pick out whatever you want to wear, and you can pack it all to take with you in the backpack." He got into the locker again. "I got some sandals too," he said and put them and the backpack on the bench. "The girl at the store said they go with everything." He put his hands on his hips for a moment and looked around taking a mental inventory. "Okay," he said seeing everything was out, "I'll just take my clothes and get dressed in the office, and you come out when you're ready." He gathered his things and headed out of the bathroom, leaving her to make her decision on what to wear.

It only took Trouble ten minutes to dress and pack the remaining clothes Mason bought. She walked out of the bathroom with her eyes lowered and rushed over to her sleeping pallet. Mason smiled sadly when he saw that she picked out the cargo pants, t-shirt, and hoodie to wear and was glad he bought them for her. It was a hard thing when you finally come to the understanding that a lot of the things you thought you were doing right were really part of the problem.

"Do you like the Taylor Swift shirt?" he asked proudly. Trouble shrugged but didn't look up at him. "Oh," he said with disappointment, "I thought all girls liked her." He leaned forward in his chair. "Well, at least the hoodie covers it, and you can get a different t-shirt later," he assured her, "one you pick out. Maybe Miley?" Trouble shook her head no. "No?" said Mason surprised. "Hmm, well, I'm not sure who the other girl singers are that you might like," he admitted. "Maybe you want the boy singers," he guessed with a smile.

Trouble shrugged but gave him a small smile.

Mason got up and went to the black insulated file cabinet and unlocked it, then opened the third drawer and took out a small protective case. He closed the cabinet then walked over and sat down next to Trouble, who had been watching him from her pallet.

"You remember I told you I was working on a new plan?" he asked and watched her nod. "Well, you're part of it," he revealed and watched her look at him warily. "I know you don't trust me. You don't have any reason to really. I mean, I paid Tony for you, so it makes me a bad guy. I get it. Any guy who does that knows he's a bad guy." Mason looked away from her. "There really is no valid excuse. Believe me, I've tried looking for one to give you." He turned to look at her again. "I'm a bad guy who wants to give something good to you, and I only have this one chance. The thing is you'll have to trust me one time to accept what I have to give you."

Trouble was holding herself close, looking down at the floor, and Mason couldn't tell what she was thinking. He hoped she didn't think he wanted her to do anything illegal or bad. He did say it was something good for her. "I wasn't supposed to be a bad guy," he said with a frown. "Everyone keeps saying I'm supposed to be the Genius Golden Child, the favorite of the reverend. He calls himself Gods Great Leader on Earth."

Mason leaned his head against the wall. "I looked up to all those guys. The Soldiers," he said puffing out his chest and saluted. "The reverend calls, and I run out to meet him so he can blow smoke up my ass, telling me how great I am, thinking it will make me want to do anything to please him. He tells me

I was called to watch and listen so I may speak the truth into the ear of God's Great Leader on Earth. So I find him some information to make him look like a god because I know it's what he really wants. Then, because he say's I'm a favorite, everyone thinks I get special treatment, and the Soldiers resent me and treat me like shit whenever they can get away with it." He frowned and shook his head. "None of it feels like I'm golden or a favorite."

Leaning back against the wall, he stretched out his muscles. "Do you remember when I told you I went and talked with the woman from the files?" he asked suddenly. "Rafe. The woman we would listen to when we had sex." He looked over at Trouble and saw her nod. "Man, I never knew someone could fuck with words." He sighed and tapped her lightly on her leg. "You liked her." He chuckled and watched her smile. "Yeah..." He dragged out the word, and she playfully hit him back. "She got in both our heads!" He hugged her and kissed the top of her head then leaned back again. "I talked to her a few times. She said some stuff that surprised me," he confessed. "She even said some stuff I've said to myself." He leaned his head back, looked at the ceiling, and sighed. "How is it people who are so different with their ideals and how they've been raised can somehow end up thinking the exact same way about certain things?" He looked over at Trouble. "I asked her about it. You know what she said?"

Trouble shook her head no.

"She said evolved thought isn't based on the limits of what we are surrounded by in tradition or even education. Evolved thought is the result of having the audacity not to recognize those things are intended to be limits." He sat silently for a moment. "At first, I thought she was being a smartass." He chuckled, but Trouble remained silent. "But then I got it. It was kind of what I've been doing here, but lately, it's been getting harder. I've been feeling the limits." He looked around at the equipment in his office. "I talked to her about technology and the future," he divulged shaking his head at the sight of the crap equipment the Stewards provided him. "She said, based on what she helps her students with, if a company doesn't update to current technology, the employees should leave, or they risk becoming less valuable in the workforce. This place has never updated the technology, as they should. So I look at my life and wonder if I'm going to be stuck in this office dealing with outdated technology and these pricks my whole life. Am I going to end up becoming just another prick or is it already too late?" He looked over at Trouble who was folding paper while she listened. "The more I think about things," he paused, "the more I think being part of the Stewards has fucked me, and my religion has fucked me up," he said softly feeling anger he wasn't sure how to interpret yet.

Mason spun the small protective case he was holding by its corners, and then looked over at Trouble. "Do you know how to read and write," he asked tentatively. He didn't want to insult her, but he had never seen her do either and had no idea if she had even been to school.

Trouble didn't look at him but nodded her head yes.

"That's good," he said relieved. "It's important because for the plan to work, and for things to be set up so you never have to go back to Tony, you'll have to follow some written instructions." Trouble finally looked at him, and Mason chuckled at the expression of disbelief on her face. "Do you have any kind of ID?"

Grabbing the small bag she had brought with her, Trouble pulled out a California ID card and handed it to Mason.

The first thing Mason saw branded across the card was the word *MINOR* in red. "Oh, man." He sighed and looked at her, "you're seventeen?" She nodded and pointed to the birthdate indicating she'd had her birthday three months ago. He shook his head, unsure what to say because Tony told him she was nineteen and legal. He decided not to say anything because Trouble probably knew Tony had lied to everyone about her age.

Mason looked at the other information on the card and saw her real name was Lorena Marie DePaz. He gave a *harrumph* as he breathed out and looked at Trouble. "Your real name is nothing close to Trouble," he said and smiled at her. "I guess you earned your nickname the hard way."

Trouble pulled her lips slightly to the side and nodded her head as she took her ID back and put it away.

"It's pretty," said Mason and turned away as he felt his face flush red, "your real name." He looked down at the protective case in his hands. "You may have to change it, and you may never see your family again," he hesitated, "so I need to know if this is something you would even want to do." He looked up at Trouble who was looking back at him suspiciously. "I'll never see mine again either," he admitted. "I'm not really sure what would happen to me if I stayed, but I know it would be bad enough I don't want to stick around to find out." He smiled and tried to laugh it off not wanting to acknowledge the fear he felt caused by the rumors he had heard about what happened to those who defied the reverend or the Stewards.

Mason watched as Trouble, who had gone back to folding paper, made another fold, and then he reached out and gently took her hand. He brought it up to his lips and kissed it then put it against his face. Trouble caressed his face and leaned into him as he turned his face to look at her. "So," he whispered, "I need to know, and I need to hear you say it. Will you be part of the new plan and follow the instructions?"

Trouble looked at Mason, her thoughts quickly clicking through her mind. She had listened to him talk a lot about people he knew and all his complaints about his job. When people showed up, she heard some of their conversations and then he would send her out for food or tell her to take a walk. Most of the time, she just listened to make sure she didn't miss the signs he wanted sex again. It was what she was here for, and if he complained to Tony, she would probably not be able to walk for days and forced back down into that dark, drugged, helpless state. She hated the feeling but could feel herself start to crave going back into the emptiness sometimes, and this wasn't a good feeling, either. It was probably one of the reasons she didn't mind staying, so she could stay clean and not have the craving again. She had considered not coming back when he sent her out. From experience, she knew running away would not end well for her. It was hard to get far on foot with no money, especially when Tony had so many contacts. It was the main reason she stayed.

As far as Mason's new plan was concerned, Trouble wasn't sure if she wanted to be part of it or not. He seemed nice enough, only because he was nicer than a lot of others who had paid Tony for her. It was unusual how he kept her for so long, but he was a strange guy. Mason was a walking, talking contradiction in her opinion, but she kept her feelings to herself. He really seemed to expect her to answer his question without knowing a single detail about his plan. There were many questions to be answered and things she needed to know before a decision could be made on a plan. She knew it might mean life or death for her.

One question would be—what exactly did Mason mean when he said he had taken care of Tony? From her perspective, there was only one thing she could do. Play to his ego and agree to follow his plan. It was clear she would be sent somewhere on her own so she would be able to look at his instructions. When that happened, she could make a secondary decision and maybe make her own plan.

The news about not seeing her family again wasn't upsetting. She had reconciled herself long ago to the possibility of leaving them behind. The first time she ran away was the year she turned ten. It was after the first time Tony had sold her. He did it when two men dragged her mother into a back room for sex while she was high on crack.

The man who paid Tony threw her over his shoulder and carried her kicking and screaming to a dirty hotel room two blocks away. When the man pushed her out of the hotel room and told her to go home, it was the last place she wanted to go. She didn't know many places, so she ended up going to the school and hiding under the tower with the slide on one side and a bridge on the other.

If it weren't for a vigilant security guard, she could have stayed in the playground all night. The police were called, and after a trip to the police station, they managed to get her name and contact her family. Her grandmother came to get her because her mother was high and Tony wasn't related to her. When she got home, Tony beat her for running away, for crying, and for talking to the police, even though she hadn't told them about him selling her. It was then she earned the name Trouble and learned how crying would only make things worse.

The next day, when she was sick in bed from the beating she'd had, her grandmother brought her food and tried to comfort her. Nan told her she thought her mother would keep her out of this kind of life and that she was sorry she was wrong. She also told her if she got the chance, she should run and never look back.

It looked to Trouble like this might be her chance. She nodded her head and cleared her throat. "Yes," she said softly.

"Great," said Mason with a smile and kissed her forehead, relieved she finally spoke. He opened the protective case he had been toying with and laid it open on the floor. Inside was a small envelope, and resting inside the foam cutouts were four USB drives, the only difference between them was their color. Mason took out the envelope and pulled out the contents. "This is a prepaid credit card for you," he said as he held it up. "I loaded it with five thousand dollars." He looked at Trouble and saw the surprise on her face. "I know it's a lot. You'll need some things, and you'll need to stay in a good hotel. One where you won't be expected to stay," he explained. "You'll have to book it online, but it's all in the instructions." He unfolded the cash. "Here is two thousand in cash to use for things right away like the bus or cab fare and food," he said and smiled as he looked at her, "and maybe a new t-shirt." He put the card and the cash back in the envelope. "The most important things are these," he said and pointed at the USB drives. "The white one is for you." He looked at her and smiled mischievously. "You know what? I forgot to add our sound files. What do you think? Would you like me to add the files we had sex to? I know they turned you on," he teased. He watched as Trouble lowered her eyes and shook her head no. "No?" he said surprised. "Yeah, you're probably right. It's just another fucked up thing. Plus, now that I talked to her, it's even more fucked up. I'll delete it all," he promised, and Trouble nodded her agreement with the decision.

"Anyway," he continued, "take the white drive to the college library, open the first document on it, and print it out. Follow the instructions. The dates are very important. I have some things I need to do, and there's a court case coming up for the Stewards. I can't leave until after it's over. They always want me around for court appearances." He closed the case and handed it to Trouble with a smile. "Keep it safe," he said softly.

Trouble nodded and looked at the case in her hands then back at Mason. "Where are you going?" she asked hesitantly.

"Me?" said Mason with a wink. "Well, I am doing something very rebellious. I'm following the advice of someone who's supposed to represent everything I should be fighting against," he confessed with a laugh, "someone who I've been recording, and Jake is assigned to pretty much fuck with her life and everyone in it." He laughed again, forcing it from himself because it all seemed so unreal. "I tried to make him back off her, but I don't think it worked. He's too obsessed with her." Mason leaned forward and looked at Trouble. "When I talked to Rafe, I told her I was hired for my job because I was a genius. Do you know what she did?"

Trouble shook her head, warily.

"She laughed," he told her wryly. "She laughed and said every kid in America is a genius. Then she asked me how many languages I spoke. I told her I could write code and tried to tell her about all the code languages, but she stopped me. She said it was great and asked again what spoken languages I knew. I said I knew a little Spanish. She told me most young people my age in other countries knew everything I knew, including computer code, plus at least two other spoken languages, and they probably were better readers and had better math skills."

He looked at Trouble angrily. "That pissed me off! I thought she was fucking un-American!" He took a breath to calm himself. "Then she started asking me if I had read a bunch of different books or heard of different theories, and I had never heard of them. She saw I was upset and told me not to worry about it because it was the state of everyone like me. It just meant since I was now aware of it, I had more limits I needed to ignore."

He smiled at Trouble's confused face again. "I know. I was confused too. So when I asked her, what limits, she explained I was limiting myself to the borders of America. She said I should go see the world and find out if I was just another American genius or if I was a world genius. She led me to her car and wrote down some information for me on a pad of paper. She tore it off, handed to me, and said it was in my hands now to set my own limits."

Mason got up and went to his desk where he opened the drawer and pulled out a file folder. He took it back to his place next to Trouble. "I applied for a paid internship at an international company on a project where we'll travel to different locations in Europe setting up receivers for satellites to help with government educational programs. Rafe actually wrote a recommendation for me after meeting me one time. Who does that?" he asked and handed her the open folder showing her the acceptance letter. "I got the job. Apparently, I was qualified because of my degree and my experience. I didn't know I could get an internship and not be in school. They're paying for my flight over and everything."

Trouble looked at the letter and felt a little jealousy creep up in her. She would love to leave the country and feel what this kind of freedom must feel like. But she had no higher education or job skills except what she had been forced into at the age of ten. She thumbed through the folder and looked at the copy of the recommendation letter and the strong, sweeping signature at the bottom, Dean Rafaella Salvaggio, Conservatory of Art and Design. She burned the name into her mind so she would never forget.

Taking the folder back, Mason closed it and stood up. He looked at his watch and walked over to his desk. "Get all your things together," he said as he put the file away. "You'll need to head out soon. I'll be right back," he said and headed to the bathroom.

Trouble looked down at the small collection of belongings she could call her own and knew it would only take her minutes to pack up. She put some of the cash in her pocket and stashed some in her purse and some in the backpack along with the USB drives and the credit card. She looked over at the bathroom door and then at the file cabinet she had watched Mason unlock. She was sure he hadn't locked it again.

Quickly, she went over to the file cabinet, pulled on the top drawer, and was surprised she was right when it opened. She reached in and took out one of the zippered bags and one of the small white boxes, then closed the drawer so it clicked softly. Her heart racing, she rushed back to her pallet, shoved her pilfered items into the backpack, zipped it closed, then sat down to calm herself. If Tony found her, one of them would be dead, and since she now had a gun, she would have a fighting chance.

3

STRETCHING BACK IN his chair, Mason Essex looked down at the origami gift Trouble had left him and smiled. It was a paper soldier standing over a girl made of paper with long paper hair. He looked up at the clock and estimated she was on the college campus by now blending in and heading to the library. He turned his attention back to the computer screen.

Originally, he had called his plan 'The Jake Off' but now it was just a subset of a bigger plan. He wanted out of the Stewards. He knew the reverend would never just let him leave. He knew too much and was too valuable of a tool—until another genius came along anyway. To leave, he would have to create a situation, one allowing him to slip away.

It was funny how one little conversation could change a person's perspective and even their entire life, but it was exactly what had happened. After talking to Rafe, then actually getting the internship, he was stunned. He couldn't believe it was all real. He had lived so long with people making promises and blowing smoke up his ass, he was sure Rafe was doing the same thing. He only sent the application in because he was pissed the Stewards had denied him funds to buy equipment again.

When he got over the shock of the acceptance letter and realized he had to find a way to leave, he started digging into the Steward database and hacked into the confidential files. It wasn't hard. They had ten-year-old security software and every backdoor and hack for it was available online if you knew where to look.

When he cross-referenced the confidential files with what everyone else was told, there were so many discrepancies, there was no doubt it was purposely done. They hadn't just glossed over a little to hide a small imperfection. They painted over them with Kilz to kill the smell. Mason couldn't help but feel a little sick when he went online and looked at what he could find about the Stewards and the things they had done, posted by the general public. The Stewards had told him not to pay attention to any of it because the public didn't know the truth, but now he realized they knew more of the truth than anyone in the actual church knew.

After a while, Mason stopped looking at random things on the database and began working on his new plan. He was sure he had covered all his bases, other than the ones you can never really cover like accidents, human error, and the unknown. Now everything was going to be in the execution of the details.

Mason hit the delete key and confirmed his action, removing the last of the sound files from the computer. He pulled out the CPU, took off the cover, and removed the hard drive. He pulled out a hard drive wrapped in a foam cover, hooked it up, and then slid it into place and secured it. After putting the CPU cover back on, he started up the computer and gave it a test drive. "Yep," he said to himself, "exactly what I'm supposedly using to get all my genius information from." He shook his head and scoffed. No one realized he had upgraded everything and just used the old CPU cover. He looked at his watch again then put the hard drive he had removed into a foam slot of one of the metal cases he had opened.

Mason was packing up all the personal gear he had installed after becoming frustrated with the outdated systems, and they had refused him money to upgrade. He had bought everything with his own money and spent two months creating hiding places and hooking everything up and installing the programs he needed. He had been happy to use his new equipment to help until people came in treating him like shit, like Jake had. Then he would play the old outdated technology card. He began making a game out of who would benefit from his personal technology. Mostly, he made sure he was the one benefiting.

Jake and Daniel had wanted him to get into the lawyer's office or hack her computers, and he was telling the truth about the Stewards technology. It wasn't good enough. But with his personal equipment, and what he knew he could buy, there would have been a chance. He could have probably given Jake all kinds of information to help his Mission. If Jake hadn't been such a prick, he might have been able to get what he wanted. Instead, Jake was going to help Mason get what he wanted. Jake just didn't know it yet—and probably never would.

Playing the game and making Jake confess on video had been a lot of fun. Originally, he was just going to keep to the confession and hold it over Jake's head for a while. But he had new plans for it now. The look on their faces when they saw him in the Commander's regalia was priceless. Mason had ordered everything at different online stores and had it for a while. He had been excited to get to use it finally. He had watched a lot of reviews and knew all the procedures and ceremonies involved, so it was easy. Keeping a straight face during the whole thing was the hardest part. He had a lot of great video of Jake, and the audio was clean and clear. He could use it all if he had more time, but it wasn't the end goal anymore.

Mason snapped closed the last metal case and began carrying all of them out to the van. He had a buyer for everything he wasn't taking with him. He was meeting soon to make the exchange. Once everything was loaded, he opened his laptop to put the finishing touches together on his plan.

4

IT FELT STRANGE to Trouble to walk across a college campus. It was almost like an alien world with some people rushing by, others walking more leisurely, and still others sitting on the lawn alone or with friends. They all were people with futures, people with a purpose much higher than she thought her purpose would ever be. Trouble watched without looking like she was watching. She kept her eyes lowered and a wide physical distance from everyone she encountered as she made her way to the library.

Trouble had followed Mason's directions and gone to the college library. She just didn't go to the college he most likely intended for her to go. Trouble felt sure he meant for her to go to the California State University campus. It was big and crowded enough to get lost in the busy waves of students. She decided to go to the college where the Rafaella woman worked—the California Conservatory of Art and Design. It was a smaller campus, and she found the library easily. The problem she had was one she probably would have had at any campus library. There was a metal detector and a security guard checking bags. She had to turn around and walk back outside. She couldn't let them find the gun in her backpack.

After walking around campus for a while, Trouble noticed the library, the campus bookstore, and the administration building seemed to be the only ones with the metal detectors and off-duty police officers at the entrances. The other buildings had security guards. She slipped into a building and walked through the halls trying to act as if she belonged. No one seemed bothered by her presence, so she kept walking. She went into a bathroom and thought about hiding the gun and bullets inside but couldn't find a place she felt was safe enough.

Trouble was almost ready to give up for the day and go find a hotel where she could leave things. She had walked into a building close to the administration offices. As she made her way down the hall, a group of students came out of a room and Trouble saw it was full of computers. She waited for them to leave, then slipped inside. There were only a couple of students in the room at their computers. She sat down next to a girl who was playing a computer game.

"Is it okay if anyone uses these computers? I'm new here and just need to print something," Trouble asked softly.

The girl didn't take her eyes off the game. "Sure," she said with a grunt and a shrug as she continued to play her game.

"Thanks," said Trouble as she moved down a chair for privacy.

Digging in her bag, Trouble took out the protective case and opened it, revealing the four USB drives. She pulled out the white drive, took off the cap, and plugged it into the USB port on the side of the keyboard. Using the mouse, she woke up the monitor and saw she would need a username and password to access the computer. She wasn't sure what to do, so she put the cursor in the first box and a list of usernames popped up. She clicked on the last one used and a password automatically filled in the lower box, so she hit enter to see what would happen. After a moment, access was granted. Apparently, someone was too lazy to type in their information each time and saved it on the computer. All the better for her.

The computer found the USB drive and Trouble chose to open the drive. A list of numbered documents with her name appeared. She double clicked on the first document and waited for it to open. It was exactly as Mason described. Instructions. Trouble hit the print button and went to get her pages. As soon as she had them, she packed everything up, logged out of the computer and then walked out quickly.

She didn't want to risk anyone reading over her shoulder or questioning her presence in the room, so she made her way outside. She walked until she found what looked like a private place. There she sat down and took out her instructions and began to read.

Here are your instructions.

Once you print them, you may consider deleting them from the drive as soon as you feel comfortable. As you saw, I named the documents *Trouble,* but neither of our real names will be in them. Now is as good a time as any to start thinking of a new name anyway.

First, use the computer and the credit card to book several hotels. You will want to change as often as you feel the need and having a place pre-booked is helpful. Don't book the cheapest ones. Try not to charge a lot of things to the room because you may need to stay in hotels for a while and you don't want to run out of money. Book three and four-star hotels, and do yourself a favor, book at least one five-star. Those are places certain people are least likely to look for you. Go to the sites listed below to book the rooms.

Second, find a place to keep the drives and some money safe NOT in a hotel. Somewhere you can get to just in case you can't get back to the hotel. Think bowling alley or bus station locker. Somewhere that has 24-hour access if possible. You don't want to wait for a place to open if you need to get away fast.

Third, I need to explain a little about the USB drives. As you know, the white one is for you. Just pay attention to the dates on the documents. The red drive is for a certain lawyer. When you open the document about her, you'll have all her information and what to do. The blue and black drives are the most important drives. They are of most value. They are your power and leverage, so keep them safe.

For now, this is all you have to think about until the next date on the document file. I don't doubt you'll read all the documents as soon as you can, and that's fine. The more prepared you are, the better. I know you're probably worried about a certain person so know he won't come looking for either of us for another month. Hopefully, it will give us both the time to get into better situations.

—Good luck. I hope someday you can consider me a good guy.

Trouble frowned as she finished Mason's instruction letter. There wasn't much to the instructions, so she would definitely be reading the rest of the documents as soon as she could. She looked up at the building where she had used the computer and knew she didn't want to go back there right now.

She got up and began walking through the campus again toward the bus stop. As she was trying to figure out what she wanted to do next, a student approached and pushed a newsprint paper into her hand. It was the school paper. Trouble was about to toss it when she saw a familiar name under a photo. The photo credit was *R. Salvaggio.*

After finding an open spot on the lawn, Trouble sat down and looked through the paper. The photo with the familiar name credit was a student who was having a Senior Show in the gallery inside the administration building. Turning the page, Trouble saw a small section where students listed items for sale. The listing catching her attention was one for a laptop and portable printer. It was for sale cheap, the ad declared. Perfect. Trouble looked around and saw a guy sitting on the lawn not far away.

"Hey," she called out and gave him a smile. "Do you have a phone I could borrow? Mine's dead, and I want to call about an ad."

The young man looked up at her and hesitated for a moment then nodded his head. "Sure," he said as he walked over and sat next to her. He handed his phone to her. "Here ya go."

"Thanks." Trouble smiled as she took the phone. "Do you want anything in return? I don't want you to think I'm just a moocher."

"How about a blowjob," he said. Then he laughed because he couldn't believe he actually said that to her.

Trouble looked at him for a moment and shrugged. "Okay, do you—" she started.

"No!" said the young man turning red. "I was kidding. You can just use the phone. I'm not a perv."

"Oh, okay," said Trouble with an arched brow. "Did you want something else?"

The young man was not sure what to make of this dark-haired girl. He wondered if she was messing with him for being such a jerk and knew, if she was, he deserved it. "No, just make your call. I probably owe you now for being such a jerk."

Trouble smiled at him then looked at the paper and dialed the number. She made arrangements to meet and then disconnected the call as she looked over at the young man again.

"Thanks again," she said and handed him the phone back.

"You're welcome," he said sheepishly. He watched as she got up to go and smiled down at her. He thought she had an incredible smile. "My name's Carson Greene. What's your name?"

"If I told you, Carson, it might get you into more trouble than you already made for yourself." She smiled and started to walk away but turned back. "Stay away from Trouble," she said and gave him a wave then turned away. She made her way across campus to buy a used computer and portable printer so she wouldn't have to worry about security and could book her hotels.

5

ACROSS TOWN, SITTING behind his desk, Jake Thompson was leaning back in his office chair inside his small graphic design company office. Sitting across from him, Melissa Aykland watched him as he read the copy of the article she had written. As she pushed her long blond hair over her shoulders, she wished he would hurry up so she could go and never have to deal with him again. The only good thing out of this, in her mind, was she got a paying gig from the L.A. Times.

She was glad, after this, her debt to Jake was repaid, and she would never have to see the sleazeball again. All she wanted was to get rid of a stalker boyfriend a year ago, and after Jake helped her, he acted as if she owed him everything including her life. This favor had pushed her to her limit because it affected her livelihood, her job. She told him this was the last favor and he agreed. She just hoped he kept his promises.

Jake finished reading then looked up at her and smiled. "If this doesn't work, nothing will. I like the fact you put all the stuff Eden told me about her in there." He laughed and sat forward in his chair. "If we're lucky, this may start a riot at the California Conservatory of Art and Design."

"So, why do you want to crucify this Rafe Salvaggio?" asked Melissa curiously. "What did she do to you, besides being your ex-girlfriends ex? She really has done something great for that school."

"She's trying to keep me from Eden, the woman I love," he insisted sounding hurt and bitter.

"You're doing this to get her back?" asked Melissa in bewilderment.

"Rafe has got Eden convinced to go back to her," Jake told her sadly. "She's practically holding her hostage!"

"I thought you two broke up ages ago," said Melissa warily. "Your relationship was so short that I didn't even get to meet the woman."

"You don't understand, Melissa. We were together for almost a year, and we were deeply in love." He looked at her sadly. "We were going to be married."

"Wow, I had no idea," she said in surprise. "But, Jake, are you seriously in love with a gay woman?" Melissa asked in disbelief. "I saw them together, and I don't think the woman is with Dean Salvaggio against her will," she said trying to find sympathy for him but failing.

"Eden is in a fragile state," Jake explained with feigned concern. "She's been seeing a therapist, is on medication and is easily influenced. I was just giving her space, and then Rafe just swooped in and started exploiting her delicate state of mind."

"So, what will this article accomplish besides possibly getting her fired?" asked Melissa doubtfully.

"It'll remind Eden about why she left Rafe in the first place," Jake insisted, "and let everyone else see Rafe for what she really is. She's a predator just as you describe. A predator preying on the woman I love."

"Okay, Jake," she said then got up and headed to the door. "You have what you want. My debt is paid, so don't call me to do anything for you again."

"Wait a minute," called Jake not finished with her yet. "When will it be printed?"

"It'll be out in the Sunday edition of L.A. Light," she said with aversion at the thought of the horrid paper, "and under a pen name. The Times wouldn't touch it, but others looking for the drama of the day will probably pick it up. The editor at the Light is so excited—he's going to broadcast it."

"Perfect!" Jake said with a smug smile.

6

RAFE SALVAGGIO HAD just finished putting together the work order for the new media lab, and with the help of her assistant Brandy, she had made changes to the design plans for the space. She was glad the week was half over. As she began checking her emails, she heard the door open and looked up to see who it was.

"Good morning, Dean Salvaggio," said Clarice happily. "Did you get our little problem taken care of yesterday?"

"Yes, I did, Clarice." Rafe smiled at her use of the words *our little problem*. "The fire is out, everyone's schedule is rearranged, and they now have flights and land transportation reserved."

"Good," she said and closed the office door for privacy. "How did the interview go Friday?"

"It went fine," Rafe assured her. "She said it should be out just before the celebration at The Kiki."

"I think I'll see if they'll send us advance copies so we can put it in our guest packets," Clarice said excitedly. She gave Rafe a sideways look. "I heard all about your exploits at The Kiki Bistro from a few students. Apparently, you're some kind of legend," she said and watched Rafe shake her head and bite her lip. "So, is it true," she asked intrigued, "are you back with your ex? What about Greer? You two seemed so happy together."

"Clarice." Rafe sighed perturbed that she had to discuss her personal life at work. "Greer and I were happy together, but she is in Baltimore now."

"So, Greer isn't coming to the celebration?" she asked with disappointment.

"Not that I'm aware of," Rafe said concerned. "Why?"

"Well, I didn't know about your ex until recently, and I sent Greer an invitation when I didn't see her name on the list," she confessed.

"Has she sent her RSVP?" Rafe asked thrown by this new information.

"I haven't seen it yet," admitted Clarice, "but she still has time to send it in."

Rafe sighed and sat back in her chair. "Well, if she has time, it would be nice if she could come, but I wish you had told me about this, Clarice. How many more people did you add to the list? I may have to give new numbers to the planning committee to make sure they have enough seats, not to mention food and drinks."

"Just Greer," Clarice assured her. "I thought," she paused and tutted, "well, Rafe, I confess I thought you needed her back since the hostage situation."

Rafe looked at her unsure why she would say such a thing. "Why?"

"Well, the students have been talking about how you're holding class outside the classroom and in some unusual spaces," she revealed. "Most of them think it's great, but there have been a few who feel like they should be inside the classroom."

"I've been meeting them in museums, sculpture gardens, and at buildings that are examples of historical architecture," said Rafe thinking it was probably the students who were failing the class or wanted to sleep at their desks who were complaining. "I think seeing the actual art instead of looking at slides and books is a better way to learn a few things."

Clarice thought about Rafe's excuse and couldn't find fault with it. "Well, anyway, I'm sorry about sending the invitation to Greer," she said earnestly. "I didn't know you were involved with someone else."

"Thank you, Clarice," Rafe said sincerely. "We've only been seeing each other again for a couple of months. She may be moving back in with me." She smiled trying to look confident and happy at the possibility. "I should know this week I think."

"Oh, my god! What have I done?" asked Clarice embarrassed. "What am I going to tell Greer?"

"Don't worry about it," Rafe reassured her. "I'll take care of it."

"I really am sorry," Clarice apologized. "I'll leave you to it," she said and walked out of the office.

Rafe watched Clarice leave then shook her head and smiled. She did not realize Clarice had even been aware of her personal relationship with Greer. She looked at her computer and composed an email.

TO: Dr.G_Noble@JohnsHopkins.org
FROM: RSalvaggio@ccad.edu
SUBJECT: Jackson-Goyer Grant Celebration Invitation

Greer,

I just found out Clarice sent you an invitation to our Jackson-Goyer Grant Celebration. I'm sorry I wasn't the one who sent it. I wasn't sure, given our situation, you would want to attend.

Eden has asked to move back in with me. I said yes last night, but with certain conditions. I know, don't lecture, teacher.

It's so hard when I keep finding out the things Jake tells me are true. She wanted to talk about why I had the affair the other day. She kept asking me *why.* Greer, I tried to explain why immediately after she confronted me. I told her why the best I could. I don't understand why she wanted to go through it again. So, instead of repeating what she chose not to hear back then, I just tried to reassure her it wouldn't happen again.

Do you think she wanted me to blame her so she would have another excuse to leave me and hurt me? Is she still punishing me? I know you can't answer these questions, and I don't blame her. It was my mistake. I hope she'll tell me everything she's keeping from me soon and won't go back to Jake. I'm doing my best to make myself irresistible.

Please let me know if you plan to attend, and I will be happy to make all of your arrangements.

Your canvas,

Rafe

Rafe had just finished her work for the day and was getting ready to leave the office when an email notification rang from her computer. She opened her email and saw it was a reply from Greer. She smiled and opened the email and began to read.

REPLY
TO: RSalvaggio@ccad.edu
FROM: Dr.G_Noble@JohnsHopkins.org
SUBJECT: RE: Jackson-Goyer Grant Celebration
 Invitation

Rafe,

You are irresistible! I can't imagine you being able to make yourself anymore irresistible.

I'm happy to hear things are moving forward with Eden. About Eden's question—she was hurting when you told her those things, so it's possible she really didn't hear you the way you hoped she would. To her, they may have just been words to be disregarded at the time. I hope, if she is sincere, your words this time help her.

It sounds like you've chosen to believe she is sincere, even though she hasn't made an effort to give you the answers you need. It's very generous of you. I don't want to lecture, but I don't want you to get hurt again. Please, be careful with your heart.

I am sorry to say I won't be able to attend your celebration, but I send my warmest congratulations.

Your artist,

Greer

As Rafe finished reading Greer's reply, Brandy's voice came over the intercom letting her know Eden was on line one. Rafe picked up the handset and punched the line button. "Eden. Hi, how are you?"

"I'm fine," said Eden through the phone. "Are you almost finished for the day?"

"As a matter of fact, I am," said Rafe. "I'm just turning off my computer."

"Good. I'd like to take you to dinner tonight," Eden said with an excited voice.

"You would?" Rafe smiled at the eagerness in Eden's voice. "Are you asking me out on a date?"

"Yes," Eden affirmed with a chuckle, "it's exactly what I'm doing."

"Well, I have to see if I can find a babysitter," said Rafe because she was supposed to have Bronte.

"Taken care of," proclaimed Eden. "Say yes. I have something for you," she said seductively.

"I love presents. Okay, yes."

"I'll pick you up at seven. Bye!"

"Goodbye," Rafe replied with a laugh. She was almost willing to believe she had her life back. Almost. She hung up then powered down her computer and left happily for home.

7

IN ANTICIPATION OF their date, Rafe Salvaggio had gone to great pains to dress perfectly for Eden. She had chosen everything carefully from the perfect scent on her skin to the perfect dress and accessories. Looking in the mirror, she put the finishing touches on her dark hair and was ready for the night. She was sure the surprise was going to be the cohabitation agreement, and it had more meaning for her than Eden could possibly imagine.

If Eden signed the agreement, it meant Rafe could keep her close, and it meant she could keep her away from Jake. It might even mean Eden was serious and she intended to stay. And maybe Eden really did love her. She looked in the mirror to check herself and saw she still had a goofy smile on her face. She would have to fix her expression before Eden got there.

Rafe went into the kitchen and fixed a drink to calm her nerves and to subdue her mood. She carried it into the living room and sat down, took a deep breath, and let it out before taking a sip of her drink. She let the alcohol flow through her body and do its job as she waited for Eden to arrive.

It was exactly seven and Eden had just stepped onto Rafe's porch. She touched her silky blond hair to make sure it was still in place. Then she looked down at her dress assessing herself. She wanted to look her best for Rafe on their date. When she was satisfied, she took a deep breath and knocked on the door. A few seconds later, the door swung open. Eden saw Rafe framed by the doorway, and the sight of her took her breath away. "Ra, Rafe," she swallowed, blown away by her tawny skinned beauty once again.

"Eden," Rafe whispered with a smile for the beautiful blonde who stood before her. They just stood looking at each other until Rafe recovered and kissed Eden on the cheek. She then held out her hand. "Are you ready?"

"Yeah," Eden said and blinked from her trance. She took Rafe's hand, and they walk to Eden's car. "It's not very often I get to drive the beautiful Rafe Salvaggio," teased Eden.

Rafe smiled at her. "You ask, you drive. I have to admit being picked up at my door by the most stunning woman I've ever seen is awe-inspiring." She leaned over and placed a careful kiss on Eden's mouth then smiled again. "We don't want to smudge anything," she winked, "yet."

Rafe and Eden had finished eating and were lingering over their drinks as they held hands across the table. They were regarding each other intensely, and the maître d' had wisely instructed the waiter to watch the table and not interrupt unless he saw them looking for someone.

Eden rubbed her thumb over Rafe's hand. "You've been very patient tonight," she said quietly. "Would you like to have what I brought for you?'

"Yes, please." Rafe smiled in anticipation.

Opening her purse, Eden pulled out a manila envelope and pushed it across the table. "I've signed and had my signature notarized. Now, it just needs your signature." She smiled and tried to wink but blinked both eyes.

"It will be signed first thing in the morning when I drop it off at Katheryn's office." Rafe tried to control her elation and suppress the bubble of wariness threatening to surface and take away the happiness she was feeling. "When," she paused and smiled as she looked at Eden, "when would you like to move in?"

Eden looked at Rafe her eyes burning with desire. "Tonight," she said softly. "I want to come home tonight."

8

WORKING FROM HOME Friday afternoon, Flynn Ogden was attempting to solve a problem with a new computer program. He had accepted a special project he could work on at home instead of taking time off work. This way he could spend more time watching over Eden and Rafe. His roommates had the rest of the day off from their jobs. They had decided to take advantage of Rafe's open invitation to the pool and were swimming next door.

Flynn heard an annoying whirring sound coming from outside, so he went out to look for its source. As he walked out the back door, the sound got louder and more frequent. He saw a figure by the fence between their house and Rafe's house. He thought it might be one of the girls at first, but quickly realized the figure was much too big.

"What are you doing?" he called out. The figure looked up, and Flynn saw that it was Jake. "Shit!"

"You should turn around and go back inside," said Jake when he realized someone had seen him. He recognized Flynn from the park and looked at him with disgust and contempt.

Flynn looked around quickly to see if anyone was with Jake. "What are you doing here? What do you want?" he demanded.

"I'm looking for Eden," he lied trying to sound innocent as he hid his camera.

"You should stay away from her!" yelled Flynn and stepping toward him aggressively.

"You don't understand. I love her," said Jake while trying to figure out what to do. "I know you think I'm a terrible person for what happened in the park." He paused to think. He had to make his story consistent since the freak was hanging out with Eden. "Those people had me totally convinced they were right, but like I told Eden, I realized my mistake. Will you tell Eden I've been looking for her and I really miss her?" he implored. "Tell her going back to Rafe is the worst thing she could do for her child. Rafe's really not someone who can be a good parent."

"You don't know anything," Flynn said angrily. "Rafe is a great parent. Eden won't go back to you, ever!"

"She will," Jake said sadly. "I know she will."

Flynn stared hard at Jake, mad at himself because his gun was in his truck. "I'm calling the police!"

"I'm going," said Jake as he started to walk away, "but please tell Eden I miss her."

"Fuck you!" Flynn called after him angrily. He ran into the house and grabbed his keys then ran to his truck. He needed to check on Eden. After trying to call her at work and being told she had taken the day off, he drove straight over to Eden's apartment.

Eden had taken off work for the day to pack her things for her move back to Rafe's house. There were boxes filled with household items and packing materials everywhere. Bronte was with their nanny Lydia for the day so Eden could work faster. A knock on the door interrupted her work and Eden went to answer it.

"Flynn," she said in surprise and could see he was in distress. "What's wrong?"

"Can I come in?" he asked restlessly as he rocked from foot to foot. "I need to talk to you."

"Sure, come in," she said as she led him inside. "Sorry about the mess. I'm moving back in with Rafe. Just into the guestroom again, but it's a start. Let's sit in the kitchen." They sat at the kitchen table. "What do you need to talk to me about?"

"I think it's a good thing you're moving back in with her," said Flynn as he looked at the boxes. "You'll be safer."

"I will feel safer," agreed Eden. "She always did make me feel safe. I guess it was one of the things we lost for a while."

"Eden," Flynn said nervously, "I mean safe from Jake."

Eden looked at Jake surprised. "Jake?"

"Yeah, I caught him between our houses today," he revealed. "He says he's still in love with you, and he wants you back, his usual lie. I think I saw a camera," he paused, "I think he was taking pictures of the girls around the pool. They didn't see him."

"Pictures of the girls?" Eden said not understanding why he would take photos of the girls.

"He says you shouldn't go back to Rafe because she isn't a good parent," Flynn added. "He may be trying to get more stuff to use against her."

"Crap!" Eden yelled and put her head in her hands. "How could I have ever been involved with someone like him? I wish there was more we could do about him besides tell Katheryn."

"The way he acted, like he had a right to be there, makes me think it wasn't the first time," Flynn said, worried he was right. "There's no telling what he's taken pictures of, and no telling what he might do now. I came over to make sure he wasn't taking pictures or anything of you and Bronte. I was really worried," he hesitated, "and scared when they told me you weren't at work. I was glad to see you were here and okay."

"I've been here most of the day," she assured him then sighed. "What can he do with the pictures of the girls? They haven't done anything wrong."

"Eden, he's a graphic designer!" Flynn said upset. "He can just Photoshop in anything he wants."

"Yeah, but we have proof of what he does so no one will take him seriously," Eden said reminding him of the package they gave Katheryn. "Besides, Katheryn says we can't do anything about him unless we can prove he's done something wrong. So far, we can't prove anything."

"I think you need to tell Katheryn to start using more of the information," suggested Flynn somberly. "I think the closer to the court date we get, the more times he's going to show up." He watched Eden as she got up to get a glass of water. "Eden, we should tell Rafe. If not, we should at least ask her about putting in a security system.

"She has a security system," she assured him. "She had to put in an expensive one for the insurance on all her art."

Well, she doesn't have a video surveillance system," he countered, "at least, not on the outside of the house. I can set one up at Jude's house too. Do you think Rafe will agree to do it?"

"I'm sure she will," said Eden. Flynn's concern and fear was feeding her anxiety. She worked to control it as she sat down and took a large gulp of her water. "She wants us to be safe. I'll just tell her it's something we really need now. I don't want to bring Jake up to her yet," she said nervously. She sat the glass down to hide her shaking hand. "We're doing so well, I don't want anything to mess things up now since she's letting me move in. We just need to be extra careful, and we both need to spend more time with Rafe."

"Okay," he agreed hesitantly. "Just let me know if you need me to help you talk to her about the security system."

"Thanks." Eden sighed already feeling exhausted from just thinking about Jake and the whole situation.

"So do you need any help here?" asked Flynn as he looked at all the boxes. "The faster you get moved out, the better."

"Sure, I'd love some help," said Eden thankfully. They went into the living room and started packing. "I'm really happy about moving back in with Rafe," she said as she worked and pushed away her troubling thoughts.

"But," said Flynn as he taped a box closed, "you said you were just moving into the guest bedroom again."

"Yeah, Rafe doesn't think I should move back into her room yet." Eden shrugged trying not to show the sting she still felt about it.

"Why not?" Flynn asked confused. "I mean you're sleeping together, aren't you?"

"We are," affirmed Eden with a slight blush, "but I think she's still hurting. I'm not sure. But I don't want to push her, and I can't blame her," she said quickly. "With the injunction and all the things I need to talk to her about, she still needs a place where she can be alone sometimes to cope. I can't believe she agreed. That must mean something, right?"

"The court date is coming up, isn't it?" asked Flynn not sure how to answer her question.

"A week from Tuesday," confirmed Eden, "and another two weeks after is the adoption court date, and Rafe will finally legally be Bronte's other parent. Maybe then Rafe and I can really start over, and she'll believe me."

"I'll just be glad when everything is settled, and we can tell Rafe everything about Jake," said Flynn as he taped up another box.

"Me too," agreed Eden. "I think everything is going to work out for us. I know there's still a lot we have to go through, and I really want things to work. I don't ever want to be without her again."

"Does she know how you feel?" asked Flynn worried.

"She knows. I'm sure she does," said Eden. "Hey, it looks like this is the last of it in here. The movers will be here early Saturday. Can you put a couple of things in your truck for me? That way I can have some of this stuff home right away."

"Sure," Flynn agreed, happy she would be right next door with Rafe. "Hey Eden, I just wanted to tell you," he hesitated, "I really like you. You've always been really nice to me. I'm glad I could help you out, you know, with this and the Jake thing. You make me feel like I belong somewhere and have a real friend. It may seem strange, but you kind of remind me of my mother. I just wish sometimes I felt as close to her as I do with you."

"Oh, thank you." Eden was touched by his words. "You're a good person, Flynn, and I really like you too. You are my friend." She hugged him. "I feel lucky to have you in my life. I really don't know what I would have done without you. I truly appreciate everything you're doing for Bronte and me," she said as she looked at him and smiled, "and Rafe."

Flynn loaded Eden's boxes in the back of his truck while Eden locked up the apartment. When everything was checked and double-checked, they got into their vehicles and began their short trip to Rafe and Eden's home.

9

THE SUN REFLECTED off the dark windows of the black SUV. Inside, Jake Thompson watched the activity in front of Eden's apartment. It was very clear to him what was happening. Eden was moving out, and he was positive he knew where she was going. He picked up his phone and dialed.

"Daniel, guess what. She's moving in with Rafe. Yes, I'm sure. I just watched her pack up some of her things. No, I'm not worried. Why?" Jake laughed. "Because the article comes out Sunday, and if the lawyers are smart, they'll have another amendment to file Monday morning. Don't worry—the pictures are a bonus. Rafe will react just like she did the last time, I promise. I'm a fucking genius!" Jake laughed confident his Mission would be a success.

Starting the vehicle and putting it into gear, Jake pulled out of the apartment complex. He had watched as Eden and her little 'boyfriend' finally left, and now he had to attend to some business. The copy of the article and some other things he and Daniel had worked on were in the seat beside him. He sent copies of everything to Mason already, and later, he had to meet with the reverend.

The article would prove he didn't have feelings for Rafe. It would take everything from her just as Mason demanded in his requirements. It may also nullify the confession Mason forced him to make. To be on the safe side, he wanted to get the tape from Mason's office. No, not a tape, a something file— whatever. He knew Mason was out on an assignment today, so he was going to make a quick stop at his office. If he found the girl there, he would figure out something to do with her too. Jake laughed to himself at some of the ideas for her as they popped into his head. He would make sure Mason wouldn't want her, or any other women like her, on the Steward property again.

Outside the shabby industrial building, Jake used his lock pick set and got the man-door open. Mason may do surveillance, but he was not so smart when it came to security. Jake chuckled to himself as he pushed the door open. He walked through the garage space noting the van was gone confirming Mason was too. At the office door, Jake used his lock picks again and easily opened the door.

10

PARKED OUTSIDE HIS assigned target, Mason Essex looked down at his phone as it buzzed. He clicked on the app for the alarm and frowned as the live video feed from his office streamed. He could clearly see Jake entering the building and going into his office. Mason tapped the option to switch cameras and saw Jake going through his office. He knew someone had been there before because a gun and ammunition were missing. He was sure it had been Jake, and now he had the proof. He wondered what Jake was looking for today. He suspected he was looking to find the video file, but he would never find it. It was stored in his private cloud account. All idiots who thought things had to be saved on USBs or CDs were so behind the times. There was no physical trace unless he had access to the account, and Jake would never have access. Besides, there was nothing left in the office belonging to Mason for Jake to take.

He watched as Jake went through his desk drawers and the unlocked file cabinets finding nothing. Then Jake went into the bathroom, and Mason tapped the screen to which cameras and saw Jake looking through all the lockers. Jake went back to the office, picked the locks on the other file cabinets. He looked through some files, and pulled out the equipment stored inside. There were guns, bullets, night vision goggles, and other surplus military items collected over the years. Mason smiled when Jake pocketed some small items before moving so his back was to the camera.

"Jakie's in trouble," Mason said in a singsong voice then chuckled. He watched as Jake closed everything up and walked out to the garage. Jake looked around at the items on the shelves and opened a few boxes. He grabbed a few things then made his way out. "I'll check to see what you took against my inventory," Mason said softly, "then we'll see what more to add to the 'Jake Off' plan."

11

EARLY SATURDAY MORNING, Eden Kingsley took Bronte and left Rafe's house to go to the apartment. She was meeting Flynn and the movers to load the last of her things to bring over to the house or send to storage. The movers were very efficient and got everything out and into the moving trucks quickly. Eden and Flynn gave the apartment a thorough cleaning and loaded some stray belongings into Flynn's truck. Before leaving, Eden took a last look around the apartment then took the keys to the management office.

Finally, they were on their way, and it took much less time than Eden had thought it would. Flynn pulled into his driveway, but Eden had to park on the street because it looked like they had company. She got Bronte out of the car then went to help get some boxes from Flynn's truck. With boxes in arms, they made their way to the house.

Eden was holding Bronte along with a small box and Flynn was carrying some larger boxes as they walked inside the house and into what seemed to be absolute chaos. In the middle of it all, shouting directions and dealing with several people at a time, was Rafe.

Eden looked around in astonishment. "What the heck?" she exclaimed. "Rafe? Rafe, what's going on?"

Rafe turned at the sound of her name. "Eden!" she called out in surprise. "What are you doing here?"

"Uh, I live here now," she said dropping her small box and trying to take in the scene.

"Oh, I know," said Rafe as she smiled. "I meant you're early." She looked at one of the workers. "Dean, you're in charge. Three hours."

"Got it," Dean answered with a quick nod then started shouting orders over the sounds of construction.

Rafe looked over at Flynn and the box he was holding. "Flynn, just hold off on the boxes until Dean is finished," she directed as she made her way to Eden.

"Sure, no problem," said Flynn. He maneuvered the boxes he was carrying, along with the one Eden dropped, to the porch.

Rafe took Bronte from Eden. "Come with me," she said and led Eden to the patio. "I wasn't expecting you back so soon. I was going to surprise you."

"What's going on in there?" Eden asked while looking over her shoulder.

"I'm just doing a little remodeling and rearranging," said Rafe excitedly.

"A little?" scoffed Eden. "Rafe, you've got an army in there. What are you doing?"

"I'm making things more," she paused pursing her lips, "comfortable. I'm freshening things up a bit."

"Are you going to tell me what you're doing in there?" asked Eden as she pointed inside the house.

"Well," said Rafe, "I'm having your room painted and your bathroom updated, because you know I haven't done anything more to the bathroom in there since I bought the house, and I know you've always wanted a steam shower. I'm turning the gallery room into a bedroom for Bronte," she kissed Bronte, "and having it decorated so you two don't have to share a room. Oh, and the paint in both rooms is safe for Bronte so she can sleep with you or in her own room tonight." She smiled proudly at Eden. "The day after you asked to move in, and I talked about the agreement with Katheryn, I had a decorator arrange everything. When you signed it, I scheduled to have it all done today. I thought it would be finished before you got here. I wasn't expecting you to pack so quickly. So," she said out of breath, and then she grinned, "what do you think?"

"I," stammered Eden, almost speechless, "I think," she shook her head and smiled, "I think it's wonderful."

"Really?" asked Rafe concerned. "I was afraid you might be a little upset because I didn't talk to you about it, but I wanted to give you a great moving-in present," she explained. "They haven't started painting yet. You can still pick another color if you want. I chose a variation of the color already there so we could keep the same accessories and things."

"No, no it's fine," Eden assured her with a laugh and kissed her. "I just didn't expect all of this. I'm surprised, really surprised. Thank you."

Jude walked out looking for Rafe. "Rafe, the designer's here, and he needs to see you."

"Oh, okay." Rafe handed Bronte back to Eden. "Don't go anywhere. I have something else I need to talk to you about," she said and walked into the house.

"I think she's been playing General Patton since you rolled out of the driveway this morning," said Jude amused. "I hope for her sake you're okay with everything. She's been worrying and asking if I thought you'd like it or if you'd think she was being controlling or whatever." She grinned and laughed. "She's really happy you're back."

"I'm happy to be back too," Eden said, unable to help returning a smile, "and I'm definitely okay with everything. I know how she gets when she's excited and trying to show how much she cares. Her surprises are legendary." She looked at Bronte with an arched brow. "This little thing was the result of her last surprise," she admitted with a soft laugh. She looked at Jude and couldn't stop smiling, though tears of happiness threatened. "I feel so lucky she's taking me back. I know I haven't made things easy for her."

"She loves you," said Jude nodding her head. "I think she really needs you, though she won't admit it."

"She needs me?" Eden laughed again. "I think you have it backward. I think I need her."

"You need each other," Jude compromised. "That's why you guys give me so much hope. The universe made you two for each other."

Rafe walked out of the house carrying a couple of drinks. "I'm back," she said and looked at Jude. "Jude, what we talked about. Will you tell Flynn to come back over? I need his help with something."

"Oh," said Jude with a jolt as she remembered their earlier conversation, "yeah, okay. Come here, Bronte," she said as she took Bronte from Eden. "We'll be next door. Bye. Say bye-bye, Bronte." Bronte gurgled and waved as Jude carried her away.

Confused, Eden took the drink Rafe was handing her. "Bye," she said quizzically. "What?" She looked at Rafe. "Why is she taking Bronte?" She watched Jude go out the side gate with her baby.

"She agreed to babysit for a while later anyway," explained Rafe, "and there's not really anywhere to put her right now while we talk." She led Eden to the double lounger then sat next to her and kissed her sweetly and deeply. "Welcome home," she whispered as she dangled a key between them. "I got the spare key back from Jude." She kissed Eden again and placed the key in her hand. Smiling, she sat back then took a sip of her drink before placing it on the table.

Recovering from her welcome home kisses, Eden looked at the key and then at Rafe. "You are the most amazing woman I know."

"Well, in that case," Rafe grinned, "I guess it means you'll agree to be my date Friday night."

"Your date?" Eden asked, curious. Then she put the key in her pocket.

"It's the Jackson-Goyer Grant Celebration being held at The Kiki Bistro," Rafe explained. "Would you like to go as my date?"

"I don't know," answered Eden mischievously. "I need to see if I can find a babysitter."

"Taken care of," declared Rafe.

"I'll need a new dress," said Eden doubtfully.

"You have time to shop," said Rafe pointedly and kissed her. "Say yes."

"Yes," said Eden with a smile just for Rafe.

"Great!" Rafe leaned over and kissed her again. "You just sit back and relax. I have to go in and make sure things are going to be done on time."

Eden watched Rafe walk away. "On time for what?" she called. "Rafe?"

Not hearing her over the sudden sound of a circular saw, Rafe walked inside without looking back. Eden shook her head, took a sip of her drink, and then lay back in the lounger. She had no doubt her questions would be answered soon.

12

THE ARMY OF construction workers and decorators had gone, and because of Rafe Salvaggio's competent command of the situation, the only evidence they were there were the changes made to the house. Eden was amazed at what Rafe was able to accomplish in such a short time. After putting more of her things away, Eden left her room and went into what used to be Rafe's art gallery. It was now an adorable little girl's room. She saw Rafe standing by the new dresser and went in to see what she was doing.

"Hey," she said softly.

Rafe turned and gave a small smile to Eden. "Hi. What do you think?" she asked. She had been unpacking Bronte's things and getting them set up in the room.

Eden saw Rafe had a small pair of shoes in her hands. They were the shoes Rafe had bought for Bronte when she was just a few months old. They were a pair of soft lace and pearl covered shoes with Bronte's name embroidered on the sole of one and her birth date on the other. The shoes came after Eden had moved out with Jake. Rafe had sent them to Eden when they arrived. "The room is beautiful. I think Bronte will really love it," she said softly.

"I hope she does," said Rafe as she put the small shoes on the dresser.

"You found her first shoes." Eden nodded toward the dresser. "I wasn't sure what box they ended up in."

"Yeah." Rafe picked up an empty box to throw away. "I was surprised to see them," she paused, "that you kept them. I always wondered if she ever got to wear them."

Eden could see Rafe was thinking about when she left and took Bronte and the sad memories the shoes brought to the surface. Her heart was heavy with regret, and she wanted to make Rafe feel better. "She did." Eden nodded. "She got to wear them. I really loved it when you sent them for her. I'm sorry you never got to see her wear them."

"It's okay," said Rafe then shrugged and turned away, "they're just shoes." She tried to hide the despair she felt at all the firsts in Bronte's life she had missed.

"No," said Eden softly as she took Rafe's arm gently so she could turn her around to look at her. "No," she said again and looked into the sad face Rafe tried to hide. "They were her first shoes, and I should have listened to myself and let you see her with them on instead of listening to," she stopped not wanting to say Jakes name. "I know it now," she said regretfully. "Bronte is very lucky to have you, Rafe. I'm lucky to have you. I love you and love everything you've done for us."

"I'm glad you like it. And I really hope you both stay," said Rafe hoping Eden's words were true.

13

RAFE SALVAGGIO AND Eden Kingsley's house was filled with their friends for Eden's housewarming. Everyone was taking tours of all the work Rafe had done to the house to welcome Eden and Bronte back home. Rafe had also arranged for a catered party banquet and a bar tended by Lexi, one of Rafe's teaching assistants, whose part-time job was bartending.

Abby and Julia took a tour of the new bathroom and then went to the bar for a drink. Abby looked around the house at everything Rafe had accomplished. "How does she find people who will do things for her like this?" asked Abby, showing her jealousy.

"I think it was the same crew who helped with the art studio remodel," said Julia as she looked around. "The owner, Dean, is in awe of her, and I'm sure his workers would walk through fire for her. She really should run for a political office. There's truly no telling what she could get done."

"I don't know," said Abby wryly. "If she ran for office, none of us would ever get any peace until the world was as perfect as she thinks it should be."

"True," Julia agreed with a stilted chuckle, scrutinizing Rafe and Eden. "Do you think they'll last this time? I know they've had a lot of bad history over the last couple of years, but they seem happy now." She wondered if she really had missed her last chance to try to make a go of things with Rafe. Not that Rafe had been any help or shown any sign of changing her mind about the level of their relationship.

"I don't know," Abby said suspiciously. "I still think something is up with Rafe even though you guys think I'm crazy."

Stacey walked up with a drink and a plate of food, and she then overheard Abby. "You're crazy too? We should form a club."

"Stacey, you're insane, and I don't want to join your club," Abby said scornfully. She looked at Julia. "I need another drink." She made her way to the bar. "I'll take a refill please." The bartender refilled her glass with a smile. "Thanks."

Eden came up beside Abby and took a glass of wine from the bar. "Hey, Abby, are you okay?" she asked seeing her unhappy look.

"I'm fine," said Abby. "I just wanted to get away from Stacey. She drives me nuts," she explained.

"Flynn says the same thing," Eden revealed with a small laugh. "Come join Rafe and me." They walked over and sat down on the sofa next to Rafe.

"Letty took Bronte to her room. She was very tired," Rafe told Eden as she sat down beside her.

"I just love the chaise lounge Rafe restored for you, Eden," said Dalia impressed once again with her colleague. "I knew she did restorations, but from what your friend Flynn told me, Rafe actually hand carved some of the missing pieces."

"I love it," said Eden warmly, remembering Rafe and Flynn unveiling the chaise lounge for her. "Rafe did everything in this house too. She showed me pictures of what it looked like before she fixed everything, and it was a disaster. She even raised the roof for the upstairs entertainment area. She's very talented."

She looked at Rafe and smiled knowingly. "It seems she's very good at everything she does."

"Flynn did a lot of the tedious work," said Rafe looking around for him. "I'm not sure where he went. Anyway, he helped me get it done much faster than I could have on my own, and he did a great job."

Eden looked at Rafe and wondered why Flynn never told her they were working on a restoration project. "So, Flynn helped you? He never said anything to me about it."

"Well, good—because it was a secret project," said Rafe with a slight smile. She had asked Flynn to keep the project a secret and was happy she could trust him to keep a promise. "I didn't want anyone complaining about me spending time on it. It really did look pretty hopeless when we took it out of the crate."

"Well, it looks like *hopeless* isn't so hard for you!" Dalia joked, laughing at her own words.

Rafe turned her smile toward Abby. "I haven't heard your evaluation yet, Abby. What do you think?"

"About the house or about you and Eden?" Abby asked cynically.

Rafe shrugged and locked eyes with Abby. "Both."

Abby tore her eyes away then glanced at Eden then back to Rafe. "I think you got things done very fast with the house and with Eden."

Rafe laughed to release the tension between them, then looked at Abby very seriously. "Things didn't go as fast with Eden as I would have liked them too," she said softly.

Looking into Rafe's eyes, Abby saw the pain she had been carrying for the past couple of years and felt bad. "Sorry, Rafe. I didn't mean—" she started.

"Abby," Rafe cut her off wanting to stay positive and not fight with her again, "let me introduce you to Dalia and Kylie. Dalia teaches Fiber and Ceramics at CCAD and Kylie works with Eden." She looked over at Kylie. "What is it you do, Kylie?"

"I'm a script researcher," said Kylie then looked at Eden. "So, why did you decide to be a roommate? Wouldn't it be better to have your own places? I mean, can't you afford your own place?"

Abby whispered to Eden, "Straight girl?" Eden nodded and tried not to smile.

Dalia smiled at Abby because she overheard her whisper. "Things are always easier with a roommate to help out. It's half the bills, half the rent, half of just about everything."

"Eden is going to be a great roommate," said Rafe with a wink. "Half of everything, right?"

"Right," said Eden slowly. "But Kylie, just so you know, we're more than roommates," she paused, "we're trying to be together again."

"Even better, roommates with benefits," teased Dalia and took another sip of her drink.

Rafe laughed and winked at Eden again, then smiled just for her. "A toast... to roommates with benefits."

The others raised their glasses as they called out, "Hear! Hear!"

"I need one of those." Abby sighed heavily.

"Oh, I'm sorry," said Kylie blushing. "I didn't know. I didn't know you were," she faltered. "Don't you have a baby? I thought," she stammered, "I thought you were dating Jake."

Eden watched Rafe's reaction with worry. "It's okay, Kylie. I'm not seeing Jake. Bronte is Rafe's baby too."

"How," started Kylie confused. "Is Rafe Bronte's real mother? She looks just like her. Did you adopt her, Eden?"

"Eden gave birth to Bronte. I'm the one who's adopting," Rafe explained. She looked attentively at Kylie. "What made you think Eden was still dating Jake?" she asked, and Eden stopped herself in mid-drink.

"Oh, he was on the lot the other day," she said frankly. "I just assumed he was there to see Eden since he asked about her."

"I see," said Rafe flatly. "Excuse me. I need to freshen up my drink." She got up and walked calmly away.

"Dang it!" Eden said softly then got up and followed Rafe.

"Did I..." Kylie hesitated, confused by their sudden departure, "did I say something wrong?"

"It's okay. Don't worry about it," said Abby attempting to keep things light but watching Rafe and Eden with concern. "Tell me about your job. What exactly is a script researcher?"

Eden followed Rafe to the bar and caught up with her. "Rafe, he wasn't there to see me," she insisted. "I didn't even know he was there. I didn't see him. I swear." She wondered how he got on the lot since she had him on the no admittance list.

"I want to believe you, Eden," Rafe said with a forced smile remembering Jake had said Eden called to meet him before.

Maybe she was filling him in on her move. Rafe looked at the bartender. "Lexi, I'll have a double scotch."

"Rafe, are you okay?" asked Eden, worried as she touched Rafe's arm. "You have to believe me."

"I'm fine," she said as Lexi handed her a double and she took a sip. "Will you excuse me? I need to check on the caterer." She walked away from Eden and went into the kitchen.

Eden watched her walk away. "Shit."

Abby made her way over to Eden. "Did you just cuss? What's going on with Rafe?"

"You heard Kylie," Eden said in misery ignoring the question about her cursing. "Jake was on the lot. I told her I'm not seeing him anymore, and it upset her he was there."

"Like you can help where the guy goes," Abby scoffed. "Overreacting a bit, isn't she?"

"It's still a sore spot," Eden explained. "She's controlling herself right now, but..." she let her words fall away.

"I need to use the restroom," Abby whispered. "The guest restroom is being viewed again, and Bronte is asleep in her room. Letty says I shouldn't go in there so other people don't go in and wake her up. Can I use Rafe's?"

"You should go ask Rafe." Eden sighed not wanting to do anything to trespass on Rafe's space, especially since she could tell she was upset.

"Okay," said Abby as she walked quickly to the kitchen where she found Rafe. "Rafe," she whispered, "I have to use the bathroom." She grimaced to show her dire need. "Can I use the one in your room? The other one is filled with admirers." She looked at Rafe in desperation.

Rafe shook her head smiling at Abby's theatrics. "Go ahead. Just be discrete. I don't want everyone in my room," she said as Abby quickly moved away and entered the bedroom.

Abby made it to the toilet just in time. She sighed with relief, reached for the toilet paper, and found the roll empty. She opened the cabinets and found a fresh roll, but in her hurry, she knocked over a couple of items. She finished her toiletry, washed her hands, and began setting things back in place inside the cabinet. As she replaced things, she noticed a familiar box toward the back and pulled it out.

"No fucking way!" she said in shock. "They were right! This is not good," she said upset as she put the strap-on back in the cabinet and closed the door. "No wonder she's acting so weird! This is so fucked up!" She primped her multi-toned blond hair as she mumbled under her breath. When she was finished, she left the restroom quickly and snuck out of Rafe's room. In the dining room, she saw Julia by the bar. "Julia, have you seen Rafe?"

"I think she went outside," said Julia pointing toward the patio.

"Thanks." Abby rushed out to the patio. She saw Rafe on the other side of the pool sitting alone in a patio chair with her eyes closed and her earbuds in listening to something on her phone. She walked over and sat in the chair next to her "Rafe," she said announcing her presence and taping her on the shoulder.

"Abby," said Rafe without opening her eyes. She had turned off the recording on her phone. It was the one from the first night she and Eden had been together. She hadn't listened to the whole recording for a while. One time, she had been listening, and she thought she heard Eden talking to Jake, but she wasn't sure if it was a dream or real because she had been half-asleep. It was difficult to be sure exactly where in the recording that she might have heard their voices. She hadn't found it again even after listening to it many times. Tonight, she tried to listen for their voices again. She then realized it was pointless. It was obvious Jake and Eden were talking—even if they weren't that night.

"I know what Eden is doing to you," said Abby agitated and no longer able to hold in her opinions.

Rafe opened her eyes and looked at her warily. "You do?"

"Yeah," Abby said hotly. "Is she like comparing you to him or something? That's so fucking sick!"

"Something like that," Rafe said hesitantly. "I guess."

"How can she do that?" Abby demanded. "I mean, it's nowhere near the same thing!" She threw her hands up in anger. "It's crazy to do that! Is this one of her straight girl games, thinking she can choose whichever she thinks is better?"

"I..." Rafe started while looking at Abby confused, "I don't know what she's thinking," she said letting out her breath, feeling deflated. *Abby definitely had a different perspective on the situation,* Rafe thought. "She's not a straight girl. She's..." she sighed, "whatever. It doesn't matter."

"Whatever is right." Abby was fuming. "She's your straight girl! I told you your thing for straight girls was going to cause you trouble. That's why you freaked about him being at the studio, isn't it?"

"I didn't freak," said Rafe calmly to try to de-escalate the conversation, "but it is what upset me. Just stop with the straight girl stuff." She knew Abby was just venting, but she felt it was insulting, not only to Eden but also to women in general, making them feel stereotyped. "I don't have a thing for straight girls—just for Eden."

"Then how can you let her do this to you?" asked Abby outraged. "She's just like a straight girl who wants it both ways!"

"You need to calm down and stop calling her a straight girl like it's an insult," Rafe said flatly. "I am giving her what she wants. I love her, and I don't want to lose her or Bronte."

"Giving her what she wants?" screeched Abby heated and flailing her arms. "At what cost to you? It isn't right! You shouldn't have to do," she hesitated, "you shouldn't be made to," she couldn't even bring herself to say it. She sat back in the chair angrily and crossed her arms. "I thought I knew her. I'm sorry for anything bad I've ever said about you. I didn't know Eden was capable of being that low."

"Abby, stop," said Rafe not wanting to deal with her escalation anymore. "Eden has been your friend for a long time. She said she needs time and patience. If I give her what she wants, I'm hoping she'll really love me, and we can work things out." She smiled sadly at Abby. "She's moved in with me, so I must be doing something right."

"Pffft. It's fucking twisted," Abby said as she shook her head. "It's wrong in so many ways. There should be a law! A law with sections!"

"Please, don't do anything stupid," Rafe begged her. "I need you to promise you'll keep this to yourself." Rafe looked intently at her. "This is serious, Abby. I could lose everything. My life with Bronte and my happiness is at risk. Can I trust you?"

"Rafe," Abby choked out, but then she saw the pain and worry in Rafe's eyes, so she looked away.

"I know you," said Rafe firmly. "You have a very hard time keeping things to yourself. Please, don't work against me on this."

"She's hurting you again," Abby objected. "I told her I didn't want to be part of anything if it hurt you."

"Don't worry," Rafe said with a small smile. "I'll be fine."

Abby looked at Rafe, and even though she smiled, her eyes and demeanor told a different story. "Will you? I'm not so sure."

14

THE LAST OF the guests were leaving the party, and Eden held tightly to Rafe as they said their goodnights at the door. Abby, the very last to leave, was looking at Eden and Rafe sourly as the blond recipient of her disapproval clung to Rafe. She looked at Rafe with concern. "You okay?" she asked wanting to help if she could.

"Everything's fine," said Rafe as she gave her a serious look telling her to stop. "We'll see you in the morning."

"Everything's very fine," said Eden as she smiled at Rafe lovingly and kissed her cheek.

Abby looked down to hide her anger. "Okay, bye." She quickly turned and left, muttering as she walked to her car.

"What's with her tonight?" asked Eden as they closed the door.

"Who knows," said Rafe as she yawned. "I'm tired. The caterer is coming back in the morning for her trays and things, and she's bringing a cleaning staff so we can leave everything." She went to the new security keypad, set the alarm, and then started walking to her room.

"Whoa," said Eden as she pulled Rafe back to her, "wait a minute." She smiled and kissed her again. "I haven't had a chance to thank you for everything you gave me tonight."

Rafe leaned her head against Eden's, still upset by the news about Jake, and the fact that somehow Abby had found out about him. "I'm so tired," she said softly hoping Eden would accept her excuse. "Let's just go to sleep. I won't be any good for you tonight."

"Come with me," Eden said invitingly as she pulled a reluctant Rafe into her newly redecorated room and sat her on the bed. She kissed her and ran her hands through her dark hair and over her shoulders. "I want to take care of you," she whispered.

Rafe closed her eyes. "Eden, I—"

"Shhh," Eden hushed her.

Silently, she unbuttoned Rafe's shirt, ran her hands inside it along her smooth, warm skin, and then slipped the shirt off her. She kissed her face, neck, and breasts, and then released her bra, tossing it aside before she pushed Rafe back on the bed.

"You've taken care of me all day long," she said softly. "Now it's time for you to let me take care of you," she added, her voice lilting upward. She kissed Rafe as she unfastened her pants and pulled herself away long enough to pull them off her. "Turn over," she whispered. "I'll give you a massage."

Rafe looked at Eden and felt like she couldn't risk refusing and upsetting her. She kept thinking about Jake being at the studio where Eden worked. Eden said she didn't know he was there. She desperately wanted to believe her. Her kisses tasted sweet, and her hands felt good running over her body. She climbed further into the bed and turned over as requested.

Stripping off her clothes, Eden climbed onto the bed next to Rafe. She began massaging her back and shoulders, marveling again at her body and the etched lines she had achieved from lifting weights. She ran her hands over her back and down along her firm hips and legs before she moved back up her body then leaned down so she could whisper seductively into Rafe's ear.

"You're so beautiful," she said seductively. "I love you."

Rafe lifted herself slightly then turned her head and looked up at Eden who kissed her. "I love you too," she said and let herself back down. Her head was spinning between the need to leave and the desire to stay. She couldn't stop hearing Jake telling her Eden loved him and how he had kissed Eden in the park. She couldn't stop herself from wondering if Eden might even be sneaking away to make love to him. She couldn't stop the memory of Kylie revealing Jake was where Eden worked. Kylie said he asked about her, not for her. She wanted to believe Eden.

"Just relax," Eden whispered as she kissed Rafe's neck, shoulders, and back.

Eden continued to massage and kiss Rafe knowing her reluctance and tense muscles were from the mention of Jake tonight. She wanted to take her tension away. Eden wished she could take away the moment Kaylie mentioned him. She straddled Rafe to get in a better position, running her hands over her head, down her neck, and then began kneading her shoulders and back firmly, taking her time while frequently stopping to kiss, lick, and suck on her body sensuously.

Rafe clung to the pillow as Eden moved against her, kissing her and caressing her. She could feel the warmth coming from between Eden's legs joined with the feeling of the slick moisture flowing onto her. She felt Eden gently bite the nape of her neck, and it drove all other thoughts from her mind.

When she felt Rafe relaxing, Eden lifted up then moved Rafe's legs apart and put her hands underneath her. Eden heard Rafe sigh as she gave in then lifted up so Eden could slide her hand under her further. She moved her hand up between Rafe's legs into her soft curls as she kissed the small of her back and ground her body against Rafe's hips pressing her into the bed and into her hand.

Rafe felt Eden's pull and knew she wanted her to rise up so she could move her hand again. She followed her silent instructions and could feel Eden then part her with her finger and slide into her. She gasped from the sensation. Eden's touches were melting her resolve against her will, her frustration released in tears she hid in the pillow because her body didn't want it to stop.

Eden felt Rafe's body respond as she gave into her love and the arousal she was creating inside her. She wanted her to feel the truth of how she felt. She wanted Rafe to feel she loved her. She poured her intent and her love into Rafe through her kisses and her touches.

Touching Rafe was always a head-spinning experience from the first time they made love to even this moment. She was so beautiful, and Eden was always amazed she just let her do whatever she wanted to do to her. Right now, she wanted to be between her legs. She lifted off her, pulling on her gently, and Rafe turned over. She climbed between Rafe's legs and pressed herself against her as she kissed her soft lips. Eden felt Rafe's hands on her hips pulling them closer, and Eden's head spun again. She took a breath so she could focus. She wanted to make tonight about Rafe and knew how easy it was to get lost in the things Rafe could do to her once she decided to take over.

Opening her eyes, Eden looked at Rafe and kissed her. "I love you." Eden kissed her again then pulled away slightly, moving her hips so she was straddling Rafe's leg. She reached down to touch Rafe. "Oh, you feel so good," she breathed as she felt how wet Rafe was for her. The sensation of Rafe under her fingers and Rafe pressing her leg into her caused Eden to be aroused, and she knew Rafe could feel how wet she was too.

Gliding smoothly through Rafe, her fingers sensitive to every texture and span, Eden delved deep, and Rafe anticipated her perfectly, pushing her hips up to meet her.

"You feel so good inside me, Ede." Rafe's voice was heavy with a yearning for more of Eden.

Eden looked up at Rafe's words and could see the pleasure she was causing her. At the erotic sight, and with those words echoing in her mind, Eden moaned as a surge shot through her, and her body reacted, spilling onto Rafe again. She wanted to give her more. She wanted to go faster. She looked down, and as she watched her fingers moving in and out of Rafe, she saw the top of her clit, and her mouth watered. She wanted to taste her. Eden moved down and tried to pull her fingers away, but Rafe reached down and held her hand.

"Stay inside me," Rafe bade her softly as she held Eden's hand in place.

"Okay, babe." Eden's voice shook with desire as she pushed her fingers back inside her. She bent over Rafe, feeling dizzy, her throat vibrating as she tasted her and rolled her tongue over Rafe's clit. She couldn't help herself. Eden knew she was relentless, but it seemed like her mind wasn't in control of what the other parts of her body were doing. Her hands were in contact with Rafe, one moving inside her the other holding onto her warm body. Her mouth had her clit entrapped, causing Rafe a beautiful torment. Her own clit was throbbing too as she flowed out and down her legs.

Eden felt Rafe put her hand on her head, holding her there. She knew Rafe was on the edge of climax, she could feel it. She focused where Rafe needed her and pushed deep inside her.

Rafe arched up, and her body tightened around Eden's fingers as she orgasmed. Eden reveled in Rafe's soft sounds of gratification, feeling the reaction Rafe's body gave to the things she had done to her. Eden slowly pulled her fingers from her and kissed her way up Rafe's body. Smiling she hovered over Rafe, kissing her as she lay weak and exhausted.

Rafe looked up at the smile on Eden's face and couldn't help but grin as she pushed Eden's hair from her face. "Humph," she rumbled. "You're pretty proud of yourself aren't you?"

"Yes, yes I am," she said and kissed Rafe again. She felt Rafe run her hands over and pull her close to kiss her breasts. She pulled away from Rafe. "Don't," she whispered, "it was just for you. You're tired. I wanted to give you something special like you gave to me."

Rafe looked at her hungrily. "I can smell you. I want to taste you," she said eagerly. She lifted herself and overturned Eden then started down her body.

Eden sat up and linked her arms under Rafe's then pulled her back up and kissed her deeply. "Just hold me," she said, "and kiss me." She felt Rafe's kisses and returned them passionately wanting her to feel how much she loved her and how happy she was to be with her in the same house again. "Hey," she said as Rafe kissed her neck, "I have something else for you."

"More?" asked Rafe into her ear then moved her kisses down to her collarbone determined to make it all the way back down. Eventually.

Eden pushed Rafe up gently and made her way out from under her. "I'll be right back," she said with a smile. Eden felt her heart thud in her chest as she noticed Rafe looking at her naked body with her blazing gray-blue eyes. She almost ran back into her arms again but recovered herself. Instead, she turned quickly and went into the kitchen. She got everything together she needed then made her way back to the bedroom. She walked in and found Rafe sitting up against the headboard waiting. "Here you go," she said and handed her a small shot glass before she climbed into bed with her. "Remember when I first moved in with you and our first night together, we made a toast with limoncello?"

Rafe laughed as she took her glass. "Yes," she said softly. "I'll never forget." She reached out and pulled Eden to her. "Come here," she said. Eden climbed over to her straddling her lap so she was facing her. "What would you like to toast to this time?" she asked and gave her a small kiss.

"Well, if we stick with tradition, we should toast to sweet drinks, long kisses, and decadent sex," Eden said with a laugh.

Rafe chuckled as she remembered when they made that toast. "We were young, drunk, and horny," she said and grinned.

"True." Eden smiled at the memory. "What do you suggest?"

Rafe held up her glass and looked into Eden's eyes. "To what's in our hearts," she said softly and held up her glass. She wondered what was really in Eden's heart but pushed the thought out of her mind, determined not to think about it tonight because she wanted to make love to her so much.

"To what's in our hearts," Eden repeated. She touched her glass to Rafe's, and they both drank. When Rafe finished her shot, Eden took her glass from her and set both glasses aside on the nightstand. She took Rafe's face in her hands and kissed her deeply. She could taste the lemon flavor of the drink on her tongue and lips. She felt Rafe put her arms around her and pull her close as she returned her kiss. Slowly, Eden pulled away. "You're in my heart," Eden said breathlessly and kissed her again "You taste so good," she whispered and kissed her once more.

Rafe ran her warm hands down Eden's back and gripped her hips, then pulled her up so that she was on her knees and her face was above her as they kissed. She ran her hands over Eden loving the feel of her naked body as it pressed against her. The small of her back, the curve of her hip, the firmness of her thigh, it was perfect for her. Eden moved her kisses to Rafe's neck. Rafe turned her head toward her ear. "So, it's just for me tonight?" she whispered.

"Yeah." Eden kissed her, and the dizzy drunk feeling came over her again.

"Well, what if there's something else I want?" Rafe asked softly and moved her hand gently between Eden's legs. She heard Eden moan as she pressed her hand up against her. She knew Eden had been very aroused just a short time ago. It probably wouldn't take much to get her back there. "I want you to come for me," she requested lustily into her ear.

"Oh, god," Eden gasped as she felt a tingling pulse run through her resulting in her body doing as Rafe commanded. "I don't know how you do this to me," she moaned as she grasped Rafe's shoulders and leaned her head against hers.

"I want you to tell me you only love me," Rafe whispered. She moved her hand to feel how wet Eden was and to test the sensitivity of the nerves she could already feel showing again.

Eden squeezed Rafe's shoulders tight as she felt Rafe's fingers flow through her. She jerked back and took a sharp breath as a short electric shock ran through her and then was gone. "I—" she panted, "I only love you," she said and let out a soft moan.

"I only love you too," said Rafe and kissed the nipple in front of her. She moved the hand on Eden's back down to her hip and pulled her forward again. Eden understood the request, pushed her hips toward Rafe, and had to hold onto the headboard. Rafe moved the hand between Eden's legs, circling and teasing the edge of her. "I want you to tell me you only want me to make love to you," said Rafe as she moved her fingers closer to their goal and waited for Eden's reply.

Eden was moving her hips so Rafe could slide inside her, but she kept moving her hand. It was driving her crazy. She wanted those long fingers of Rafe's inside her now. "Oh, god, Rafe," she begged, "please!"

"Say it," whispered Rafe then leaned her head forward and blew a breath down onto her open nerves while sliding her fingers around the edge of where she knew Eden wanted them to go.

Pushing her body against Rafe at the sensations running through her, Eden arched and cried out as she felt her body give Rafe more without her having to ask. "I—I only want you to make love to me," said Eden softly and felt Rafe slide inside her. "Oh, yes," she called out and moved her body to the steady rhythm Rafe had set for them. She could feel it building inside her, and it felt so good. She could feel the warmth radiating from Rafe, and a fine sweat had broken out on each of them because of it. Then she felt the push Rafe gave, and suddenly, she was deeper inside her, and every nerve was firing. "Oh," was all Eden could utter because Rafe had moved the rhythm to a hard deep push Eden knew would give her what she craved.

"Eden," said Rafe breathlessly as she pushed into her, "Tell me when you come it's for only me."

"It's for you," said Eden without hesitation as Rafe began to move faster against her. "It's all for you." She panted, and before she could take another breath, she felt Rafe brush the sensitive place deep inside. She felt herself begin to tighten as Rafe pushed and hit her mark. She continued hitting it, pushing Eden further toward the edge each time. Sparks flew in front of Eden's eyes and her arms wrapped tightly around Rafe. She couldn't control the sounds of ecstasy as her body trembled from the pleasure Rafe had caused to overwhelm.

Rafe held Eden close as she trembled and flowed over her hand and arm even though Rafe hadn't pulled out yet because Eden still clenched tightly. Finally, Eden's grip around Rafe's neck loosened, and her fingers relaxed enough to untangle them from Rafe's hair. Rafe put her free hand up high on Eden's back and gently helped her lay down beside her. She kissed her as she slowly and carefully removed her fingers. She made a trail up Eden's body with her wet fingers and kissed her again.

"I'm going to go get what's mine now," said Rafe with a grin and began making her way down Eden's body. She knew she would get there sometime.

"Oh, my god, Rafe. I don't know if I can take any more." Eden's voice quaked because of what Rafe was doing to her, and she was still throbbing. She put her hands on Rafe's head and ran her hands over her hair as Rafe kissed her quivering body.

"You said it's for me," said Rafe breathing onto Eden's skin making goose bumps appear. She took Eden's breast into her mouth, and she arched up into her. She knew Eden liked the feel of her tongue circling her sensitive nipple and the electric shock it caused when she engulfed it with her mouth and sucked with just the right amount of pressure. She smiled when Eden arched against her, and she heard the small gasp meaning shock waves had run through her body delivering Eden pleasure.

Eden was already starting to writhe under Rafe's attention and lifted her arm to put it over her eyes. "You're killing me," she moaned as Rafe kissed her way down further. She felt Rafe take hold of her legs and spread them, then run her hands down them slowly toward her vagina. Eden bit her lip as she turned her head, and then couldn't believe Rafe had made her come again, but she was definitely dripping. She felt Rafe's fingers wipe the drip and rub it lightly over her. Eden couldn't help but moan because her touch felt so good.

Eden's arms flew down to her sides slamming into the mattress hard, and she gripped the sheets as she felt Rafe's tongue lick over her. "Ah," Eden cried out at the sensation and then the sensation came again. "Oh, god," she gasped and lifted herself instinctually.

She felt Rafe hold her hips tight and take control of her as her tongue ran over her swollen clit. Eden knew Rafe could keep this game up for hours and drive her mad. She hated it because it was so frustrating, she loved it for the same reason, and she had missed it when she couldn't have it. She only wanted it from Rafe. She was torn between wanting her to keep doing what she was doing and wanting her to just fuck her and make her climax. Rafe was circling her clit with her tongue, and it felt so good. She wanted to arch into her, but Rafe held her in place and controlled every movement. Rafe would build her to the edge and back off then tongue her until she was wet and aching with the need for her to be inside her. Then she would just lick gently until she started all over again. It was driving her crazy. She picked up her arm to put it over her eyes, and suddenly, Rafe's tongue was on top of her clit, and her hand was sliding through the wetness for lubrication. Eden gripped the sheets at her sides again. Rafe slid her fingers close to the edge of her and pulled back teasing and keeping her from having what she wanted. Eden, covered in sweat, had clutched Rafe's hair again. She wasn't sure if she could take any more. Suddenly, Rafe had gone too far, and she knew this time it had to be coming.

Eden felt Rafe suck her clit into her mouth as she slid her fingers deep inside her. "Yes, I want you to fuck me," she begged her. "I only want you to fuck me!" She knew Rafe heard her because Rafe sucked harder on her clit. She then felt Rafe's tongue move against her relentlessly as she began to fuck her hard and deep until she arched up and cried out again as she came hard for her. For good measure, Rafe fucked her and sucked her sensitive nerves until Eden lost her mind. Eden could do nothing but laugh uncontrollably as her body jerked at the slightest touch on her clit.

Rafe climbed up Eden's body then pushed Eden's hair from her face so she could look into her eyes. She smiled as she saw the gold spots in them had grown large. It always amazed her when it happened.

"You're very beautiful," she said and kissed her sweetly. "I love you," she whispered and kissed her again. She slowly pulled away and started to get out of bed.

Eden clung to Rafe, barely able to hold onto her because she was so weak. "Whoa, whoa, whoa, what are you doing?"

"I've got to go to bed," she yawned. "It's getting late, and we need to sleep."

"You're not going anywhere," Eden growled softly and pulled Rafe back down on the bed rolling herself on top of her using her entire body because she could barely use her trembling limbs. She looked intently into her eyes. "This is my first night in my new room. The one you made for me. I want you here." She kissed her. "I want you here all night."

Rafe looked away and sighed. "Eden, I think—"

Eden covered Rafe's mouth with her hand. "No, you don't think right now. Remember, I'm taking care of you now."

Rafe turned her head to get Eden's hand off her mouth. "Well, I think I took pretty good care of you," she said with an arched brow. "And I thought it was about what I wanted tonight."

"You're staying," Eden said with finality. She smiled down at her and kissed her then spoke between her kisses, "I love you, you're mine, and you're staying with me—all night." She held tight to her, laid her head on her shoulder, and sighed. "You better still be here in the morning." She felt Rafe put her arms around her and sigh. "I love you," Eden whispered again. "Thank you for loving me too. Oh, and for all the other things you did too." She laughed softly against her. "And you thought you wouldn't be any good for me tonight."

"As long as we have all night," Rafe purred and overturned Eden holding her hands above her head, "I should see what else you might yell out, telling me what you want only me to do to you." She took her breast in her mouth.

Eden pulled a hand free and ran it over Rafe's head. "I only want you for everything," she whispered. "I don't think I can take anymore," Eden said softly as Rafe moved up to kiss her.

"I have more things I can do to you," said Rafe as she moved her warm hands over her body and then kissed her neck.

"You've been doing a lot of things to me lately you never did before," Eden said as she laughed softly enjoying Rafe's attention.

"I can always stop," said Rafe and arched her eyebrow.

"Oh, I don't think so." Eden chuckled. "I think it's in the cohabitation agreement how you can't ever stop."

"Hmm, I don't remember that part," said Rafe with a grin. "I'll have to ask Katheryn to send me a copy on Monday."

"I have a copy," said Eden quickly and tried to wink but blinked both eyes. "I'll get it for you."

"You do that," said Rafe and kissed her. "In the meantime, you said it's about what I want tonight, and I want more of you." Rafe reached over, grabbed the shot glasses, and poured the last drops of limoncello over Eden's breasts and stomach, and she then leaned over her to taste.

Eden looked at the clock on her nightstand and saw it was after midnight. "It's morning." Eden laughed as Rafe ran her tongue over her, tasting her body as she started moving her warm hands over her. "Rafe, it's morning! Oh, god," she moaned. "Rafe, it's," she lost her words for a while. "Ah, yes," she gasped and squeezed Rafe's hand tight, and then Eden let Rafe take her where she wanted into the morning.

15

ABBY VAN FALKOV WAS sprawled out in her bed sleeping heavily. The mobile phone laying on her nightstand rang, and she gave a jolt but refused to wake. The phone continued to ring, and she opened one eye and looked at the clock as it showed six o'clock. The phone stopped ringing, and she closed her eye again.

After a while, the phone began to ring again, and Abby sat up angrily. She fought her way to the edge of the bed and grabbed the phone off the nightstand.

"Who the hell is this?" she answered angrily. "Do you know it's six o'clock in the morning on a Sunday?" She listened to the caller. "What? Sonia, why are you calling me? Who? Yes, I know Rafe Salvaggio. So, she has stuff written about her all the time. Is that what you're calling me about?" She listened again. "How bad can it be? I mean she's a college dean now, for fuck's sake! That bad?" She got out of bed. "Okay, okay, I'm going." She stomped over and turned on her computer then opened her email. "I have the file. Yes, I'll read it right now," she said and threw the phone on the desk.

She yawned, opened the attachment, and began to read. "What the! Who the fuck wrote this?" She read more. "Oh, fuck, this is bad."

She pushed the print button and picked up the phone and dialed back L. A. Magazine. "Sonia? Hey, I just read it. When's this coming out? What? It's out now? This morning? Fuck! What publication? The what? What the fuck is that? No, I'll find it." She hung up and sighed. "This is so fucking bad. I have to call a meeting."

16

AFTER SEVERAL VERY early morning phone calls harassing everyone, Abby Van Falkov finally convinced them to meet her for an emergency meeting at The Kiki Bistro. On her way to the meeting, she picked up copies of the magazine with the article about Rafe.

Everyone sat together with their coffee, each reading their own copy of the scandalous article and trying to figure out the best way to handle Rafe after she finished reading it.

"What's 'deific rule?'" asked Jude reading the article.

"Oh, it means she has a god-like rule," answered Julia absently looking in her copy of the magazine.

Jude looked up puzzled. "So they think Rafe lords over everyone?"

"Well, the TA who was bartending last night sure thought Rafe was the greatest thing since creation," said Stacey sarcastically. "She went on and on about her. Dean Salvaggio this, Dean Salvaggio that," she mocked. "I tried to talk to her about my work, but it seemed like Rafe was all she could think about, so I just walked away."

"Thank god for her," said Abby as she looked at Stacey menacingly, "or maybe thank Rafe for her." Jude snickered as Abby raged on. "Her students like her so much because she gets things done and gives them opportunities," she declared protectively of her friend.

Jude laughed knowing anything she said that even resembled being on Stacey's side would wrankle Abby. Their feud was one Jude still didn't really understand. "Well, the work crew yesterday sure jumped when she spoke."

"The workers seemed happy about it. She didn't treat any of them bad or anything," said Flynn tapping the table nervously as he read, knowing the girls were right and Rafe was not going to be happy. He was glad Rafe had agreed to the new security system and had cameras installed around the house. If

Jake showed up again, the security cameras would have it all recorded and saved to the cloud.

"You know Rafe, she never demands, she just," Abby hesitated then shrugged, "expects."

"What's 'bane' mean?" asked Jude.

"It's because she's so smart," added Flynn. "And she's a really good teacher too. When we hang out, she always teaches me something new and fun."

"Bane is like evil or curse," Julia explained, and Jude grimaced.

Stacey looked over at Flynn as if she had just met him. "You hang out with her?"

"Sometimes," admitted Flynn as he fidgeted with his hands then looked away from her.

"When?" she asked in disbelief.

"Guys, we have to figure out how to help Rafe through this," said Jude as she threw down the magazine.

"Can't Eden help her?" asked Stacey. "Oh, I guess she can't," she said as she read the article. "Rafe is going to blow a blood vessel when she sees this."

Julia looked up and gave Abby a shove. "There she is with Eden and Bronte."

"Rafe, Eden, over here," Abby called with a wave. She looked over at Julia. "Eden's already on my shit list."

Julia shook her head at Abby. It seemed like, at any given moment, Abby could vacillate on who to like or who to be mad at. She was like an Ali Baba carnival ride sometimes.

Eden and Rafe saw the girls and waved back at them. Eden left Rafe at the counter to order and happily joined the girls with Bronte.

"Good morning," she said and yawned. She literally had only about three hours of sleep, but it was worth it. She smiled to herself. As she looked around the table, she wondered why everyone was being so quiet. She sat down with Bronte. "What's going on?"

"Eden, something's happened," said Julia looking at her somberly and noting the dark circles around her eyes, "and it isn't very good."

"What happened?" Eden was suddenly anxious as she looked at all their worried faces.

"It's about Rafe," said Abby irritated with her. "You may want to start running now." She threw a copy of the article in front of Eden. "It's bad, and we aren't sure what to do. It's all over town this morning."

"Maybe we should let Rafe eat first before we show it to her," suggested Julia unsuccessfully trying to hide her discomfort. She wondered if she should leave before the explosion occurred.

"Why would I want to run?" Eden asked confused.

"Show me what?" asked Rafe as she sat her coffee and Eden's tea on the table and sat down. She smiled at Eden. "I got you a dirty chai tea to help you stay awake. The waiter's bringing Bronte's juice with our order."

Julia watched as Rafe stared into Eden's eyes. It was hard to miss the possessive almost greedy look Rafe had as she looked at Eden who had flushed red under her gaze. *Good god,*

Rafe, don't be such a prat this time, she thought as she looked from Eden to the article. Julia was sure, after reading the article, Rafe would definitely smarten up and move on from Eden as she had advised her so many times.

Rafe looked around the table and frowned. "What's going on and why are you all so quiet?"

"Rafe," Eden started and looked anxiously from Abby to Rafe, "Abby just told me there's an article out about you."

"Oh yeah," Rafe affirmed with a smile, "the one going in the L. A. Times about the Jackson-Goyer Foundation Grant. It's good, I know." Rafe nodded and took a sip of her coffee. "We put copies of it in all the guest packages." She looked at everyone and saw they weren't happy. "What?"

"Rafe, this article is in the L. A. Light, and it's definitely not good," said Abby as she hesitantly handed her a copy of the magazine.

"L. A. Light? Never heard of it," said Rafe with a slight shrug. She took the small magazine from Abby, and her face went dark as she saw the title and her anger grew as she read the article.

The Art of Shame: Dean Rafaella E. Salvaggio
By M. Land, Special Reporter

Controlling, immoral, predatory, homosexual, perverted, antagonistic, arrogant, and demonic. These are just some of the words used to describe the newest and youngest 'Dean of Arts' at California Conservatory of Art and Design, Dean Rafaella E. Salvaggio.

California Conservatory of Art and Design (CCAD) has been a symbol of hope and promise for our community, a reason for pride in the students who would become our future neighbors and leaders. But now this image might be tarnished with shame.

Dean Rafaella Salvaggio, the former owner of the construction and restoration company, Eroina Conservazione e Design, is best known for making hostile real estate deals to obtain American historical properties. She then would hold them hostage from the American people for unprecedented amounts of money after using taxpayer money to renovate the properties.

With her new position, she is now using her diabolical business practices to subject our CCAD students and community to perverted and pornographic materials and ideals. She currently proves her shame in the CCAD Gallery Show of Student and Faculty Art. She has made it her agenda to seek out the most offensive art, the most immoral art, and the most perverted art and bring it into the public eye.

In addition, she came to the aid and defense of Wade Delchus, the very man who held her and a class of students hostage. She convinced and encouraged Mr. Delchus to create the alarming and disgusting art he produces and sells from his prison cell and arranged for his show, Diesel Therapy, in a New York gallery.

This is proof she can do nothing less than corrupt and morally debase the youth and the weak-minded at CCAD, in our community, and potentially, across America.

So, why was the bane to all that is good even considered for a position at CCAD? The answer to this question is money. In her short time at CCAD, she has been able to raise over one million dollars for her department, almost half of which comes from the Jackson-Goyer Foundation of New York. Her ability to raise money rivals top political lobbyists. So, what it begs to question—is the money she raised as corrupt and debased as the art she promotes, the hostile business deals she has struck, and the shame of her homosexual agenda? This question can only be answered by demanding a review of her practices and an audit. We can only hope the Board of the California Conservatory of Art and Design takes this action immediately.

Dean Salvaggio walks through the grounds of California Conservatory of Art and Design where she has a deific rule over her department from instructors to students. She encourages fellow professors and grad students to use unethical business practices to exploit private and government programs for personal gain, not unlike she has done throughout her career. When she issues orders, enthralled students line up to fulfill them and her every whim. They idolize her and dedicate time and energy to promoting her on websites, attending her special lectures, and in signing up for her special topic classes. She emboldens her students to involve themselves in situations from exploring immoral sexual expression and to breaking with good and sound values and to turning their backs on convention by perpetuating unpatriotic ideals and inciting propaganda against our great country and other countries where she has worked.

When asked about her views on art, she said,

"Art cannot be judged by any one person or one group's moral compass; it is ever-changing and growing through the human experience. Whether the experience is divine or earthly to the person who views it is subjective. However, by looking at art for art's sake, without judgment or preconceived ideas, we can learn so much about humanity and ourselves."

With this stance, she justifies her subversive agenda and tries to make us believe she is a friend to our community.

What proof, you may ask, does this humble writer have to substantiate these claims? Fortunately, the proof is well documented through company records, and we only need to visit the gallery on campus or download her pornographic online lecture* to see how her dangerous agenda is influencing our community.

Off campus, the infection continues. In her own 'lesbian' community, Ms. Salvaggio is described as a predator legendary for using her influence and power for the wanton and gratuitous seduction of women both homosexual and heterosexual. Her ex-partner, who was heterosexual when she was unfortunate enough to meet Ms. Salvaggio, has described her as controlling, emotionally abusive, self-involved, and domineering— not to mention she is also guilty of infidelity to her ex-partner, which shows she can make even the most perverted situation into an even more inconceivable abomination.

For a short while, Ms. Salvaggio's ex-partner saw the error of her ways and pulled herself out of the depraved lifestyle she was coerced into. Regrettably, the unfortunate woman, after being seriously scarred by the actions of her subjugator, has been pulled back into the same world of debauchery and sin—we are sure against her will.

After visiting local establishments, (not to be named here to prevent the free advertising of immoral dens), and speaking to the people who frequent them, it is apparent Ms. Salvaggio is legendary for her exploits and used what several patrons called her 'wildling soul-stealing powers' to seduce and ensnare her ex-partner, putting her back under her power and control.

Ms. Salvaggio is currently using her power and control to obtain parental rights to the child to whom her ex-partner gave birth. Her ex-partner is a fair-haired, light-skinned white, wholesome American woman from the Heart of America. Ms. Salvaggio forced her ex-partner to be artificially inseminated with the sperm of a man who was not only a stranger but also not an American so the child would emulate Ms. Salvaggio in her darker-toned appearance and foreign lineage. This was just one more way for Ms. Salvaggio to control her relationship with her oppressed ex-partner. Though the ex-partner has tried to stop the adoption and has been fighting it for over a year, it is still currently on the dockets for hearing. We can only hope the birth mother wins in her battle to keep the deviant Ms. Salvaggio from encroaching into her life and controlling the relationship with her child by obtaining adoptive parental rights. This is not the type of person who should be raising an impressionable child, so let us hope the legal system will do our community justice by denying the adoption petition.

Sadly, there are too many examples of Dean Salvaggio's exploits to list in this small publication. We must act—we must not fail our community. We must demand Dean Salvaggio be taken to task for the harm she is doing to our youth, our community, and by extension, to our country. We cannot allow money to be what binds her to our community. Dean Salvaggio is morally corrupt in business, her personal life, and in her public life, and this community must stop her depraved and morally debased agenda. If allowed to continue her work at CCAD, Dean Salvaggio will pervert and shame the fine traditions the school has strived to build since opening and cause strife and anguish to the minds and souls of the students who must come in contact with such a tainted person.

We must call for a review of Dean Salvaggio based upon the values by which our community lives. When she is found wanting, which she surely will, we must demand she be removed from her position of power over the young minds and souls at California Conservatory of Art and Design.

To voice your opinion or report reliable information regarding Dean Rafaella E. Salvaggio, call 888-555-SINR. (888-555-7467)

*Note: As of publication, this pornographic site has been taken down pending litigation.

Rafe gripped the magazine tighter as she read it. Her jaw clenched, and the vein against her temple throbbed as she barely controlled her fury.

Looking up from reading the article, she scanned each of the faces in front of her and then her gaze settled on Eden. "You," she said with an unnervingly calm voice, "stay away from me." She looked at everyone again. "Excuse me," she said as she got up, shaking with the effort to control her anger. She walked out the door and threw the magazine furiously into the trashcan as she walked down the sidewalk.

Eden snatched up a copy of the article, and as she skimmed through it, she paled. "No," she choked out as she looked at Julia shaking her head. "This is—" she could not find the words.

"Did you say those things about her?" asked Julia with concern. "That she forced you to inseminate with the donor sperm?"

"You did say Bronte was her last surprise," Jude reminded her. "Did you not want to do it?"

"I—" was all Eden could get out before she broke out in tears. "I didn't at first," she admitted as she sobbed, "but it was my decision. I wanted our baby!"

"Did you change your mind about the adoption—again?" asked Stacey sarcastically. "You're fighting it now?"

"No," Eden said shaking her head in denial. "I'm not fighting it! I never—" she stammered. "I want Rafe to adopt. Bronte is her daughter!"

"What about all those other things," asked Julia cautiously, "I don't understand. I thought you loved her."

Eden looked at everyone with worry and dread. "I do love her," she whispered.

"Right!" said Abby cynically as she looked angrily at Eden. "I'm going to find Rafe."

Eden followed Abby out the door shaking with shock and horror and holding Bronte close. She stopped just outside and looked at Flynn who had followed her. She pulled out her cellular phone. "I have to call Katheryn."

17

WALKING DOWN THE street, Abby Van Falkov looked into every doorway trying to find Rafe. She finally found her sitting on a bench in a small memorial park. She sat down next to Rafe and looked at what she was drinking. "A Slurpee?" she asked surprised.

Rafe looked at her drink then at Abby, "No bars are open, so I went for the brain freeze."

"I'll write another article and put it in L. A. Magazine," said Abby trying to be helpful. "I'll tell them where they can shove it."

"Please, don't dig me into a deeper hole," Rafe said as she rubbed her temples.

"You have to respond, or everyone will think all the stuff is true!" Abby insisted. Abby knew how the game worked: She with the last word wins.

Rafe took Abby's copy of the magazine from her hand and opened it. "Let's see," she said as she scanned the article, "looks like it must all be true, Abby. I am a Satan wannabe who oppresses her wife, turns people into sexual deviants with immoral art, and who wants to create beings in my own image, and was out to steal all the American historical properties and take down governments." She tossed the magazine back to her. "My life is fucked now. I'm going to lose my daughter, Eden, my job, my pride, and whatever else they decide to take. Plus, the business my father and I built may now be tarnished. I'm just lucky they didn't mention my father's real estate business by name. You want to know what the worst thing about this is?" she asked trying not to release the manic laugh wanting to explode from within her. "I fucking sold both the businesses. I sold them for the very fucking things I'm losing."

"Tell me how I can help," offered Abby upset and feeling guilty because she had been the source of some of those rumors around the club. However, she felt it was one thing to say the harmless things she had said at a bar and another to say the hurtful things Eden had said. She just couldn't understand why Eden would say things like that to people. "Why," she fought her own anger, "why would she say those things?"

Rafe sighed pushing down her anger and grief. "You can't help. I guess she said them because they're true." Her shoulders slumped. "Why would she lie?"

"I don't believe it," said Abby at a loss. "We were all there when we met the guy, and you introduced us all. She looked like she liked the guy," she said remembering when they all met Rafe's Italian friend. "I mean, he didn't speak much English, but he was great, and he sang all those Italian songs. She didn't look like she was forced."

"I can't take anymore," said Rafe barely hearing Abby's words. She was feeling numb except for the pain building in her head. The only thing she could think of was getting away now, maybe back to Italy. Gabri had been asking her to come, and he would be happy to see her. "I'm at my breaking point. This is it for me," she said as her phone rang interrupting her. She looked at the phone and saw it was Katheryn. "Hello," she answered. "She did? I don't see how it will help." She looked at

Abby. "It's Katheryn. Eden called her, and now Katheryn wants to see me at her house."

"You have to go," said Abby and saw Rafe question her with her eyes. "You have to go," she encouraged her.

"Katheryn," Rafe said into the phone, "okay, what time. No, I don't want her there. I don't want to fucking see her right now! I don't care," Rafe said firmly. "If she's there, I'll leave. I'll bring a copy. Bye." She ended the call and sighed. "Abby, will you go with me?"

"Sure," said Abby with a nod. "Can I have some Slurpee?"

Rafe looked at her cup and handed it to Abby. "You can have the rest."

"Thanks." She took a sip of the drink and stood up. "Come on. Let's take your car. I'll drive. I promise not to peel out or speed," she said as she smiled hoping to get Rafe in a better mood.

18

PULLING UP TO the gate of Katheryn Hardam's imposing home, Abby Van Falkov reached out and pushed the buzzer at the entry as Rafe sat quietly in the passenger seat of the car. They were buzzed in, and when the gate opened, she drove up the well-maintained driveway toward the large stately home. They parked in the vast parking area in front of the house. They walked up the stairs to the large ornate front door. Abby rang the doorbell with Rafe standing silent and numb beside her.

Abby took in the large mansion and the grounds, and then whistled, impressed. "Do you think she'd like a roommate?" she asked. "Her guest house looks incredible."

"I wouldn't want to even imagine what her cohabitation or rental agreement would look like," said Rafe flatly.

The door opened, and Katheryn looked at them somberly. "Rafe, Abby," she greeted them, "come inside." They followed her down the hall toward her office. "I'm sorry, Abby. I need to talk to Rafe privately, client confidentiality and all. You make yourself at home, and we'll be out in a little while."

"Thanks, Abby," said Rafe as Katheryn ushered her into the office then closed the door.

"So let's see a copy of the article in question," said Katheryn. Rafe offered her the copy Abby's had given her earlier in the park. Katheryn took it, then went to sit behind her desk to read it.

Rafe sat in one of the large leather chairs facing the desk and waited patiently while Katheryn read the article. It wasn't long before she saw the attorney was finally at the end. "So, do I throw in the towel?" Rafe asked forcing herself to be calm.

Katheryn leaned forward and threw the article on the desk. "No, Rafe. We're throwing down the gauntlet," she proclaimed.

"What?" Rafe asked confused. "What gauntlet?"

"The libel gauntlet," said Katheryn pragmatically. "You and I know that none of this is true or, if it hints at truth, it has been distorted to do harm to you. I'll call the judge today and let him know about this and that we're filing a lawsuit. We'll make a motion to suppress so this can't be discussed or used at the injunction hearing since we're claiming libel."

"It's not libel if their source is the person who said those things happened to them, and they maintain those things are true," said Rafe sadly.

"You really think Eden said those things?"

"She did say those things," said Rafe with a frustrated sigh. "She didn't want to use the donor sperm."

"But she changed her mind and was inseminated by her own hand," Katheryn reminded her. "Rafe, if she said something about her initial apprehension, it looks like someone else took it out of context and has made it sound like she was forced to do something against her will. Do you believe she was inseminated against her will, meaning that she felt she had no choice and felt she had to use it on herself?"

"I just don't know what to believe anymore," Rafe said with apprehension. "I don't want to think she felt that way. It wasn't my intent to make her feel like she had no choice. We talked about this, we did," Rafe insisted sadly, "but she told me she didn't remember talking about it specifically."

"I'll settle it today," Katheryn contended. "I'll draw up an affidavit she can sign refuting the statements in the article. She's worried you won't come home. She said she would sign anything you wanted her to sign. She said things were going well until this article."

"She did?" Rafe laughed bitterly. "She really thinks things are going well? Then why the hell are these things still happening? I can't take any more. My whole life may be ruined with this article."

"I'm going to take care of it, Rafe," Katheryn swore. "Do I have your permission to take whatever legal action I deem appropriate?"

"Do I have a choice?" Rafe asked defeated and threw up her hands.

Katheryn watched her client's reaction and knew this was the time she had to disclose the information she had received from Eden. She just hoped it wasn't too late. She looked at Rafe and took a breath to focus.

"Rafe, I've received some information from a reliable source that affects your case," she said somberly, "possibly with both cases, as I think they're linked. Unfortunately, I have to be careful about what I tell you so I can protect my source." She paused so Rafe could take in in her words. "If I use this information, the federal government may have to be brought in, and you will lose some privacy. I think the group that filed the injunction, the Stewards to the Protection of the Innocence and Morals of Youths are involved in more situations like yours, and I think they got your information through the internet and by getting inside one or more of your computers."

"What?" Rafe exclaimed appalled. "When did you find out about this?"

"Not recently," admitted Katheryn. "I've suspected for a while, but I had to convince the source to allow me to go forward before I could talk to you. I have their consent now if you would like to go in this direction."

"Of course, do it," insisted Rafe. "I can't allow anyone else to go through this hell. I'll talk to whoever I need to talk with."

"They may want to take all of your computers for analysis," Katheryn revealed, "including Eden's since she is your ex-partner and current girlfriend."

"You'll have to ask Eden about her computer," said Rafe surly. "I don't think she's my girlfriend or anything anymore. I think she'll be leaving me soon and, whether or not this injunction is upheld, Bronte will be gone too."

"Rafe, you do know she isn't fighting the adoption. She made it clear in front of me that she wants to fight the injunction, and she wants you to adopt," Katheryn reminded her.

Rafe just looked at Katheryn and swallowed back her anger. "I've heard her threaten to stop the adoption more times than her promise to have it go through. I really... I just don't know what to believe anymore or which of the things she's said carries the most weight. She told whoever wrote the article that she never wanted the adoption."

"That's not the impression I got when I talked to her," said Katheryn concerned.

"Really? Make her sign an affidavit for that too then," Rafe snapped.

"She signed the cohabitation agreement," Katheryn reminded her. "Is that why you weighted it so it would be easy for her to leave and get out of the agreement?"

Rafe just looked at her silently as she held back her emotions.

"I think you're just upset and you need to go home and talk to her," suggested Katheryn. "Don't let this article break you down, Rafe. I'm going to do my best for you."

"Do you think I'll still have a job Monday?" Rafe asked. "If I lose it, you'll have a client who won't look good for either of your cases. I'm not sure I want to pay you for something I'm going to lose anyway."

"I'll warn them Monday of the consequences of firing you over a libelous article." Katheryn smiled confidently choosing not to delve into the possibility Rafe would fire her from the case. She knew Rafe was upset and was most likely talking out of hand. They had come too far on the case and too close to a court date to quit now. "Who's your boss?"

"The CCAD President, Clarice Biggalow," answered Rafe.

Katheryn wrote the name on her pad. She didn't know why Rafe was so concerned with her job because it wasn't like she needed to work. "If you do lose this job, it won't hurt the case," she reminded her. "Since you inherited," she stopped herself at the look on Rafe's face. It was a cross between hurt and anger. "What?" she asked.

"I really like what I'm doing at the school," she said evenly. "I don't want anything else taken from me. I don't do it for the money. Originally, I got this job to keep me busy and close to home for Bronte. But it's turned into more for me. It's the only stable thing I feel like I have right now, and I don't want to lose it."

"Okay, here's what I need you to do," said Katheryn as she stood up and started around her desk. "Go home, talk to Eden, relax, and let me take care of this. It's what you pay me for. I'll set up an appointment with Eden in the morning and get the affidavits for her to sign."

"What about the rest?" Rafe asked. "The predator stuff and the agenda and corrupting souls," she shook her head, "and then the corrupt business deals and other accusations. I can't put that kind of shadow over my career or mine and my father's businesses. I'm under contract to not damage the companies in any way per the sales transfer agreements."

"Well, you don't have any lawsuits against you for those things, so that's a plus," said Katheryn positively. Rafe looked at her unamused. "Sorry," she said. "Those are opinions of people who know of you but don't know you. You and I both know all your business dealings were legal and above board. If you want to answer those things, we can, but let's see what happens Monday first. Our priority is the adoption. If any actual harm is done to the businesses, we will handle that matter separately, and we'll sue them all out of existence."

"Fine," said Rafe her head beginning to throb with more pain from holding in her anger. "Call me and keep me updated."

19

RIDING IN SILENCE, Rafe Salvaggio pressed her hand to her temple to try to stem her headache. Abby was at the wheel again, and it was surprising she was able to hold in her opinion on the situation all the way home. They pulled into the driveway, and Rafe just sat there and didn't get out. She could tell Abby was getting impatient by the way she shifted in her seat, but she was not ready to face Eden yet.

Finally, she looked at Abby. "Eden can take you back to your car if she's home, or maybe Flynn or Jude," she said evenly. "Thanks for going with me and driving me home. I just wish a lawsuit could take my anger and hurt away."

"Maybe this will help," said Abby and held up a notepad she had pilfered from Katheryn's house. "I wrote an article while I waited. Do you want to read it?"

"Okay." Rafe sighed as she took the pad from Abby and read the draft of her article. "No, Abby, you can't attack Eden like this. It'll give them fuel," she said as she read. "And you can't go into detail about Bronte or our personal life. You have to be careful." She handed the notepad back to her.

"When I'm careful, it sounds like fluff!" said Abby flustered.

"Then I guess you can't write the article," said Rafe firmly.

"I'll think about it today and make some revisions," she countered. They got out of the car and walked to the house. "I hope she's not here. I'm really pissed at her," said Abby with a scowl.

"She lives here now, and remember," said Rafe looking at her hard, "you promised to keep your mouth shut."

"I know, I know," said Abby, and she stopped on the stairs agitated. "I can't go in," she said upset. "I'm going next door to wait for Jude. I'll see you later, Rafe."

Rafe watched her walk away. "Thanks again, Abby," she called then walked into the house. She looked around for Eden, finding she wasn't there. Rafe didn't know if she should feel sad or relieved.

20

AFTER MEETING WITH Katheryn, taking Bronte to Letty, and stopping by the store, Eden Kingsley walked in the door with a couple of grocery bags, deposited them in the kitchen, and then went to look for Rafe. She found her out on the patio asleep in a lounger with a half-empty bottle of scotch and a bucket of ice. She sighed and took the glass out of her hand then took everything inside. She put the groceries away and made some sandwiches. She took the sandwiches along with some ice tea to the patio and set them on the small table next to the lounger. She sat on the edge of the lounger next to Rafe and reached out to touch her lightly.

"Rafe," she said softly. "Rafe, wake up." Rafe opened her eyes and looked at Eden then closed them again. "Wake up please," she implored gently.

Her emotions numbed by pain, her temper anesthetized by the alcohol, and in her drowsiness, Rafe opened her eyes and looked at Eden. "Where's Bronte?" she asked then closed her eyes.

"She's staying the night with Letty," said Eden. "I barely got away from everyone, especially Letty, over the article," she said anxiously. "I spent a long time listening to her tell me I better not be 'fucking' with you. I can't believe someone would publish something like that about us. Have you eaten anything?"

"I had a Slurpee," Rafe mumbled with her eyes still closed.

"A Slurpee?" Eden frowned and shook her head. "I made you a sandwich. Will you wake up and eat it? After all that scotch, I think you may need it."

Rafe waved her away. "You don't have to wait on me or make me food," she said sullenly. "You're not my slave."

"I know," Eden said annoyed. "I did it because I wanted to, and because I care about you."

Rafe opened her eyes and looked at Eden with emptiness in her eyes. "I may lose my job tomorrow."

"It'll be okay," Eden reassured her. "I talked to Katheryn, and I'm going to see her again in the morning. I don't think you'll lose your job, and if you do, we'll still be okay," Eden said confidently. Rafe gave a bitter laugh. "What?"

"Just thinking about what things will be like with me without a job," she said impassively.

"If that happens, there are a lot of things you can do," Eden assured her. "You have a lot of passion and drive. I have faith in you."

Rafe turned her head away and sighed. "Great, so I'll be passionately unemployed." She could feel her head begin to throb again and felt a weight pressing down on her chest. "I don't think you should be with me if I don't have a job."

"What's that supposed to mean?" Eden asked anxiously.

"It means I can't do what you did after you quit your job," explained Rafe remembering how Eden was angry with her all the time back then. She also remembered Jake's suggestion of how it was possible everything going on back then was the reason her relationship with Eden had fallen apart. "I'm no good without a job or project. I've worked since I was thirteen in my father's business. I've always supported myself since I moved out of my father's house and started my company back in college."

Rafe remembered the deal she made with her father to start the restoration business. The year she started her master program, he gave her startup money, but then she had to stop using his money for school and living. Luckily, she already had an account with money in it she could use for school. She had either earned or been gifted the money in her account, so she was able to use it as needed, and her father couldn't touch it. His only concession was the apartment in Milano she lived in, but she had to manage the property for him. The first few years of the business was like a competition on how hard he could make her work. She had to balance carefully between him, as co-CEO for the company, buying properties to restore, and her education and its demands on her time with classes and teaching in both Italy and France. She met every challenge, though, and made a lot of money. It felt good to win against him. Now she didn't know what she would do without the stability of work and something to do.

"I'm pretty sure you can't handle being the only one with a job with me staying home all the time. I wanted to slow down because of what happened to us when I was working all the time, but not stop completely."

"There were other things going on besides your working all the time back then," insisted Eden, unsure why she was bringing things up from back then now.

"There are other things going on now too," said Rafe tersely. "I'm not cut out for staying home. I can't cook, I don't do house cleaning, I barely do my own laundry or pick up my dry cleaning." She paused to reign in her frustration. "I write checks. I manage people who do all of those things for me while I'm off being passionate about other things."

"I know." Eden laughed softly.

Rafe closed her eyes again not liking the fact Eden was amused with her situation. "If I don't have a job, you'll expect all of those things from me. Then when I fail, you'll..." she did not finish the thought.

"What?" asked Eden. "Leave? Rafe, I won't leave you because you don't do the laundry."

"Maybe." Rafe shrugged, certain she was right. There were other reasons she would leave but she would only use them when it would hurt the most. It would be better if Eden left because of an excuse she gave her, one where she could maintain control. "But you were angry all the time about everything when you stayed home. I couldn't do anything right," she looked sadly at Eden. "Frankly, when you're in charge of the house, it's scary." She sighed as she looked away. "This situation is one reason why we needed the cohabitation agreement," she said. "If I'm fired, and I don't find a job in the time allotted, you and Bronte will have to move and take the dissolution of agreement money. Maybe you should just go now," she suggested and waved her away.

"I'm not leaving," insisted Eden unsettled by Rafe's lack of anger or emotion. "Just so you know... I have been living on my own for a while, and I've got the hang of how things work. I was scared back then, Rafe. I never expected to be the one who took on everything while I stayed home on top of going to fertilization treatments and doctors' appointments while you were gone all over the world. I was overwhelmed. I had no idea all the things you did for us or what I was taking on. You made it look easy, but it wasn't easy at all. I was angry with more than you being gone or how you were spending money. Those things were just easier to use against you then. I'm sorry I was angry for so long."

"I still have no idea why you were so angry with me then," said Rafe softly. "I just wanted to make you happy, and I thought you were telling me you wanted me home more. That's why I sold everything... to be with you and Bronte."

Eden looked away as guilt ran through her. "I'm sorry, babe. I really am." She looked up at her again. "I realize now it was very hard for you to give up your father's business and then walk out of your own with no planned direction." She took a breath to steady herself. "I was just so," she paused, "so messed up and confused back then. Even I don't really know why I did a lot of things. I'm trying to figure things out, though. I really am working hard to be able to talk to you about all those things."

Rafe closed her eyes again and didn't respond. After a long silence, she looked at Eden again. "Did I really trick you into loving me? Did I prey on you and keep you with me all those years against your will?" she asked calmly.

"What? Trick me?" Eden shook her head. "Babe, you definitely didn't trick me. I was scared after the first time we kissed, but then I realized I shouldn't be because I felt something I had never felt before—or since. I was falling in love with you. I'm the one who practically attacked you, remember?

I could have just never called you again. But I really wanted to see you. I'm not as innocent as you try to make me seem."

"You were innocent," Rafe said unemotionally. "I was doing everything I could since I laid eyes on you to make you see me and want me." After a short silence, Rafe continued, "Do you really think I'm all of those things you said about me in the article? Controlling, emotionally abusive, self-involved, and domineering?"

"You can be all of those things sometimes," Eden said hesitantly. "You're definitely controlling. Just look at what you did yesterday."

"I didn't control anyone," said Rafe irritated. "They were paid well."

"Rafe, that was your tool to control them to get what you wanted," Eden pointed out amused. "Just think about it, you got the cleaning crew to work on a Sunday."

"They were happy to do it," Rafe insisted.

"Well," said Eden as she touched Rafe's hair, "you're also very good at making people feel good about being controlled."

"But not you," Rafe retorted as she pushed Eden's hand away from her. "Do I really control you?"

"Oh god, Rafe." Eden laughed anxiously. "You control just about everything and everyone. You planned things without me, you changed plans without telling me, you decided where we went on vacations, and when we would go, you made lists and itineraries for everything," she said animatedly. "Yes, you did control me. I really didn't mind because it was easier to just let you handle things, but after you," she hesitated, "did what you did, everything about you made me angry."

Rafe sighed at the reminder of her crime again. "Well, what about now?"

"Now, you're still very controlling," Eden confirmed. "But you have changed. Now you can let someone else be in charge. And now, I know I can actually take charge when I need to," she said releasing a short laugh trying to be positive. "I think it's painful for you, though. You let me do the dinner party on my own, and you didn't drive Abby completely mad when she was in charge of her dinner party."

"How am I," Rafe started uncertainly, "emotionally abusive and domineering? I already know I'm a self-involved asshole," she said dryly. "I learned that the hard way."

Eden looked at Rafe, uncomfortable with the question. "Sit up and eat your sandwich," she said not wanting to argue.

Rafe sat up carefully and put her hand to her spinning head. "Dizzy," she mumbled. She looked at the sandwich Eden made her and picked it up. "Thank you," she said and looked at Eden. "Are you going to tell me?"

"Maybe emotionally abusive is too harsh," she admitted apprehensively. "I know I told you one of the reasons I left and was unsure was because I thought I needed to be with a man. I know now it was a mistake. But now I think what I really needed was to find 'me.' My world was in turmoil, and I felt lost, and really just felt disregarded sometimes, and the affair," she exhaled heavily, "it compounded those feelings."

Rafe frowned. It was yet another reminder of her transgression, and she was confused how anything Eden said had to do with the accusation of being emotionally abusive or domineering.

Eden saw Rafe's confused look and continued. "One example of something that made me feel disregarded was how you would walk in the door and then vent and rage about everything. I never got to tell you about my day and what happened. It was like what happened in your day was much more important than mine. When I tried to tell you how I felt, it seemed like you always had something else on your mind, or you would get a phone call you had to take and then I was forgotten. It seemed like I was always second. I think it's why I was spending so much time with Abby and online back then. I could say all the things to them because you didn't seem to have time to listen to me."

Rafe took a drink, and then sat it back down beside the sandwich she had only taken one bite from. "I didn't realize..." she said sadly because she always thought she had put Eden first. It was why she worked so hard back then. To make sure she and the baby they were working so hard to have would have everything.

What Rafe remembered from then was coming home to silence or unreasonable complaints. She knew Eden was having anxiety problems, and she thought the only way to keep her calm was not to be there to upset her sometimes. Rafe knew she would try to talk to Eden about work, but didn't know it was so hard for her to hear about what was going on with the company at the time. Everything at her company, good and bad, affected Eden too, financially and personally.

"You were always the only person I could talk to and say what I really thought," said Rafe softly. "I thought you wanted me to talk to you about the company. You always gave me good advice and could calm me down. You were like my after work drink, I guess." She shook her head. "That's sad. I don't want to use you like that. I didn't know you wanted to tell me about your day. I'm sorry."

"Just so you know," said Eden, "when you decided to give me your full attention, I was in heaven." She smiled at her. "Just like you've been doing lately." She laughed at the feeling of fullness she had in her heart now and the knowledge she was where she belonged. "Having the full, undistracted attention of Rafe Salvaggio is like going to the fair in the spring. Everything smells good, everything tastes better, the colors are brighter, excitement is all around, and you don't ever want to leave."

Leaning back in her lounger, Rafe wasn't responding or smiling like Eden hoped she would.

"What about the domineering part?" Rafe asked evenly wondering if Eden would leave her again if she couldn't keep up with giving her all the attention she seemed to need.

"You know you are," Eden said with a slightly nervous laugh.

"But did I really force you to..." Rafe looked at Eden grimly, "to use the donor, to use Gabri's sperm?"

Shaking her head, Eden ran her hands over her face and through her hair anxiously. "No, definitely no," she said. "It was my decision. I knew the decision would make you happy, but I didn't just do it for that."

"You said you didn't want to, and it seems now like you changed your mind very quickly," Rafe said unemotionally. "Why the sudden change of heart?"

"The more I thought about it, the more I couldn't believe I was so afraid," Eden said reassuringly. "My fear about the donor sperm coming from a donor you knew personally but one I didn't know, was just," she looked up to find her words, "just me not thinking clearly."

The memory of Rafe and Gabri together, and how they looked like a pair of beautiful angels who had come down to visit earth and were speaking with each other in a language she literally didn't understand, filled her mind. She remembered how she felt like an outsider.

"It wasn't like picking from the donor catalog where I could read all the stats and have a sort of distance," Eden continued. "You knew him, and I didn't. I didn't know anything about him except what you told me. It just hit me this was a real person who I knew nothing about, and I guess it suddenly became real," she explained as she lost the fight to control her tears. "When you told me he had agreed to be the donor and you..." she hesitated, "you just made the decision without me, I felt trapped. Then I asked myself, what if you were a man, would I have the same feelings about not having a choice about your sperm? My answer was no. I wouldn't be scared at all because I love you. So I realized you picking the donor without me shouldn't matter at all as long as we would have a happy and healthy baby together. And we did." She smiled through her tears.

"We did," Rafe nodded very calmly. She wasn't sure she liked how Eden had to think of her as a man before she was okay with using Gabri's sperm. "Well, I'm sorry I'm not a man," she said evenly but unable to hide the dripping sarcasm.

Eden looked up at her with a frown and wiped her eyes. "That's not what I meant. I don't want or need you to be a man," Eden said softly. "I love you, Rafe." She looked at Rafe worried about how unnervingly calm she was being.

"Who did you tell all of those things to?" she asked without emotion. "Why would you say those things if you're telling me now they aren't true, or really that bad?"

"I..." she started hesitantly, "I really don't remember who I told. I was probably just angry when I was talking about you," she said wishing she had never met Jake. "But I never said you forced me to do anything," she said desperately. "Whoever I said things to they took my words and twisted them."

"So you're still angry with me, and you're talking about it to..." she looked up doubtfully, "whoever—to strangers you don't remember. What is it that keeps you with me? Stockholm syndrome or something?"

"Rafe, don't," Eden said shaking her head. "I'm not your prisoner or here against my will. I love you and want to be with you. I haven't said those things about you for a long time. It had to be someone I talked to months and months ago," she said as she waved the time away. "I'm not angry with you."

"You can tell me if you don't really want me to adopt Bronte," she said sadly. "I don't want to drag her through court and put her at risk. I'll do whatever you want."

Eden looked up as she ran her hands through her hair anxiously. "I'm not fighting the adoption. I made a promise to you, and I'm keeping it. I know I may have said things when I was with..." she stopped not wanting to say Jake's name out loud. "I said things in anger and fear I should never have said. I'm sorry. I absolutely want the adoption to go through."

Rafe looked up at Eden desolately. "When are you going to tell me the things you're keeping from me?" she asked softly.

'I—" Eden stopped. "Soon. I'm still working on things. I still need you to give me a little more time and patience." She could see Rafe wasn't happy with her answer. "I love you," she said again. Rafe didn't respond, and Eden swallowed nervously. "I've made a new rule," she announced trying to sound positive.

"You what?" asked Rafe as she looked at her crossly.

"I've made a new rule," Eden repeated. "I don't think it's fair only you can make the rules."

"Eden." Rafe pinched the bridge of her nose, shook her head, and then continued, "I'm not making rules to just—" She was cut off.

"Just listen to my rule," Eden interrupted her. She watched as Rafe looked at her then looked away. "The rule is if my bedroom door is open you can come in if you want. But," she paused, "if you come in, you have to stay all night." Rafe didn't look at her or respond. "Okay?"

"Okay, I guess," Rafe said impassively, thinking it meant she might not be going in Eden's room anytime soon.

"You believe I love you, don't you?" asked Eden anxiously.

Rafe hesitated. "I want to."

"You always say that." Eden took a deep breath and delivered her challenge. "I want you to think about it tonight," she said calmly. "If you believe me," she paused, "I want you to come into my room. If you don't yet, I'll understand, and you can go to your own room. I just need to know."

21

IT WAS MIDNIGHT. Eden Kingsley woke up and looked at her clock. Rafe hadn't come into her room. She sighed and got out of bed. She went to Rafe's room and was surprised when the door was open. She looked inside and saw she wasn't there. She walked through the house to see if Rafe was still awake somewhere. She finally found her in Bronte's room asleep on her new sleigh bed. Eden pulled up the sheet and climbed in beside her. She touched Rafe's warm face and pushed back a dark curl damp from the sweat along her hairline.

"Rafe," she said softly and kissed her warm temple, "you're so warm." She could see Rafe was troubled in her dreams. She kissed her forehead lightly and looked into her eyes when she opened them. "Leave it to you to find a loophole," she whispered.

"Neutral territory," Rafe mumbled with a frown and couldn't control the shiver that ran through her. She then closed her eyes with dread.

"You drive me mad, you know," Eden said softly and wrapped her arms around Rafe's warm body hoping to reassure her things would be okay.

Rafe turned her face away. "Go to sleep."

22

MONDAY MORNING LIGHT shined through the window and found Rafe Salvaggio in her own room and bed again. She woke up, still tired from lack of sleep, worried about what the day would bring. She showered then dressed carefully in her favorite white power suit in preparation for being fired. She hoped the pure and heroic color would help soothe flaring tempers. She was still numb from the article and its implications. Purely out of emotional self-preservation, she was keeping her distance from Eden.

Eden was already up and in the kitchen after turning off the alarm and opening the patio doors. She had breakfast on the table and poured coffee for Rafe and tea for herself. She was upset because, after she had fallen asleep in Bronte's bed sometime in the night, Rafe had gone into her own room. She wasn't sure what else to do except try to reassure Rafe and try to help her feel better.

She looked up and saw Rafe as she walked in the kitchen. "Wow! You look great." She smiled trying to be positive and supportive, which wasn't hard. She admired the contrast of Rafe's white suit against her swarthy skin and black hair. She looked like an angel with eyes burning with angry gray-blue fire.

"Well, I at least want to look good if I'm being fired," said Rafe absently and a bit harshly. "Thanks for making the coffee," she said softly trying to make up for her tone.

"No problem," Eden said trying to be upbeat. As she stirred honey into her tea, the doorbell rang. "I'll get it." She smiled when she opened the door. "Hey, Abby."

"Is Rafe still here?" asked Abby coldly as she pushed past Eden and walked inside.

"She's in the kitchen," Eden answered shocked at Abby's attitude. She closed the door and followed her to the kitchen.

"Rafe, I'm glad I caught you," said Abby all business as she entered the kitchen. "I just wanted you to know I did it. I wrote the article and showed it to Katheryn yesterday, and she said it was fine. I got it in just in time. It's not in L. A. Magazine. It's in the L. A. Perspective," she said quickly. "I know it's more of an opinion rag, but it's popular, and they were really excited to buy it."

"What article?" Eden asked confused.

"Abby, I wish you would have talked to me first," said Rafe annoyed.

"I had to make deadline," she said as she pulled out a copy of the paper. "Here's your copy."

"Shit," said Rafe angrily as she snatched the paper from her. "I'm already going to be fired this morning. I don't need more problems." She sat down at the table with her coffee and read Abby's article.

Dean Rafe Salvaggio: Turning on the Light
By Abigale Van Falkov

Wake up, people! Turn on the light and step out of the darkness! This is not the dark ages! Recently a truly offensive article was written and published in the L. A. Light (I had never heard of it before either) about the new, and youngest, Dean of Arts at the California Conservatory for Art and Design, Dean Rafe Salvaggio.

That article set out to crucify her for being a strong, independent and opinioned lesbian, things she has never hidden nor denied since moving to this community many years ago. In the article, they have called for Dean Salvaggio's dismissal at CCAD as well as a review and audit of her fundraising accounts to show how she was able to raise over one million dollars for her department. The article implied Dean Salvaggio thinks she is some sort of demi-god who is out to steal the job of Satan and corrupt the souls of the innocent and the weak-minded. (That is you, dear reader, by the way—they really have nerve saying that about you.) I'm writing this article to share the truth, and I'm using my real name, unlike 'M. Land' who no one claims to be or to know.

Take a look at the picture of Dean Salvaggio on this page. I see you finally ripped your eyes away to continue reading. You have to admit she is one of the most beautiful women you have ever seen, and it doesn't matter if you're straight or gay or a man or woman, people are drawn to beauty. But there is more to her than physical beauty. She is driven, aggressive, and confident. Traits that in a straight white male are exalted, but in Dean Salvaggio, they have been vilified. She used those traits to help her raise money for her department so the students and faculty would have the best facilities in the state and maybe the country.

Because of her efforts, more students will attend CCAD, and this will benefit our community by bringing in more consumers and fresh ideas so we can grow. She worked hard to win the grants and donations. They didn't just give them to her because she's beautiful. She spends hundreds of hours researching and writing grant proposals and creating and making presentations. In other words, she does her job, and she does it well.

Let's talk about this so-called agenda. Since when did wanting to listen to new ideas and learn about ourselves become unpatriotic? That's what America is all about, freedoms. If it weren't, the offensive article about Dean Salvaggio wouldn't have even been published. It's called freedom of the press. So why are those people using this freedom to take away the freedom of another? (Aren't they the moral watchdogs?—Sarcasm intended.) They need to watch out, or they may have to warn everyone against themselves.

That article was more offensive than any of the art they claim is part of Dean Salvaggio's 'agenda' to corrupt the community. Remember, people, Dean Salvaggio didn't create the art, but she understands it is an important human expression shared to create understanding and tolerance for humanity—even when someone is paying a debt to society and trying to become a productive citizen.

I know for a fact Dean Salvaggio realizes some of the art out there is offensive to some people, including herself, but to suppress or censor an artist's freedom of expression is not, and has never been, her policy. For this, she deserves credit and respect by the art community and by all those who cherish the freedoms given to us by our constitution. There is no agenda corrupt or otherwise. Let's look at Dean Salvaggio's quote again:

"Art cannot be judged by any one person or one group's moral compass; it is ever changing and growing through the human experience. Whether the experience is divine or earthly to the person who views it is subjective. However, by looking at art for art's sake without judgment or preconceived ideas, we can learn so much about humanity and ourselves."

I'm not really into art, but it sounds like she's just saying everyone is entitled to his or her own opinion, and we should give new ideas a chance, even if, in the end, we decide they aren't ones we particularly want to embrace. I can live with that. Can you, reader?

As for her god-like walk through campus, I'd say her students understand this idea of freedom of expression as she has allowed them to explore ideas others may have oppressed. For this, they respect and admire her. They show it to her by their willingness to learn and be part of what she is trying to teach them. If it is god-like to have people want to help and be part of your programs and projects, then we have many gods in America. I for one will be worshiping at Dean Salvaggio's feet because I know when she is involved in a project, it will be nothing less than divine, and our community will be better for her commitment and involvement.

The most offensive part of the article in question was the attack on Dean Salvaggio's personal life. I am not sure where the author got his/her information, but it is so far from the truth, I'd be surprised if a lawsuit isn't filed against them. It is true and public information Dean Salvaggio is seeking a second-parent adoption for her and her partner's child. I have seen Dean Salvaggio with the child, and she is a wonderful parent. She is dedicated and caring and would lay her life down for the child. What mother wouldn't? She has been part of the child's life from the years of planning and preparing for the conception to the current legal proceedings. Not granting the adoption would be a travesty. As far as the conception and the accusation Dean Salvaggio coerced her partner into it, this is also a tragic lie. They discussed every detail, planned for years, and it was ultimately up to her partner whether or not to use the donor sperm in question. They filed for the second-parent adoption together, and they both want it approved. They are both proud of their child and have no issues or regrets about her conception or birth.

Like all couples, Dean Salvaggio and her partner had problems, and like all people, Dean Salvaggio and her partner have their shortcomings. They were in a four and a half year relationship, and they were tried and tested.

While they were apart, they both became involved with people who they thought would be right for them or they just dated. Dean Salvaggio was accused of being a predator, but I can assure you (look at the picture again) that her prey had no problem with being captured, and her influence or power just makes her more desirable. As far as her being a soul-stealing wildling—well, who wouldn't want a wildling lover? I mean come on, think about it. Things like that are said about people out of experience, desire for the experience, or a little bit of envy. What do the ladies (or men) call you?

Currently, Dean Salvaggio and her partner are working on getting their lives back to a place where they can be happy. Isn't that all we can hope for, a little happiness? Dean Salvaggio and her partner's decision to work on their relationship again (i.e., the seduction at The Kiki Bistro—I don't mind giving out a little free advertising) was not one-sided. They both knew what they were doing; they are adults. And since when is it a bad thing to be seduced by someone you love? Would you think differently if Dean Salvaggio were a man going after a woman? If you would, you need to get out more and open your mind. Couples break up and get back together all the time. They say hurtful things about each other in anger, some true, some perceived, and Dean Salvaggio and her partner are no different. Words said when in pain, should never be used as fodder by others to crucify and vilify another person for any reason. We can all only hope they make it through this new roadblock and find happiness in their love and respect for each other.

So I say, go ahead and do your audit and review. You'll find Dean Salvaggio's ethical standards are just as high, if not higher, as the next persons, and there is no wrongdoing, morally or otherwise. The students at CCAD have not lost their souls to her. They know she has given them the gift of freedom to see and think for themselves.

Oh, just a side note, when you find out all of this is unfounded and a waste of good paper and Dean Salvaggio is exonerated, I suggest you give her a new title: Maestro Salvaggio or Goddess Salvaggio, or—well, you get the picture.

Dean Salvaggio is not harming our youth, our community, or our country in any way; she is, in fact, doing her part to better them. I call on the community to show your support for Dean Salvaggio and the work she has done and the opportunities she has created. Call CCAD, call the mayor, call the governor, call your senator—but don't call the president because that would just be silly—or call me at the WLEZ station, and we can talk about this on air.

———————————————

Rafe looked up in horror and anger. "Damn it, Abby. You told them to call the school and the radio station!"

"Yeah," she said proudly. "I talked to one of the producers yesterday, and she's setting up a special line for me. We may combine my blog to some special segments. I'm on my way in now just in case she wants to do a special segment today. I know it's mostly fluff, but Katheryn made me take a lot out, like stuff about your business and Bronte, and with your restrictions...." She rolled her eyes and smirked toward Eden.

Rafe stood up and looked at Eden. "This is turning into a circus," she said and shoved the paper at Eden absently. "I am so fucking fired!" she said angrily and walked out the door, not understanding why Katheryn would encourage Abby.

Eden watched Rafe leave and was upset she had left without even a goodbye—or eating. She looked at the article then at Abby. "This is good, Abby. Thank you," she said sincerely. "I'm sure if Rafe weren't so upset, she'd say thank you too."

"She doesn't deserve this shit," said Abby as she looked at Eden coldly. "I did my best to make you look good to help Rafe because she didn't want me saying anything bad about you. Believe me," she fought to keep her temper in check, "that is more than you deserve." She turned and walked out the door, leaving Eden stunned her friend would say such things to her.

23

UPON ARRIVING AT the California Conservatory for Art and Design, Rafe Salvaggio pulled into her parking spot and got out of her car. It felt like the one place where she could come and feel like things were going well in her life instead of like someone was trying to snatch it away. When she first took the job as dean, she wasn't sure if she would be able to work behind a desk all day or deal with students. Her experience teaching as a requirement while getting her master's degrees and doctorates weren't the best because she was also trying to run her company at the same time. It worried her how she might be as frustrated and unhappy with a job as dean as she was as a student teacher. However, as she got to know the school, the teachers, and the students, she found it was nothing like her other experience. It seemed exciting and easy for her to do her job.

She enjoyed solving problems and helping teachers and students get the things they needed to enable them to enjoy their work and education. She even enjoyed teaching, just not the grading. She loved seeing all the advancements and strides the departments had made, and in turn, the growth of the students in their work and their educational experiences.

She hated how it was all being taken away from her, but she mostly hated knowing she was probably going to be fired. She had never been fired from a job, and it made her angry how, on top of fucking up her personal life, now Eden and Jake had to move on to her career and livelihood.

She straightened her clothes and grabbed her briefcase from the car, then started walking to the building. On the way, she saw her TA, Lexi, running up to her.

"Dean Salvaggio," called Lexi, "I've come to meet you and warn you."

"Warn me about what?" Rafe asked, then saw the problem as they approached the building. There was a large group of picketers marching in front of the building holding up signs demanding her dismissal and warning of her immorality. There were also several news crews filming the picketers. "Shit!"

"Don't worry. A bunch of us are here to get you through," Lexi called as she ran ahead to get other students and faculty.

"Hey, Dean Salvaggio," said Dalia as she came toward her. "Making the news again, I see."

"Professor Harris, I can't seem to outrun my apparent depraved reputation," she said grimly.

"Well, just come with me." Dalia laughed despite the seriousness of the situation, knowing that this was nothing compared to other protests she had attended in the past. She led Rafe across the campus toward a group of students and faculty. "We were going to sneak you in the back, but that entrance is being covered by picketers too right now. Even David is here to help us with his students. I think it's the first time he's ever participated in anything but his sculpture class. Get in the middle of the group, and we'll power you through."

Rafe nervously looked at the angry crowd. "Take care of me, Dalia. The last time I was involved with a protest, I was sixteen and skipped school to hang out with my cousin Letty. We were almost arrested and thrown in a Bronx jail."

"I've talked to the officers," said Dalia confidently, "and they know you're coming. It's good to have friends in law enforcement," she added with a wink.

Rafe got into the middle of the large group of faculty and students. They moved forward and broke through the angry picketers who were shouting for her head as they tried to grab at or hit Rafe and the people helping her.

Adding to the pandemonium were the news reporters, who were shouting questions, and photographers and camera crews, who were trying to get shots of everything. The police kept a close eye on things and pulled away a few of the more violent picketers who were using their signs to pummel the charging group.

The group powered Rafe up to the building entrance and lost a few of the guards as they pushed through, but they made it past the picketers. Rafe was rushed up the stairs, and they finally made it to the door.

Dalia worked to fix her hair and clothes as she laughed. "Well, you made it this far. I hope you can make it the rest of the way on your own. We're all pulling for you!"

"Thanks," said Rafe as she pulled herself back together. She looked at the group who had helped her as they took up all the space on the stairs and sidewalk below. "Thanks, everyone. I really appreciate your help and support," she told them all.

Dalia, still laughing with adrenalin, turned to the group. "Okay, guys. Let's show those protesters what we think!" she shouted.

The group, as one, fell to their knees and bowed to Rafe. "We worship you, oh, exalted Dean Salvaggio!" they chanted loudly. "We worship you! Dean Salvaggio!" They exalted her. "Dean Salvaggio!" Cameras rolled and clicked, and the news crews captured the moment.

Laughing with relief for the first time since she read the article, Rafe pointed dramatically at the faculty members. "Instructors, back to work!" she shouted then pointed dramatically to the students. "Students, back to class! And if you don't have a class—go create!" The group jumped up, cheered, and laughed. Then they broke up, moving back down the stairs, disrupting the picketers as much as they possibly could. Rafe walked into the building as the press ran to get their newest story out.

Inside, Rafe took a deep breath and started her walk toward her office. She shook her head as she overheard the mutters of *soul-stealing Salvaggio* and *control freak* from the less supportive at the school, but she fixed a hubristic smile on her face and kept walking.

She made her way through the school and was close to her office when some of her students approached her. "Dean Salvaggio, I've brought you some coffee," said Mark. "We think you're great!"

"Thank you," Rafe said as she took the coffee.

"And here's a blueberry muffin," offered Tera. "We weren't sure what you liked, but everyone likes blueberry."

"Thanks," said Rafe as she took the bag with the muffin inside it. "I do like blueberry." She smiled hoping to reassure the students.

"Can we carry something for you, or do you need us to do anything for you?" asked Robbie as she followed her closely.

"I think I'm fine for now, Robbie," she said appreciatively as she made it to her office. "Leave your names with Brandy, and I'll let you know if I need you." She looked at Brandy who had a stack of papers on her desk. "I'm ready whenever you are." She straightened her posture then walked into her office and took off her jacket.

"I'll be right in," said Brandy and started to take the student names. When she had finished, she went into Rafe's office. "Okay, messages," she said as she started putting stacks on Rafe's desk. "This stack is news people, this stack is parents, this stack is good people, this stack is crazies, and this stack is President Biggalow."

Rafe sorted through the messages. "Fuck," she said under her breath and looked at Brandy. "Did they really say this shit to you?" Brandy nodded with disgust at the messages. Rafe handed them back to her. "Sort out the parents who want me dead from the ones who just want to hurt me," she said warily. "Get their addresses from the student files and send the ones who want me dead a letter thanking them for their concern and a CCAD bumper sticker. The ones who just want to hurt me get a pen. If you get any who support me," she smiled doubtfully, "send them a jacket. Ignore the crazies, unless they sound seriously violent. Put them on a list for the police. Make a list of the good people and give it to President Biggalow. Tell the news people they have to go through the public relations department for comments."

"Got it," said Brandy as she gathered everything. "President Biggalow wants to see you right away. Shall I just tell everyone else you're not in?"

"Yes." Rafe rubbed her temples as she sighed. "I really may not be in after I talk with Clarice."

"Well, I think you're a great boss," Brandy volunteered, "and they would be stupid to let you go."

"Thanks, Brandy." Rafe smiled despondently. "I know I'm probably not the easiest person to work for, and I do appreciate you, but Clarice 'the Beast' Biggalow may rip my head off today." She got up, put her jacket back on, and smoothed it down. "Okay, I'm ready."

"Good luck," said Brandy as she gave Rafe an unexpected hug.

"Thanks." Rafe shook her head and chuckled as she recovered from the hug, and then walked out and headed for Clarice's office.

24

THE SECRETARY WAVED Rafe Salvaggio into the CCAD president's office where she saw Clarice was on the phone. Rafe sat in the chair in front of her desk and waited patiently as she finished the call. Clarice hung up the phone and looked at Rafe with a troubled expression. "Rafe, I'm glad you made it through. I saw the antics of your students and some of the staff this morning. It's already all over the news and has apparently gone viral."

"Sorry," said Rafe with concern. "They were just showing their spirit and support. I hope you won't discipline them for helping me."

Clarice looked at her and pursed her lips, unhappy with the thought of taking disciplinary action against so many faculty and staff. Luckily, it wasn't something she needed to discuss with Dean Salvaggio. "As you might expect, I've had calls from everyone imaginable," she said somberly. "Including several of your former clients, who were quite determined you are being vilified. Others believe your department should be reviewed."

"I raised all my money ethically, Clarice," Rafe defended herself.

"I know you did," said Clarice grimly. "I was there at the Jackson-Goyer Foundation Grant presentations. I also met most of the donors when they toured the school with you. But the board wasn't there, and they've called a meeting to decide what to do."

"Should I be there?" asked Rafe thinking she might have the opportunity to talk with them.

"No, it'll be a closed meeting," said Clarice. "Don't worry," she said as she picked up a stack of messages. "All of these donors have threatened to withdraw their pledges or not give again if you're fired based on the article. Not to mention, your lawyer called to warn us if you're fired, a lawsuit will follow." She looked at Rafe and shook her head. "But don't get your hopes up too high. Just as many people have called with the opposite opinion."

"So, what am I supposed to do?"

"I've recommended to the board we give you a paid leave of absence until things can be sorted out and everyone calms down," Clarice revealed grimly.

"A leave of absence," Rafe repeated. "What about the Jackson-Goyer Grant party? What about the projects I'm working on?" she asked with frustration.

"The party is Friday, and I think you should still come," Clarice decreed. "You are the one who made it possible, after all. The projects you'll have to pass on to someone until we know what the board wants to do. Who do you recommend?"

"Ask Professor Harris first, then Professor Bach." Rafe sighed as she thought of all the projects and details to be passed along. "You may need them both, but Brandy has all the information."

Clarice got up and walked around her desk, and Rafe stood. "Rafe, I'll do my best for you, and hopefully, you'll get the chance to talk to the board," she said and shook Rafe's hand. "I still believe you're the best thing that's happened to this school in a long time."

"Thank you, Clarice," said Rafe evenly. "How long do you think this leave of absence will be?"

"It could be anywhere from a week to a few months," said Clarice, "depending on the direction the board wants to go."

25

A FEW HOURS later, Rafe Salvaggio had finished lining out her projects with Dalia and Brandy. As they watched, she put everything she needed to take home with her into her briefcase. She looked around her office for what may be the last time, then ran her hands through her hair and rubbed her temples.

She took a breath and resolved to walk out with her head held high.

She looked over at Dalia and smiled apprehensively. "Do you think the protesters are still out there or do you think they've taken a lunch break?"

Dalia laughed just enough to let Dean Salvaggio know her attempt at light heartedness was not missed. "Let me call Bobbie," she said then dialed her phone. "Bobbie, look outside and tell me what you see. Oh, really?" She twisted her lips at the news she was hearing. "Well, gather everyone at the back of the building, and we'll sneak Dean Salvaggio out that way. Ten minutes," she said then hung up and looked at Rafe. "She says it looks like they've taken the opportunity to hold a revival. She checked it out earlier, and there's some reverend speaking to the crowd. It may turn nasty if you go out the front entrance, but the back entrance is fairly clear. They'll meet us out back, and we'll get you to your car."

"I can't believe this is happening," groaned Rafe.

"Don't worry," said Dalia with a warm smile. "The board will see the light, and this whole thing will blow over before you know it. Then you'll be back here making things happen again."

"Thank you," said Rafe, hoping she was right. She knew not everyone understood, including Katheryn, but she had come to enjoy her job and the people. She hated losing what she felt was the last stable thing she felt she could count on. "Let's get out of here." She put on her jacket, picked up her briefcase and laptop, and then they headed out the door.

With the help of Dalia and a few students and faculty, Rafe Salvaggio made it out of the school and to her car without incident. The students had surrounded her casually and made her look like one of them, and then they just walked out the back door. Her students and even a couple of professors gave her a tearful goodbye, and they promised to help her as much as they could. Rafe had no idea so many people were supporting her and appreciated her.

She felt humbled.

26

IT WAS JUST before two o'clock when Rafe Salvaggio arrived home. When she walked into the house, she threw her briefcase in her office and then sat her laptop on the kitchen counter. After changing her clothes, she fixed herself a drink and took it and her laptop out to the patio. She opened her computer and composed an email.

TO: Dr.G_Noble@JohnsHopkins.org
FROM: RSalvaggio@ccad.edu
SUBJECT: I'm in the news again.
ATTACHMENTS: hands.jpg; Article1.pdf; Article2.pdf

Greer,

Things keep spinning further and further out of control and I'm not sure what to believe. There are so many things happening I don't know which way to turn anymore. Eden is telling me that the article 1, attached, was a surprise to her and she's telling me things I hope are true. But how did they get this personal information without her? She is the only one who could have said those things. She says her words were twisted. Is this part of her plan? The rest they could have found anywhere, and the quote was definitely the one I gave to the reporter I told you about. There were other things in the article I know I told the reporter that day too. I should have known she was trouble by her handshake. And Eden's reaction to her—I'm not sure if it was genuine anymore or if it was all part of her plan too. Maybe it was a bad idea to let her move back in after all.

Katheryn says the federal government may be getting involved in my case. I don't know if Eden knows about them. I may ask her tonight. To top everything off, I'm now on a leave of absence from my job because of the article. If she did plan this, Eden couldn't have done a better or more thorough job of fucking up my life. I'm just so numb from it all. I want to run to you and get away from all of this madness, but I know I have to see this through.

The court date for the injunction is next Tuesday, and I'll know if my dream is ending then. It's been about a week since I've heard anything from Jake, so either he's giving up, or he knows things are coming to an end. I'm so tired of finding out Jake has been telling me the truth and waiting for Eden to tell me whatever it is she's hiding. I'm tired of being angry, tired of hurting, and tired of playing what I consider a game. I'm at my breaking point. I can't take much more. I may be losing Bronte, Eden, my job, and who knows what else. I do love Eden, and I wanted to spend my life with her, but I'm just not sure if it's going to happen. I don't know what to believe anymore or what she really wants.

The only thing keeping me sane now is my photography. I've sent a new photo to you. It's from a study of hands I've been working on. I was inspired by you. I remember your hands being magnificent. I may be putting myself into your hands again soon, and I hope if that happens that you'll still have me, even if it's just as a friend. I miss you.

Your canvas,

Rafe

After sending the email, Rafe wasn't sure what to do next. She had never been in a situation where it seemed like everything in her life had just stopped. She took the last sip of her drink, and then she got up and carried everything inside. She made another drink and took it and her laptop into her room. There was another project she could work on for a while.

She went to her closet and got out a small box. The box used to hold stationary for her old company, but now it held other things. She took the box to her bed, opened the document on her computer, and began to make updates to it. It was not long before the stress from the past few days mixed with the scotch caught up with her, and she fell asleep.

27

AFTER HER UNPLANNED nap, Rafe Salvaggio had gone into the bathroom to wash the sweat from her face. The nap wasn't restful, and she woke with a reality as bad as her dreams. She changed her shirt and took her computer into the living room to check her email finding a message from Greer. She opened the email immediately hoping whatever was in it would make her feel better.

> REPLY
> TO: RSalvaggio@ccad.edu
> FROM: Dr.G_Noble@JohnsHopkins.org
> SUBJECT: RE: I'm in the news again.

> My sweet Rafe,
> I remember you telling me how you always get in trouble when you play games, and it sounds like you're in trouble. Life is much harder than any game, and your life is definitely not a game. I know you're afraid to do anything to jeopardize the injunction hearing, but if Eden is lying to you, it may be already decided. I hope for your sake she's telling you the truth and you don't lose your dream.
> The article was appalling, and I can see why you have the feelings you described. Abby is a good friend for defending you the way she did. I wish I could be there to help you. I'm sorry your job is in jeopardy. I know you love it, and it will be hard

for you to stay home. Just keep up your photography and get through the next week. Hopefully, everything will be fine.

I love your photo. I'm happy my hands were such an inspiration. I know I'll never forget yours. You are truly a Maestre! I would love nothing more than to take you and your heart into my hands for safekeeping, but let's not go down said path until you are absolutely sure you can live with a different dream.

I miss you too.

Your artist,

Greer

Rafe had just finished reading Greer's reply to her email for a second time and was just about to begin composing another email when the doorbell rang. Rafe got up to go answer the door, and when she opened it, she found Ephraim and Letty with Bronte. "Hey, B Girl!" Rafe smiled as the baby reached out to her and took Bronte from Ephraim. "I didn't realize it was five already. Was she a good girl? "

"Of course she was," Ephraim assured her with a smile. "We're a bit early."

"She's always a good girl," insisted Letty. She looked seriously at Rafe. "I need to talk to you."

"Okay, come in," she said worried something else had happened. She led them into the living room where they sat down as Rafe put Bronte on the floor and she toddled over to her toys. "What's up?"

"I don't like the article and what Eden said in it," said Letty angrily. "I told her yesterday what I thought of her. If she didn't want to have this baby, then why did she do it?" she asked in distress. "And if she thinks you're so terrible, why is she coming back around? You let her move back in, and now shit is starting again! I don't like it! I thought she was different now. But she's just like she was before. She's just like every other sorry ass shallow bitch out there trying to bring you down again."

"Letty," Rafe said sadly, placing her hand on Letty's arm to calm her, "she says the article isn't true, and she's signing affidavits denying she was forced into anything."

"She can sign any fucking thing she wants to sign!" Letty said with venom. "This shit is still out there, and she put it there! How can you just sit there and let her get away with saying things like that about you? How can you just let her hurt you again?"

"I talked to her last night," Rafe said distressed.

"And she what? She made up excuses like she told me?" asked Letty angrily. "It doesn't matter what her excuse is—she shouldn't be telling everybody your business like that. If that article makes you lose this baby, I'll kill her!"

"Letty, please," said Rafe trying to remain calm. "Katheryn is trying to stop it from being used at the hearing, and she's having Eden sign affidavits. I'm not sure what else I can do right now."

"You can tell her you're keeping this baby and kick her ass out!" she said hotly. "That's what you can do!"

"I can't do that," Rafe shook her head. "I can't do it to Bronte."

The front door opened, and Eden walked into the living room. "Hi, I'm home," she called happily. She saw the serious faces of everyone in the living room and lost her smile. "Is everything okay?"

Rafe looked at Letty with worry and then at Eden. "Everything's fine." She smiled weakly. "They're just bringing Bronte home."

"Everything is not fine!" said Letty as she stood up angrily. "I don't know why my cousin is keeping you around, but I'm warning you! You'd better not fuck with her life anymore!" she fumed. "She loves this baby, and so do I! She already missed a whole lot of time because of you and went through hell! If you don't want this baby, you can just leave her with us and get the hell out!"

Eden looked in shock at Rafe. "I-I...," was all she could get out.

"Letty, please," Rafe said quickly and looked at Ephraim. "Please, you should go."

"Screw you, Letty!" Eden shouted recovering from her shock. "I told you the article was a lie! I never said I didn't want my baby! I'm not leaving my baby with you or anyone else! She's my child! Mine!" she screamed and picked up Bronte then took her into her room.

"I'm warning you, bitch!" Letty yelled back as she started to follow Eden. "Don't fuck with my family! Don't fuck with Rafe's life again!"

"Letty, stop," growled Rafe as she held Letty back. "Don't do this, please." She seized her and hugged her. "Thank you, thank you for caring about Bronte and me so much. Please,

Letty, don't make a bad situation worse," she pleaded and released her. "Please."

"Rafe, I'm just so pissed, and I don't understand why you're not," said Letty shaking with barely controlled anger. "I remember what she did to you and how it affected you. I don't want to see you like that again. I can't watch you go through hell again and not do anything."

"I am upset," Rafe confessed. "There's just so much, and I'm so tired of it all," she said. "I feel like my life is being drained out of me every day."

"Oh, Cugina," Letty said as her anger deflated seeing the distress in Rafe and hugged her. "I'm so worried about you. It's like a bad dream come to life. Why are you letting this happen again? Why is she doing this to you?"

"Please," Rafe begged. "I have to keep it together just a little while longer. Don't make her want to leave me again."

Ephraim gently pulled Letty away from Rafe. "Come on, Letty. We should go."

"It's just not right!" said Letty her anger building again. "It's not right, Rafe!"

"You should go, please," she said as she pulled herself away. "Thank you for being here for me," she said and walked them to the front door, locking it behind them.

Rafe leaned against the door trying to control the swirl of emotions running through her. When she had herself under control and could be calm again, she walked to Eden's bedroom door and knocked softly. "Eden?" she called out. "Eden, are you okay?"

"Come in," Eden sobbed.

Rafe opened the door and saw Eden sitting on her bed holding Bronte and crying. "I'm sorry," she said as she sat next to her on the bed.

Eden looked at Rafe in misery through her tears. "I want my baby. I love my baby! I've never said I didn't want her," she said angrily.

"I know," Rafe reassured her and put her hand on Eden's shoulder to comfort her.

"How," she cried, "how can you stand it? You have these people writing things and saying things about you all the time. You just take it." Her voice caught as she looked at Rafe. "I can't, Rafe," she said desperately. "People were calling me things and talking behind my back and… and…," she stuttered then a new flood of tears broke from her eyes and ran down her cheeks. "People like Letty threatening to take my baby away," she sobbed, "our friends and other people I know. Even strangers are angry with me, calling me things, telling me to leave you or leave you alone. I can't face them," she said in misery. She couldn't tell Rafe about the people who offered to rescue her. She was afraid they were part of the Stewards. "I'm scared, I'm so scared." Sobbing and shaking, she turned away from Rafe and held Bronte close to herself protectively. "I won't let anyone take my baby! She's mine, she's my baby," she claimed defiantly in tears.

Hesitantly, Rafe put her hand gently on Eden's back not sure what to make of her words and actions. "I'm sorry you had a bad day," she whispered as a feeling of numbness consumed her.

28

RAFE SALVAGGIO WAS spending the first full day of her leave of absence from the school alone by the pool. She had asked Eden to stay home with her, but Eden insisted she had to go back to work no matter how upset she was by the things that happened yesterday. She claimed she had too much work to do, and she didn't want to be intimidated by anyone.

To Rafe, it seemed like Eden was just determined not to stay home and spend any more time than necessary in her presence. To add to their problems, Eden was now also upset with Letty. Rafe tried to tell Eden Letty was just reacting to the article like everyone else, and she would talk to her, but Eden wasn't in the mood to listen. Eden was also angry because Rafe didn't sleep in her room last night, but Rafe just couldn't bring herself to do it. *It most likely means she's going to spend time with Jake*, Rafe thought, because she probably really just wanted to be with him anyway. Rafe figured, for all she knew, Jake was meeting Eden at work or something and was why she was so determined to leave the house.

Ephraim came by and picked up Bronte soon after Eden left. Rafe was supposed to call and tell him not to come because Eden was angry at Letty, but she forgot to call and make arrangements with Lydia. So she sent her with Ephraim since he was already there. He took her to day school, said Letty would pick her up after work, and they should call when they were ready for them to bring her home. She didn't mention to him how Eden was feeling about Letty.

Rafe spent most of the morning organizing her negatives and photographs. She also made a list of things she would need to set up a basic home darkroom and ordered them from an online supplier since she wouldn't be able to use the one at the school for a while. She called to check on the projects at school, and everything was fine with them.

Finally, she ran out of things to keep herself busy. She planned to go out and take photographs after lunch, but after she sat down, the chaos of her life crashed into her mind, and suddenly, she couldn't eat. Instead, she sat by the pool and coated the turmoil with a steady supply of alcohol while she listened, off and on, to the recording she made the night she brought Eden home for the first time. She finally gave up listening to the sounds of static, unsure if the things she heard were really there or in her imagination as she drank. Soon the numbness had set in, and it was fine with Rafe as she stared at the nothingness in front of her. She heard the back gate click closed and knew someone had come in, and she really didn't care who it was.

Jude and Abby walked over to where Rafe was sitting. "Hey, Rafe," said Jude.

"We thought we'd see you at The Kiki for lunch since you don't have to go to work," said Abby as she made herself comfortable and sat in the chair beside Rafe.

"I just thought I'd stay home today," said Rafe still looking straight ahead.

"Is there anything we can do for you?" asked Abby worried.

"No," said Rafe flatly.

"We got a really good response to my article about you on WLEZ," Abby told her, trying to be positive. "Did you get to hear any of it?"

"No," said Rafe flatly still staring straight ahead.

Abby looked at Jude who shrugged. "What'd you have for lunch?" she asked and Rafe held up her glass of scotch. "Has Eden called to check on you?" Rafe turned her head and looked at Abby with squinted eyes. "I guess, no," she said. "Fuck her."

"Abby, don't," said Jude chastising her.

"Why not? She's the reason for all this," said Abby, obviously irritated as she leaned back in her chair and crossed her arms.

Jude sat next to Rafe and looked at her closely. She could see Rafe wasn't herself, and it concerned her. "Rafe, how are you feeling?"

Rafe looked blankly at Jude. "Numb."

"Okay." Jude nodded thoughtfully. "Wait here," she said and left the way she came in.

"Letty said you talked to Eden about the article," said Abby hesitantly. "What'd she say?"

"She said her words were taken out of context about the insemination," Rafe said despondently.

"But," Abby swallowed her anger so she would not have an outburst, "not about you?"

Rafe took a sip of her drink, "I'm all of those things."

"Fuck, everyone is all of those things." Abby laughed bitterly. "You're just better at it."

Rafe knew Abby was trying to cheer her up and gave her a small smile. "Thanks for helping me and writing your article."

Jude returned through the gate carrying a small box. She went over and sat on the ground beside Rafe's chair. "This will take away your numbness and all your worries at the same time," she promised. She opened the box, took out a joint, and lit up.

"Jude," said Abby smiling, "you're just what the doctor ordered."

29

THE TRIO WAS feeling very good after a few fat, superior quality, well-rolled joints, and there was a blue haze over Rafe Salvaggio's patio. The music was up loud, and the indie rocker Kristie Stremel was singing about a best kiss. They all were laughing and having a great time sprawled out by the pool. There were plates, food wrappers, and empty bags of chips strewn about in and outside the house. They had raided Rafe's cupboards and then raided the pantry and refrigerator at Jude's house. Other food containers were all around too because they had ordered food from two different restaurants, Thai and Pizza. Rafe bribed the Thai food guy to deliver with a hundred dollar tip. Abby thought it was the greatest thing ever. Rafe was the cheapest rich chick she knew, except when it came to women and booze—and now the magic weed. Rafe had eaten more in the short time than she had in the last three days.

Abby and Jude were drinking beers, and Rafe was drinking a 'special' bottle of champagne and eating gelato from the carton. The effects of the marijuana had opened Rafe up and made her relaxed and extremely talkative. It was all a great amusement to Abby because Rafe's Italian accent became more pronounced.

Rafe held the latest joint they had lit and looked at it as she smiled. "Mary Jane, I don't love you," she said seductively to the joint in her Italian accented English. "I just want to fuck you. But don't tell my wife!"

All three of the stoned friends cracked up laughing.

"You don't have a wife, Rafe," squealed Abby as they all laughed.

"I," Rafe laughed, "I know." She took a hit. "But I used to!" She laughed again uncontrollably.

"Pass her over. I want some of that too," said Abby. Rafe passed the joint to Abby who took a toke and spoke as she held in her smoke. "I'm the one who loves you, Mary Jane," she said and passed to Jude.

"I'm with Rafe." Jude released her smoke. "I just want Mary Jane to fuck me up!" They all laughed again, and Jude passed it back to Rafe who took another drag.

"Do you want to listen to the recording again?" asked Rafe as she fumbled with her phone.

Eden walked out of the house and onto the patio, finding the three by the pool surrounded by a food mess and a cloud of smoke. She turned the loud music off irritably. "What do you think you're doing?" she asked angrily.

The three looked at Eden in surprise and started laughing.

"Rafe! You've been busted!" screeched Abby, and they all roared with laughter again.

148

Rafe was doubled over in laughter. "It's," she wheezed, "it's okay," she caught her breath. "I think Mary Jane has fucked me good by now!" They burst out into uproarious laughter. Rafe took a breath as she tried to control her laughter and looked up at Eden. "*Ciao, mia dolce,*"[1] she slurred, "come over here." Eden walked closer to her, and Rafe looked at her innocently. "How was your day?" she asked. They all burst into laughter again, and Abby rolled onto her side.

"Rafe, what is this?" Eden demanded not amused. "You're getting stoned now?" She looked at Abby and Jude. "How could you guys let her do this? Where's Bronte?"

Thinking through the haze, Rafe smiled at Eden. "She's with the Letty spaghetti, of course."

They all laughed again.

"I told you I didn't want her to go over there!" Eden stomped her foot angrily.

"Rafe needed to relax, Edy," said Abby as she tried to breathe and stop laughing so she could take a toke. "It's okay," she said as she held in her smoke, "we turned off the surveillance cameras," she exhaled, "we think." They all laughed again, and Abby passed it on.

"We don't want no big brother watching us," Jude said, and they all kept laughing.

"I think it's time for you two to go," Eden fumed with an angry scowl. She looked over at what Rafe was drinking and grabbed the almost empty bottle of champagne from her. "How could you drink this?" she asked, shocked and hurt.

----

[1] Hello, my sweet,

"You can have some too, Ede," Rafe said as she smiled up at her. "We didn't make it to our ten year anniversary, and I didn't want it to go to waste. It's good with gelato too." She grinned and took a toke then handed the joint to Abby.

"Rafe," she angrily choked back tears and put the bottle back on the table.

"Don't be such a drag, Edy!" Abby laughed taking another hit before passing it to Jude who just smiled and took a drag.

Rafe took the joint from Jude and pulled a toke. She held the smoke then spoke as she let it out. "Come on, Ede," she said as she held out the joint to her, "do your democratic duty and take a hit with us," she encouraged her with a stoned smile.

"No, Rafe, she," Abby said as she laughed before Eden could say anything, "she should join our new political party. Edy, we've decided to form our own political party. It's the *Gaymocratic* party!"

They all laughed uncontrollably until they had to stop for air.

"Rafe," Abby wheezed, "Rafe is our candidate because," she laughed, "because she has pissed off more people and caused more riots than anyone we know."

Rafe took a toke and smiled. "I'm like the gay Clinton," she said as she let out her smoke and winked.

"Yeah, except you admit you inhaled and you did fuck the girl!" said Abby, and they all burst out laughing again.

"And I can be a very nasty woman," slurred Rafe seductively then winked at Eden.

"Rafe for President!" Jude cheered with boisterous laughter. "She's, she's like two Clintons in one!"

"Rafe, Rafe," Abby said excitedly, "show her your muscle! She's got real fucking muscles!"

Rafe flexed her arm showing off her bicep while Abby and Jude cheered and passed the joint. Through her laugh, Rafe let out the smoke from her last toke. "I want you guys to hang out with me some more," she slurred happily.

Eden snatched the joint from Rafe and threw it on the ground then watched in frustration as Abby picked it up as they kept laughing. "Rafe, stop it," she begged her, "please. What are you doing?"

Looking through half-closed eyes, Rafe smiled at Eden. "I'm having an affair with Mary Jane," she said with a deep dope infused chuckle. "Do you want to know why?" Eden crossed her arms with an angry sigh as Rafe picked up a lighter and another joint then looked at it lovingly. "I can see her," she said smoothly. She held the joint up to her ear and rolled it between her fingers listening to it crackle. "I can hear her," she said then ran the joint under her nose. "I can smell her." She smiled and put the joint in her mouth and lit it, taking a pull. "I can breathe her in," she said as she released the smoke, rolling it on her tongue. "I can taste her, so sweet," she said softly and held up the joint. "I can touch her," she looked up at Eden, "and hold her tight, but still let her go," she smiled, "and not worry one bit about where she's gone." She offered the joint to Eden.

Abby let out her smoke. "Hey!" she said with a croak. "That sounds like the line you used on me!" she recalled with a laugh.

"I think I used the same line on everyone." Rafe laughed then looked up at Eden somberly. "Except you," she said then shrugged and started to take another drag.

"Rafe, please stop this," pleaded Eden and took the joint away from her.

Abby looked at Rafe, and Rafe looked back with raised eyebrows, and they burst out laughing. "I don't think Rafe is ready to stop her affair just yet!" Abby squeaked, and they all laughed.

"Yeah, I don't know if Jayne Eden can fuck me as good as Mary Jane!" Rafe laughed at how clever she was to use Eden's name in her joke.

"Stop it!" screamed Eden furious and hurt by her words and how she was making light of having an affair. "Abby, Jude, get out! Now!" she demanded and pointed toward the gate.

"Hey, it's cool, Eden. We'll go," said Jude through her cloud of smoke. She started to pack away her little box, and Rafe put her hand over a couple of joints. Jude looked at her then nodded. "Okay," she said quietly.

"You know, Edy, if you stopped hurting her and doing shit to her and making her—" Abby stopped herself from mentioning the strap-on secret and looked at Rafe then put her finger to her lips. "Shhh," she shushed herself and looked at Eden. "Maybe then she wouldn't need to drink and fuck Mary Jane to forget her pain."

"Damn it, Abby!" Eden screamed at her angrily. "Get out! You're stoned!"

Abby laughed with Rafe and Jude. "I'm going." Abby kept laughing. "I am fucking stoned, and you're just one sick fucking straight girl!"

They all burst out laughing again. Abby and Jude got up then walked next door laughing all the way.

Rafe watched Jude and Abby leave. "Fuck, now everyone is leaving me." She chuckled then picked up a joint and the lighter and lit up. "Mary Jane, I need you to fuck me some more tonight." She laughed and took a drag.

"When did you start smoking pot?" asked Eden as she looked at Rafe with tears running down her cheeks and in disbelief. "This isn't you."

Rafe looked over at her smiling. "The best thing about my Mary Jane is she takes control of my mind and makes it so I don't have to think or worry about a thing," she said and looked at Eden through sad glassy eyes. "Can you do the same for me? Can you take control and lift away all the shit in my life? Can you stop my world from spinning out of control?" She took a drag and held it. "Can you stop me," she said as she let out her smoke, "from spinning out of control? Can you do it even if it's just for a little while?" She looked at Eden and winked. "I think you can," she whispered.

Eden took the joint from Rafe then put it on the table with the others. She sat down on the lounger next to Rafe and held her face. "Rafe, everything is going to be okay," she said as she looked into her red-rimmed gray-blue eyes worriedly.

Rafe leaned forward and kissed Eden. "Tell me," she breathed, "tell me to stop," she said softly as she kissed her. She moved her hands over Eden and kissed her deeply then moved her kisses to her face and neck. "Tell me you want me to stop," she whispered in her ear.

"Rafe," Eden said breathlessly as Rafe kissed her, "I love you," she said, "I don't want you to stop if you need me." Rafe sucked hard on the top of her breast and Eden pushed her back in shock from the pain. "Shit, Rafe!" she yelled.

"Tell me your secrets," Rafe said as she lay back in the lounger with a glazed smiled. "Tell me what you want from me."

"What are you doing?" asked Eden upset and unnerved as Rafe just smiled at her. "I don't think I like this. I'm going inside." She got up and went inside, leaving Rafe alone by the pool.

30

PICKING UP THE champagne bottle, Rafe Salvaggio drank the last of it and smiled. She dropped the thick empty bottle to the ground, happy with the deep clanking sound it made. She clumsily gathered her phone then made several failed attempts to stand up. Rafe thought she might be able to record Eden again with her phone. She finally made it to her feet. She smiled at her success as she carefully put one foot in front of the other and headed toward the opening of the doorway. She needed to know where Eden had gone. She needed to see if she could take away the pain threatening to engulf her. Jayne can play her game, she thought, and then chuckled to herself.

As she made her way to the door, her world spun and tilted, and her body made the perceived adjustments. A light sweat broke out over her body from the exertion. She laughed as colors and shapes jumped in front of her eyes and thoughts spun in and out of her mind disjointedly. At the doorway, she grabbed hold of the door and the doorframe and tried to focus on her next goal.

She found her target, released her hold of the doorframe, and took two steps forward and stopped. She suddenly had the thought it may be safer to be on all fours, making it so she didn't have as far to fall. She slowly lowered herself down and began crawling toward her goal while laughing at her own cleverness. She made it to her goal, pulled herself up by the bedroom doorframe, and staggered into the room and sat on the bed. She sat for a while gripping her phone and smiling as her eyes focused in and out on nothing.

Eden walked into her room from the bathroom in her bathrobe to get some things she would need after she took her shower. "Rafe, what are you doing?" she asked when she saw her on the bed.

"It was your rule," said Rafe smiling.

Eden sighed then walked over and sat down next to her. "My rule?" she repeated.

"Your rule. If the door is open, I can come in," Rafe reminded her as the phone slipped out of her hand and onto the bed.

"Oh, okay." Eden smelled the marijuana on Rafe and wrinkled her nose. "Rafe, you need to go take a shower or go to your room. I can't take that smell."

"I can't leave," she said grinning and then placed her head against Eden.

"Why not?" asked Eden as she rolled her eyes.

"Your rule. If I come in, I have to stay all night," she reminded her again then looked down and started trying to unbutton her shirt.

Eden watched Rafe and sighed as she fumbled. "Let me help you." She stood then unbuttoned Rafe's shirt and took her bra off. "Stand up," she directed her. Rafe looked at her and gave a smile just for her then stood up and leaned over Eden, putting her hands on her shoulders, and then kissed her. Eden unbuttoned and unzipped her pants, letting them slide down her. Eden tried to push her away, but Rafe pulled her onto the bed. "You have to get in the shower now," she said as she sat back up pulling Rafe with her. "We have to hurry before Bronte and dinner get here."

Rafe leaned into Eden and looked at her face. "Okay," she said but just stayed in place unable to move.

Eden stood up, taking Rafe up with her, "Rafe, you're so freaking stoned. Why did you do this?" Rafe just smiled at her and tried to kiss her. "No," she avoided the kiss, "let's go to the shower."

They made their way to the new steam shower Eden had already turned on. The steam filled the bathroom. Eden opened the shower door and led Rafe inside where she sat her on the shower seat.

"Eden," Rafe said panicky as she tried to stand, "Eden, why the hell is it so hard to breathe in here?"

"It's just steam, babe," Eden told her, and she held her down on the shower seat.

"Steam," Rafe said in alarm. "You have to put in my conditioner," she slurred to her. "You have to do my hair, Ede, or it will be shit tomorrow! You have to go get my stuff!"

Eden sighed with frustration. "Okay. Just sit right there, and I'll go get it." She left Rafe in the shower and went quickly to get the hair products.

"There's too much steam," Rafe said to no one as she looked around herself. "I can't see anything. I've got to turn this fucking steam off, or my hair will be shit." She stood up looking for the controls. Her leg gave way as she stepped forward, and she slipped on the wet tile. She landed hard on the shower floor and hit the back of her head on the edge of the shower seat. "Shit!" she cried out and laughed. "*Che cazzo del male!*"[2] She shook her head to clear her vision and rubbed the back of her head. "*Ohi, merda!*"[3]

Eden walked back in with all of Rafe's hair products and other things she would need. She opened the shower door and saw Rafe on the floor with blood swirling around her and on the shower seat. "Oh, God, Rafe!" she yelled in fear. She turned off the shower and grabbed a towel.

"Thank god you turned off the steam, Ede," said Rafe from the shower floor. "I couldn't reach it."

Eden knelt down next to Rafe and put the towel on the back of her head. "You're bleeding! I told you to sit down."

---

[2] That fucking hurt!
[3] Oh, shit!

Rafe put a hand on each of Eden's arms. "You need to be put back together," she said as she blinked her eyes until Eden was all in one piece again. "There, that's better," she said then smiled at her success.

"Shit," Eden said worried, "do you have a concussion or is it the damn pot?"

Rafe grinned up at her. "You're cursing a lot." She chuckled at her own magnificent observation. "I'm still rubbing off on you."

Eden sighed and rolled her eyes. "You just scared the crap out of me."

"You have to wash my hair," said Rafe as she held out a piece of her wet hair. "Get my stuff."

"I don't think we can wash your hair," said Eden still holding the towel to Rafe's head. "It may hurt your cut."

"Ede," said Rafe, looking at Eden as if she were crazy, "it'll hurt worse to have shitty hair. Get my stuff," she insisted.

Hiding her frustration, Eden pulled the towel away from Rafe's head. "Okay, it's not bleeding as much now. I'm going to turn on the water," she told her.

"But not the steam," Rafe said in a panic.

"But not the steam," Eden assured her, "and I'll wash your hair." She turned the water on, got Rafe's shampoo and conditioner, and washed her hair as carefully as she could. "Okay, do you think you can stand up and sit on the seat again?"

"Yes." Rafe pulled herself up with Eden's help and then sat on the seat. "I think I may have broken my ass, Ede." She laughed at the hazy thought.

"You did break your ass," she assured her and couldn't help laughing. "Your ass and your head." She grabbed a body sponge and put some soap in it. "Here, use this." She handed her the soapy sponge.

"Okay." Rafe took the sponge and looked at it then smiled. "Where do you want me to start?"

Eden rolled her eyes. "Anywhere you want." She grabbed another sponge for herself.

Rafe reached out and ran her sponge over Eden's lower back and hips. "I'd start higher, but I can't reach."

Eden looked up at the ceiling and shook her head. "Use it on yourself."

"No," said Rafe as she ran the sponge over Eden's lower back, "this is your soap. I have to use it on you." She put her arms around Eden's waist and ran the sponge up her stomach and back down over her thighs. She pulled her down so she was sitting in her lap and moved the sponge up to her breasts and neck as she kissed Eden's back. "Tell me if I miss anywhere," she said huskily.

"Rafe," said Eden as she broke away and took the sponge from her. "I want you to use my soap." She began to use the sponge on Rafe covering her body with suds.

"Ede," Rafe said smiling crookedly, "I like it when you do that." She reached out for Eden, but her arms slid down her soapy body. "*Ti amo.*"

"I know you like it," said Eden as she grabbed the showerhead to start rinsing off Rafe, pushing her hands away. "I love you too." She finished rinsing Rafe and then washed herself quickly.

C. L. CATTANO

Rafe looked around confused. "Why is my shower so small, Ede?"

"It's not your shower," Eden reminded her as she rinsed herself off. "It's the new one you had put in for me."

"Oh, yeah, the steam shower," said Rafe. "Did you put conditioner in my hair?"

"Yes." Eden sighed and turned off the water. "Okay, let's get out and dry off." She pulled Rafe to her feet.

Rafe leaned against Eden and kissed her, and then began licking the water off her shoulder. "I want to drink the water off you, Ede," she whispered. "*Bellissima*, Ede," she said as she moved her tongue to her chest and breasts.

"Rafe, we need to get out before you slip and fall again," Eden said as she pushed Rafe's head back gently. "Stop," she told her firmly. She opened the shower door and stepped out, quickly grabbing the towels and wrapping Rafe in one. She helped Rafe out of the shower and sat her on the toilet seat. Eden dried herself off and put on her pajamas as Rafe watched with glassy eyes. "Let's comb your hair out, okay?"

Rafe put her hand to her hair. "Okay, you need to put my stuff in it."

"I know," said Eden as she squeezed out some hair product into her hand and worked it into Rafe's hair trying not to get any in her cut. When she got it all in, she started to comb out her dark curly hair.

"*Ohi*," Rafe complained. "Ede, be careful. Start at the bottom."

"Sorry," Eden said trying to be careful. "I know how to comb your hair." She finally got all the tangles out and got out

160

the liquid Band-Aid, the Neosporin, and a washcloth. "Okay, I'm going to clean your cut and see how big it is," she said and looked at the wound. "Good, it's not too big, but you're going to have a big bump." She dabbed some blood away.

Rafe flinched away. "That fucking hurt, Ede. *Basta*!"

"Sorry," she said with a grimace, not wanting to hurt her. "Okay, I'm going to put some medicine on it, so hold still." She applied the Neosporin and the liquid Band-Aid. "There. That should help stop the bleeding." She put everything away, and then she prepared Rafe's toothbrush and handed it to her. "Here, brush your teeth."

"Is this mine or yours?" she asked as she looked at the toothbrush. "I only like my toothpaste. I don't like the stuff you use."

"It's yours," she said annoyed. "I know you don't like the kind I use."

Rafe smiled at her. "I just don't like brushing my teeth with it, but it tastes good when I kiss you," she said and tried to kiss her.

"You brush your teeth, and I'll brush mine, then you can kiss me and taste it, okay?" asked Eden as she held her back.

"Okay," Rafe agreed and brushed her teeth.

They finished brushing their teeth, and Eden picked up Rafe's pajamas. "Now, I'm going to put your things back in your bathroom, okay? You put your pajamas on," she said and handed them to Rafe. "I think I better call Ephraim and let them keep Bronte tonight if they can. I don't think I can take care of two babies tonight." She turned and walked out with Rafe's things.

"I'm not a baby." Rafe frowned then looked at the pajamas Eden handed her and smiled. "Put them on what?" She dropped them on the floor and walked into Eden's bedroom naked.

After Eden had called Letty, she went back into the room and saw Rafe sitting on the bed. "Where are your pajamas?" she asked in dismay. "You were supposed to put them on."

"I did," said Rafe with a smile. "I put them on," she paused, "the floor." She laughed at her own joke.

"Rafe!" Eden hissed in frustration. "You're driving me crazy!"

Rafe grasped Eden's hand and pulled her onto the bed. "*Ti voglio da impazzire?* Do you want me to fuck you like crazy?" she asked and started to pull off Eden's pajama bottoms and ran her hands under her shirt.

Eden closed her eyes at her touch. "Oh, my god, Rafe," her words were cut off as Rafe covered her mouth with her own.

"Tell me to stop," Rafe whispered as she moved her kisses to Eden's chin then sucked hard on her throat.

"That freaking hurt!" screamed Eden as she pushed Rafe back and slapped her face in reaction to the pain. "Stop!"

Rafe smiled at her then looked puzzled as her pupils dilated. She slid off the bed down to the floor where she knelt and put her head on the floor as tears of blinding pain flooded from her eyes. "Ede," she cried out in pain, "my head hurts," she moaned, "I think," she started shaking, "I think something happened."

"Rafe, I'm sorry," Eden said in a panic when she realized she had hurt her head. "I'm so sorry," she said in misery as she knelt next to her. "I didn't mean to. I forgot!"

"Ede," she whispered in pain, "what's that ringing? Make it stop," she begged.

"It's the doorbell," Eden told her. "It's probably the food."

"I'll get it," Rafe said and started to get up then stopped suddenly. "Ede," she moaned in pain, "I can't move! It hurts."

"Okay," Eden said anxiously, "Okay, just don't move. I'll go answer the door. You don't have any clothes on." She looked at Rafe and saw her start to shake. "Rafe, what's wrong?"

"I can't move, Ede," and her body shook with painful laughter she couldn't control.

Eden looked anxiously from Rafe to the door. "Shit!" she hissed as she got up, pulled the sheet off the bed, and put it over Rafe.

"You cussed again." Rafe laughed then groaned in pain.

Eden just shook her head as she grabbed her robe and ran out of the room, slipping on her robe as she ran to the door. When she opened the door, she saw she was right about it being the pizza guy. "Sorry," she said quickly, "can you stay here on the porch for a minute? I have to run next door." She took off before the guy could answer. She ran over to Jude's and pounded on their door. "Jude! Abby!" she screamed over and over until she got a response.

"Hey, Eden," said Jude as she opened the door wondering if they were going to get a lecture.

"I need you," she said in a panic. "Rafe needs you." She pulled on her arm. "Come on." She ran back to the house pulling Jude as Abby and Flynn followed.

"What the fuck is going on?" asked Abby as they got to the house.

"I think we have to take her to the hospital," Eden said, her voice shaking in fear. "I have to pay for the food. She's in my bedroom." She went to pay the pizza guy, and Flynn followed her.

Abby walked into Eden's room, Jude close behind her, and they saw Rafe naked on the floor with a sheet half over her. They knelt down beside her. "Rafe, what the hell happened?" asked Abby freaking out.

Rafe opened her eyes slightly. "You're back," she whispered.

"Dude," Jude snickered, "what are you doing naked on the floor?"

"My head," she laughed and then groaned, "my head hurts."

"Okay, we have to hurry," said Eden as she ran back into the room worried. "Flynn will drive us to the hospital. Just let me get my clothes on. You guys put her pajamas on her, and we'll take her to the hospital."

"Eden," Rafe called out, "Ede," she said and reached up to her.

"I'm sorry," cried Eden as she knelt next to Rafe and tried to comfort her. "I'm so sorry."

"What the hell did you do to her?" Abby demanded.

"Ede, just help me get back on the bed," Rafe said as she shuddered in pain again. "I can't go to the hospital."

"Is she going to be okay?" asked Flynn as he stood in the doorway concerned.

"Abby, help us get her up," said Jude as she took Rafe's arm. Rafe held her head as they lifted her onto the bed.

They finally got Rafe's pajamas on her. Abby sat next to her and moved Rafe's phone to the night table while Jude sat on the end of the bed. "What happened?"

"She slipped in the shower," Eden said anxiously as she stood between the bed and the door trying to think about what she should do for her. "This is your fault, you guys," she said hotly. "You got her stoned, and now she's hurt! She needs to see a doctor!"

"Stop yelling," Rafe begged as she held her head. "I can't go to the hospital."

"You have to," Eden insisted. "You may have a concussion or something."

"I'll be fine," said Rafe as her head throbbed. "My head just hurts. They've already crucified me. If I show up at the hospital stoned, they'll want to stick a sharpened stake up my ass. I'm not going anywhere."

"Impalement?" Abby laughed. "You are so fucking funny, Rafe!"

"Rafe, please," Eden pleaded as she paced. "You almost passed out from the pain." Rafe just looked at her and smiled but then grimaced in pain. "I'm calling someone," Eden snapped and left the room with Flynn close behind her.

"You fucking slipped in the shower?" Jude laughed at her plight. "Classic!"

"Why the hell did you almost pass out?" asked Abby curiously.

"Eden," said Rafe as she tried not to laugh, "slapped me across the face."

"She what?" screeched Abby. "Why?"

"I was doing an experiment, and it went wrong," Rafe explained.

"Experiment?" asked Jude with a laugh.

"Yeah, I was trying to see if Jayne Eden could replace Mary Jane," said Rafe. They all started laughing until Rafe had to stop because her head hurt. "Stop laughing. It hurts," she said, her face twisted in laughter and then pain.

"You're definitely more stoned than I am." Jude declared and laughed. "You're such a featherhead."

"Much, much more stoned," Abby said through laughter, too.

"I think she could have replaced Mary Jane if I hadn't slipped in the shower," Rafe said in fuzzy logic. "Fucking steam shower," she mumbled.

"I'm going to go see what she's doing," said Jude smiling. She walked out of the bedroom and found Eden at the kitchen table on the phone, and Flynn sitting with her.

"She's talking, and she's been up, but she's back in bed now," said Eden into the phone. "No. She has a bump, and it's just a small cut. I cleaned it and put Neosporin and liquid Band-Aid on it. Okay. Okay. Should I give her something like Aspirin or Tylenol? I'll check for swelling. Ice, right. Thank you. I will. Thank you." She hung up the phone and laid her head on the island counter "Flynn, why did she do this?" She looked up at him. "They turned the surveillance cameras and the alarm off, and I can't get it working. Will you look at it?"

"Sure, I'll fix it. Don't worry." Flynn left to fix the security system.

Jude sat at the island next to Eden. "She'll be okay," she said reassuringly.

Eden looked at Jude in despair. "Why did you have to get her stoned?"

"She was drinking herself numb, and you said she had barely eaten in three days," said Jude with a shrug. "She needed to relax."

"She drank our champagne," said Eden as a couple of errant tears ran down her face. "She's not acting like herself."

"Is that why you slapped her?" asked Jude cautiously.

"No, she hurt me." Upset, Eden showed Jude the mark on her neck that Rafe made. "It hurt, and I slapped her to make her stop. She kept telling me to make her stop." She wrung her hands. "She's out of control, Jude. She's being cruel. That's not her." She stood up and got a glass out of the cabinet.

"She said she was doing an experiment to see if you could take the place of the marijuana," Jude informed her with a chuckle.

"What?" asked Eden, confused as she filled the glass with water.

"Eden, the marijuana was easing her pain," said Jude casually. "She probably realized she couldn't smoke it forever and wanted to see if you could take some of her pain away. It's crazy, but she is high." Jude shrugged as if everything should be clear. "Her life is fucked up. She's fucked up right now."

"I just don't understand," said Eden as she ran her hands through her hair. "I told her if she needed me, I would be there for her." She pulled ice from the freezer and put it in a freezer bag then wrapped it in a dishtowel.

"Well, you weren't there," Jude pointed out. "She told us she asked you to stay home with her today. Maybe she needed something more."

"More what? What does that mean?" asked Eden frustrated. "Why did you have to get her stoned?"

"Think about it," said Jude thoughtfully. "Since the article came out, she hasn't screamed, yelled, broken things, or anything. That's not Rafe. Remember when the injunction was first filed? She tore the art studio apart. It was scary. Now she just—" Jude lifted her empty hands. "Nothing, no reaction at all. She's fucked up and stoned, but she's laughing. She might be acting a little cruel, but she's talking and joking. I'll take that over her having no reaction at all because no reaction is even scarier. Her life is fucked, Eden, and she just sat there. I had to do something. I couldn't stand seeing her just shutting down."

"You still shouldn't have done it," Eden insisted. "What if this was more serious? Then her life would be even more fucked up. Even if she wasn't hurt, it affects more than just her. I had to leave Bronte with Ephraim and Letty. You guys made a big mess out there, and you messed up the security system. I've been dealing with this shit too, you know, and her being stoned out of her mind has made it harder on me!"

"Yeah, but those things aren't so bad. I mean, we can fix those things, and Bronte is fine with Ephraim and Letty," reasoned Jude. "I know you're dealing with things too, Eden, but you aren't losing anything. Rafe may be losing her job. The article may make her lose Bronte, and the person she loves said the things in the article. From the way she was talking today, I think she may be questioning whether or not you really do love her. Maybe that's why she's being cruel."

"I do love her!" Eden snapped angrily. "I told you the article twisted my words!" She stormed off to her bedroom with Jude behind her.

"I'm sorry, Eden," said Jude as she followed her. "I know you say you love her, and they may have twisted your words, but you did say those things, and she has to deal with that on top of everything else."

Without looking back, Eden went into the bathroom for Tylenol.

Abby was lying in bed next to Rafe and laughing so hard, she had tears in her eyes. "Do another one," she begged.

"Okay," Rafe laughed softly. "You, sir, are a scatophagous malefactor," she said dramatically.

"That sounds great," said Abby trying to control her laughter. "Now, tell me what it means."

"It means he's a shit eating criminal." Rafe smiled but had to close one eye because of the pain it caused.

"That is so fucking funny," Abby cracked up. "Rafe, when you're high, you're a genius!"

"What are you guys doing?" asked Jude as she sat on the bed.

"Rafe is proving you can…" Abby started as she tried catching her breath, "you can cuss someone out without," she laughed, "without using cuss words. It's so fucking funny! She does it much better than Eden!" She cracked herself up again.

"How does it work if no one knows what it means?" asked Jude puzzled.

"Who fucking cares if the idiots don't know what it means? I know what it means," reasoned Rafe and laughed softly trying not to cause more pain.

"Yeah, who the fuck cares!" Abby laughed. "It's funny!"

"*È esilarante!*"[4] Rafe laughed softly then groaned.

"What's that mean?" asked Abby shaking her head. "Maybe she needs more Mary Jane."

"I don't think Eden is gonna go for that," Jude said looking askance at where Eden had gone.

Eden came out of the bathroom wiping away tears and sat next to Rafe. "I talked to a nurse, and she said you have to stay awake for at least another hour, and I have to watch you," she reported with red-rimmed, puffy eyes. "Here's some ice for your head and some Tylenol."

Rafe took the pills and washed them down with the water. "Thanks, Ede," she said. "I don't want the ice on my head," she complained. "I have a real ice pack in the freezer."

"Well, you have to use this one because I didn't know about the other. This is made, so put it on your head," she said firmly. "It'll keep any swelling down." She held the ice pack to Rafe's head and looked at Jude and Abby. "Thanks for coming over, guys."

_____

[4] Is hilarious!

"No problem." Jude smiled at her sympathetically. "Hey, we should go. Come on, Abby."

"Oh, we were just getting started," whined Abby with disappointment as she climbed out of bed. "Once she comes down, she won't do crazy things anymore. We have to take advantage of it while we can."

"I hope she comes down soon," said Eden with a frown.

"It's too bad." Abby sighed. "She probably won't remember anything about this in the morning. We should have left the cameras on." She looked a Jude and they laughed at the memory of what they could have relived through security footage.

"Jude, please don't give her any more," Eden begged.

"Hey, she was a friend in need." Jude shrugged away Eden's concern. "I'm always there to help my friends." She turned and walked out with Abby close on her heels.

"My head is feeling a little better now, Ede. You can take the ice off now," Rafe said as she looked up at Eden with shiny eyes. "It's too cold."

"I'll take it off for a while, but I may have to put it on again later," said Eden as she took the ice pack and set it aside.

"I'm getting sleepy," Rafe said as she laid her head back.

"You can't go to sleep yet," said Eden as she climbed into bed beside her. "You have to stay awake."

"No, I'm going to sleep," said Rafe as her eyes started to close.

"Talk to me for a while," Eden said as she moved closer and brushed Rafe's hair back from her face to try to keep her awake.

Rafe looked over at her and smiled. "Okay." She reached out and pulled Eden to her then ran her hands over her. "You're very beautiful," she said softly, "so soft." She kissed her face and mouth. "Your toothpaste tastes good too." She chuckled as she kissed her.

"Everything will be okay, you know?" Eden whispered as she stroked Rafe's hair and felt Rafe's warm hands on her body and her warm lips as she kissed her. "I just wish the article was never written."

"It's okay, Ede," Rafe whispered. "I won't ever let anyone take Bronte away from you. I know you love your baby. Don't be scared," she said looking at her with glassy-eyed concern. "I love you both. *Mi sono innamorato di te.*"[5]

"We love you too," said Eden softly and kissed her forehead. "Talk to me some more."

"What do you want me to talk about?" Rafe smiled goofily at her.

"Tell me why everyone is calling you a wildling." Eden smiled at her expression.

"Fucking Abby." Rafe frowned.

"Abby?"

Rafe laughed softly then leaned back against the headboard and closed her eyes. "She thinks I stole part of her soul," she said imitating a vampire.

Eden laughed and shook her head. "What?"

Rafe grinned carefully with her eyes closed. "I used my line on her and some technique," she said and yawned. "I think she

---

[5] I fell in love with you.

falls in love with everyone she has sex with," she mumbled sleepily.

"Stay awake and talk to me," said Eden as she lifted Rafe's head gently. "So you think she's still in love with you?"

"She has to be," she said mischievously. "So *che i segreti dello zingaro*."[6] She chuckled as Abby's confused face floated before her mind's eye. "I stole part of her soul."

"You're so full of it." Eden laughed loving hearing her speak Italian even if she didn't understand.

"Hey," Rafe said as she opened her eyes and smiled at Eden sleepily. "I don't hear you complaining. Even Greer loves Wildling Rafe."

"She does?" asked Eden finding it was suddenly not so funny.

"Did you know she can speak with her hands?" Rafe asked and closed her eyes again. "Not like Italians but really talk." She grinned as Greer's face popped into her mind.

"Oh, you mean sign language," Eden realized, her head spinning from the subject change. She shook Rafe gently to keep her awake.

"She does this thing that heals me," Rafe said softly. "She talks to me with her hands, and she sees me."

"She sees you? What does that mean?" asked Eden confused and trying to keep her anxiety pushed down.

"I don't know," Rafe said with a wrinkled brow. "I can't explain it. But it's what she does, you know. She heals people."

"She's an art therapist," Eden clarified.

---

[6] I know the secrets of the Gypsy.

"That's right." Rafe nodded sleepily. "She's really smart. She's a real doctor, not like me. I don't really help people. Have you seen her heal people too?"

"No," said Eden looking at Rafe and realizing again just how close she came to losing her. "You help people all the time, babe."

Rafe opened her eyes, smiling as she looked at Eden. "You use to see me. Do you want me to teach you some sign language?"

Eden ran her hands through her hair troubled, unsure what Rafe meant when she said she used to see her. "I'll bet it's hard to learn sign language."

"Yeah, it's a lot of work," Rafe said earnestly. "It's lucky we have email."

"You email her?" Eden was shocked and felt a tightness in her stomach at the unexpected news.

"Sometimes," Rafe nodded groggily, "she tells me about her day, and I tell her about mine." She looked over at Eden. "We should email each other more."

"Why do we need to email each other when we can just talk?" asked Eden with a small laugh as she tried to hide her discomfort.

"That's true." Rafe yawned. "But it would be fun."

"Let's talk about something else." Eden pulled Rafe so she was sitting up. She needed her to stay awake a while longer.

Rafe wrapped her arms around Eden. "What do you want to talk about now?"

"Do you love her?" Eden asked hesitantly. "Greer." She tried to fight it, but she couldn't help asking the question even though she was dreading the answer.

"Yeah," Rafe said in her smooth, soft voice. "She loves me too, just like you and Abby. I think you'd love her too."

"No, I love you," said Eden possessively.

"I love you too," said Rafe softly.

"What about Greer?" Eden asked anxiously.

Rafe tilted Eden's face up and smiled, "I love you both," she said and tried to kiss Eden, but she turned her face away.

"I don't want you to love her," she said jealously.

"I can't help it," said Rafe confused because she really couldn't help that she loved Greer.

"You have to choose one of us. I don't want to share you," Eden said covetously.

"You're so funny." Rafe laughed softly. "I already chose you."

"But you still love her?" Eden pressed.

"Yes, just like you love Jake." She sighed sleepily. "When you leave me, she'll help me."

"What are you talking about?" asked Eden as a shot of anxiety ran through her. "I don't love him. I only love you," she insisted. "Rafe, what do you mean she'll help you when I leave you? I'm not leaving you. I only love you."

Rafe reached over Eden for her phone. "I think I heard you," she said as she tried to pull up the recording she made.

"You heard me? What are you talking about?"

"It's on my phone."

"What's on your phone?"

Rafe looked up from her phone and frowned as her hazy mind saw Eden was looking at her suspiciously. Paranoia swept through her. "Nothing," she said and pulled her phone up so that Eden couldn't see the screen.

"Rafe, what did you hear? What's on your phone?" Eden asked again. "Did Jake say something to you?" The fear he was talking to her again or leaving her voicemails ran through her like ice in her veins. "Let me see," she said trying to be calm and reaching for the phone.

"No." Rafe held her phone out of Eden's reach. The mention of Jake tweaked at her paranoia, and she deleted the sound file. "It's nothing. It's gone." She smiled, feeling clever again.

"Rafe, I love you," Eden said as she ran a hand through Rafe's hair. "I don't love Jake or anyone else. I'm not going to leave you."

"That's good," said Rafe and touched Eden's face as she looked into her eyes. "I'm the one who really loves you," she said softly. "I love you more than anyone else, so you should stay with me."

Eden was drawn to her and kissed her. "I will stay with you," she promised.

"*Sei la mia anima gemella*," Rafe said softly.

"I know," she said with a smile as she stroked Rafe's face. "You haven't said that to me for a while. You're my soulmate too," said Eden as she pushed Rafe's hair back from her face again.

"*Non potrò mai smettere d'amarti,*"[7] said Rafe as she looked at Eden with her glassy eyes. "*Non posso vivere senza te,*"[8] she said, and her heavy eyelids started to slide closed.

"Rafe, English. I don't know what you said," Eden whispered. "Talk to me, babe. Don't go to sleep."

Rafe slipped into Italian again when she opened her eyes and touched Eden's hair. "*Amo tutto di te,*" she whispered. "I love everything about you," she repeated in English and leaned in to kiss her.

"What things do you love about me?" Eden smiled as their kiss opened up a rush of love for Rafe that flooded through her.

"I love how you can't wink," said Rafe as she touched Eden's face lovingly.

"What?" Eden laughed. "I can wink!"

"No, you can't." Rafe chuckled. "You try, but you always blink both eyes and scrunch your nose. It's cute," she said and put her head against Eden's and smiled into her eyes. "I love to watch you try to wink."

"Cute, huh?" she said wryly, and Rafe nodded against her head. "Okay, what else?"

"I love your eyes," she said. "I could look into them forever."

"I know," said Eden and could not help her smile. "You've told me many times they fascinate you."

"They do," said Rafe as she looked into her eyes. "They're so beautiful, and I get lost sometimes when I look into them. They're like a beautiful painting."

---

[7] I'll never stop loving you

[8] I can't live without you

"You and your art," said Eden and kissed her sweetly. "I'm glad you love my eyes. Tell me something else."

Rafe laughed softly. "You're going to get conceited."

"No." Eden kissed her. "I just like to hear you tell me what you love about me."

"*Conceeeeited.*" Rafe smiled and ran her hand over Eden then pulled her close. "I love how I feel connected to you," she whispered. "It's like you're the other half of me, the good half of course." She laughed quietly and buried her head in Eden's shoulder as she winced in pain.

Eden pushed Rafe's hair back, lifted her face, and kissed her on the lips softly. "You feel a connection, huh? I feel it too. I think your half is good," she said and kissed her again.

Rafe pulled away and sat back while she shook her head slowly. "No, I'm not the good half. I fuck up too much. It'll be sad if I can't keep you with me."

"We both fuck up," she said anxiously, "and I told you I'm not going anywhere." She looked at Rafe and could see she was falling asleep again. She pulled her up so she was sitting up again. "But speaking of fuck-ups, why did you have to drink our champagne?"

"I was thirsty, and it was good," she slurred groggily. "Did you taste it?"

"No, you drank the whole bottle," said Eden exasperated.

"Oh," Rafe said drowsily. "That's okay."

"I wish you hadn't," Eden grumbled. "It was special."

"Don't worry, Ede," said Rafe as she stroked her hair. "I have more. I'll get you some."

"You have more?"

Rafe nodded and looked at her with one eye opened. "I have a whole case."

"You do?"

"Yes." Rafe tried to push Eden back so she could lie on her stomach. "It's at the wine sellers in their wine cellar." Rafe chuckled. "Doesn't that sound funny? English is funny sometimes."

Stunned, Eden pushed Rafe back up, ignoring her raving about English, and looked into her eyes. "You bought a whole case? It was over three hundred dollars a bottle back then."

"I know," agreed Rafe with a nod and a smile. "But I had to buy a whole case. What if there was an earthquake and the one we had here got broken?

"An earthquake?" Eden looked at her in disbelief then remembered earthquakes were something that worried her. "Rafe," she shook her head, "you bought a whole case, and you've had it in storage for almost six years?

"Plus the one I drank." Rafe nodded. "I have a lot of things stored there. Hey," she slurred with a smile, "why don't I get it out of storage, and we can have a party and drink the rest of it."

"You have other things there?" asked Eden as she shook her head in wonder. "More champagne and wine?

"Yes, I'm collecting it," Rafe said and closed her eyes, "special vintages," she mumbled, "you know."

"I didn't know," said Eden as she shook her head.

"You know," Rafe said slowly, "I told you. I started it with my Papa. You just forgot."

"I'm sure I would have remembered that," Eden insisted knowing it was probably another thing Rafe had done with her father and never thought to say anything about it to her. Rafe was always doing those sorts of things and always acted surprised when she didn't know about it. It was always one of the things she would point out when she was angry. This time, though, she was glad Rafe had done it because they still had some of their champagne. "Let's wait a little bit longer before we take our champagne out."

"Okay." Rafe yawned and laid her head on Eden. "I didn't think you wanted it. You didn't take it with you when you left. You left all of me behind."

Eden was heart struck but accepted the pain. She knew it was true. She left many things behind so she wouldn't constantly be reminded of Rafe. "I'm sorry," she whispered. She saw Rafe was nodding off to sleep. "Rafe, talk to me," said Eden as she held Rafe's head up. She just had to keep her awake a little bit longer. "Jude said you were doing an experiment on me."

"Really?" asked Rafe as she opened her eyes halfway.

"Yes, really," said Eden "Were you?"

"Yes," said Rafe smiling as she leaned in and kissed Eden. "Do you want to try again?"

"I'm not sure," Eden said apprehensively and gently pushed Rafe back. "Why do you want me to take the place of the marijuana?"

"I told you why." Rafe sighed. "You forget a lot. *Vieni qui e baciami.*[9] She leaned in again to kiss Eden and closed her eyes. "I remember everything you say, Ede," she whispered.

---

[9] Come over here and kiss me.

"Will you tell me again?" Eden asked as she pushed Rafe's hair back again and tried to keep her awake and talking.

"No, it's okay," said Rafe as she yawned and shook with exhaustion. "I hurt now," she said softly. "I'm sleepy," she sighed, "so tired," she mumbled. She leaned forward and put her head on Eden's chest. "You can keep me warm," she slurred. "Please, don't let go."

"I'm sorry you hurt," said Eden worried about her head. "Stay awake, Rafe," she said trying to push her back up, "just a little longer."

"I can't make it a little longer Ede," said Rafe as she nuzzled into Eden. "I'm bleeding," she moaned.

Frightened, Eden looked over Rafe's head at her cut. "No, you're not bleeding, babe," she said relieved. "The bandage is still good."

"My heart is bleeding now," Rafe slurred. "It won't stop," she said sadly.

"Rafe," Eden's voice caught as she was struck hard by her confession.

"I hurt," mumbled Rafe with her glazed eyes half open. "Kiss me, Ede. Make it go away."

"You have to stay awake," said Eden as tears ran down her face, and she shook with sadness for Rafe. "Sit up. Come on," she encouraged her.

"I'm sleepy," Rafe slurred as her eyes slowly closed. "I need to sleep, Ede. I can't," she mumbled incoherently.

"Rafe, I'm sorry," said Eden in tears. She kissed her softly. "I'm so sorry for everything," she whispered. She ran her fingers through her dark hair and kissed her, then watched as Rafe fell asleep.

31

THE DARK CIRCLES around Eden Kingsley's eyes attested to the fact she hadn't had much sleep. Between waking up every few hours to check on Rafe, and all the things running through her mind, sleep eluded her. She was up early and ready for work but was very worried about Rafe and the things she had said last night. She wasn't sure what to do about it all. She called Flynn, and he came over as she was making coffee and toast.

Eden sat down at the counter and gave Flynn a plate of toast with honey. "I've made some coffee for when she wakes up," said Eden as she began giving him some instructions for the day. "The only thing in the house they left to eat last night is some bread and a couple of pieces of fruit. There's a cold pizza I ordered last night but didn't eat." She sighed and shook her head. "I doubt she'll eat it, though. I'll pick up some groceries on my way home. I'm going to take off work early today and pick up Bronte so we can spend time with Rafe. Jude said Rafe was upset because I didn't stay home with her yesterday. I should be home around one o'clock or so."

"Do you need me to do anything?" asked Flynn then took a bite of his toast.

"Do you know how to retrieve something from a phone?"

"Well," he hesitated, "if I have the passcode, maybe. Why?"

"Rafe deleted something off her phone last night. It might have been something from Jake."

"Like a voicemail?"

"Maybe, I don't know." She looked at Flynn with worry. "Never mind. Just keep an eye on Rafe and help her if she needs it," said Eden as she ate her toast. "I talked to Abby this morning. She's still mad at me, but she said she would stop by later." She sighed and brushed crumbs from her hands.

"Abby and Jude were both mad when they came back last night," said Flynn anxiously as he remembered Abby's high-pitched complaints and Jude's measured comments to try to hide how upset they really were at the situation.

"Everyone's mad at me," said Eden upset. "That stupid article!"

"It was Jake who told them all of that stuff, wasn't it?" Flynn asked. It sounded like a guess, but they both knew it was the obvious truth.

Eden swallowed and held back her tears. "I confided in him," she whispered trying to keep her voice low. "I trusted him. But I never said Rafe forced me, or I didn't want Bronte."

"I know you didn't," Flynn assured her. "I'm glad you told Katheryn to use everything and to tell Rafe about the FBI. But," he hesitated uncomfortably, "I think you better tell Rafe about things before the FBI does. Once they start asking questions, she'll figure it out and if you haven't told her," Flynn looked at her with worry.

"I know, I know," said Eden trying to control the shaking of her hand as she held her coffee cup. "It's going to be bad. I just want to win in court next Tuesday." She looked at Flynn in torment. "Last night, she told me her heart was bleeding. She's still hurting, and I can't hurt her again by telling her those things right now. When we win in court, she'll be on more solid ground," Eden tried to say confidently. "She'll know Bronte and I aren't leaving, and we love her. Then I can tell her everything."

"I just hope you win," said Flynn worried about what might happen if they lost. "That article made it sound like you're fighting the adoption."

"We have to win," said Eden firmly. "It was Jake who wanted to fight it, not me. I told Katheryn we have to win." She looked down at her watch. "I need to go. Don't let Abby or Jude give her any more pot," she instructed him. She then gathered her things and left for work.

Flynn finished his toast and turned on his computer to work at the kitchen counter. He thought about what Eden said about the possibility of Jake calling Rafe. Without the passcodes, it would be hard to get into the phone, but he knew of something he could do, and he wouldn't need a passcode.

Sneaking into Eden's room, he took Rafe's phone back to the kitchen and hooked it to his computer. He had done this with Eden's phone when he was at her house setting up her computer. He uploaded the special software to Rafe's phone then carefully placed it back where he found it. He went back into the kitchen and worked for a couple of hours.

Abby and Jude came in through the patio. "Where is she?" asked Abby as she walked into the kitchen.

"She's still asleep in Eden's room," answered Flynn as he closed his laptop.

Abby turned around and made her way to Eden's room. She sat on the bed next to Rafe. "Hey, wake up, sleepy head," she said playfully and shook her awake.

Rafe opened her eyes and squinted up at Abby. "What are you doing here?" she asked annoyed that Abby was hovering over her.

"Good morning to you too." Abby smiled unfazed by the question. "I'm here to make sure you stay conscious. Oh, and to clean up the patio. Eden was really pissed." She laughed because otherwise her anger at Eden would return.

"She was? Why?" asked Rafe with dread.

"You have no idea what I'm talking about, do you?" asked Abby, finding the whole situation humorous.

"Sure I do," said Rafe shifting her eyes trying to remember. "You're talking about," she tried to think. "No, I have no idea, sorry. My head hurts," she said and put her hand to her head.

"Is she decent?" asked Jude as she walked in the room.

"Decently in oblivion to what went on last night," joked Abby. "I told you."

"Get me some aspirin or something," said Rafe as she sat up slowly.

Abby opened the Tylenol bottle on the nightstand and handed a couple to Rafe, along with the glass of water that was beside them. "You slipped and fell in the shower last night," Abby informed her cheerfully.

"Do I have amnesia? Is that why I can't remember?" Rafe asked with a frown as she took the pills.

"No," said Abby amused. "You can't remember because you were too stoned to really care."

"Oh, yeah." Rafe grimaced in pain as her head throbbed. "I remember you guys came over asking me about lunch."

"You were so fucking funny last night, Rafe!" Abby could not help her grin. "But Eden was pissed."

"Why, because we didn't save any for her?" Rafe asked annoyed, this time because Eden was now pissed again about something she had done. "What paper is she going to announce it in?"

Rafe was obviously grumpy, and Abby snorted her laugh.

"No, because you were so fucked up," Jude said through her laughter.

"Yeah," Abby said teasingly, "she'll probably put that on a billboard on Sunset Boulevard, anyway. I can see it now 'Salvaggio Stoned' and a photo of you on the shower floor. There'd be a caption at the bottom saying, *She tried to fuck Mary Jane, but the girl plays rough with lightweights*." She and Jude laughed, but Rafe only frowned.

"My head feels like it is ten times too big," groaned Rafe as she put her hand to her head.

"You hit your head on the shower seat," Abby told her. "Eden had to wash your hair." She looked at Rafe evaluating her head. "You do have a big head."

"I know." Rafe smiled wryly at Abby. "I have a giant head, and the whole thing hurts."

"Come on," said Abby and held out her hand. "You should get up and move around." She pulled Rafe out of bed. "Get dressed," she told her once she was standing. "Jude and I have to go clean up the patio."

186

32

WHILE CLEANING UP the mess on the patio, Jude Atwood and Abby Van Falkov were joking around about the events of the previous night. As they were discussing who was going to fish out what fell into the pool, they looked up in surprise when Flynn ran outside freaking out.

"Jude, Abby, something's wrong with Rafe!"

"What happened?" Abby asked alarmed.

"She's in her room, and the door's locked," Flynn said panicking. "She's screaming and cussing and yelling something in Italian. I think she said she was going to kill someone." He swallowed. "I think she said she was going to kill Eden."

"I'm glad I'm not Eden!" Abby laughed and looked over at Jude.

"We," Jude started as she was bent over with laughter, "we should have told her," she caught her breath, "told her about her hair before she went into her room."

"I wasn't going to tell her!" Abby laughed shrilly.

"You shouldn't have told her Eden washed her hair," said Jude as she held her side, "or that she had a big head."

After calming Flynn down, and laughing hard at the whole situation, Jude and Abby went back to work on the patio mess. When they had finished, they went inside to wait for Rafe. About a half hour later, Rafe came out of her room dressed and ready for the day. She found Jude, Abby, and Flynn sitting in the kitchen at the island.

"You okay, Rafe?" asked Abby trying not to smile.

"Fuck you, Abby!"

"Hey, be nice. I didn't do anything," said Abby innocently. "Your hair looks good."

"Fucking Eden," snapped Rafe. "*Lei deve rovinare la mia vita e miei capelli,*"[10] Rafe mumbled. "I'm starving." She started opening cabinets and the refrigerator looking for food.

"What?" Abby said, annoyed Rafe was speaking in Italian again. She looked at Jude. "She's doing it again!"

"We looked, there's not much here," said Jude holding back her smile. "Just cold pizza."

"Eden said she was bringing groceries home later," volunteered Flynn trying to be helpful. "She said she'd be back with Bronte about one."

"I can't wait that long," she said and slammed the refrigerator. "Let's go get something from Letty at The Kiki." She grabbed her keys and walked out the door.

"See, Abby," said Jude as they watched Rafe walk out. "I told you we helped. Eden doesn't know what she's talking about. The Rafe we know and love is back." She grinned with the satisfaction of a job well done. "Let's go keep her company."

"She was still much funnier stoned," Abby quipped as she got up to follow Jude.

"I'm going to stay," Flynn told them. "I have to finish my work and email it in. I'll let Eden know where you guys went."

---

[10] You have to ruin my life and my hair.

33

RAFE SALVAGGIO WALKED into The Kiki Bistro just before the lunch crowd started to show up, finding a table by the window. Abby and Jude followed close behind and joined her. They ordered lunch, and as they ate, Abby and Jude were doing their best to improve Rafe's bad mood. They were also trying to keep away the crowd of people who recognized her and had found the courage to approach the table. Some people who approached were sympathetic, and others were making no secret they would be happy to have a baby for Rafe if she would only ask. Still others offered to take her home for the chance to ease her pain. Rafe was watching one of the offers walk away with a hungry lecherous look.

"Rafe!" Abby said and smacked her on the arm. "Stop looking at her like that."

"What?" said Rafe annoyed.

"What if Eden walks in?" asked Abby and gave her a look. She was unhappy with Eden, but she didn't want anything else to happen that could be used against Rafe.

"Then she can add another complaint about me to her fucking list," Rafe said as she stabbed her salad.

"She's not doing anything wrong, Abby," said Jude as she watched the girl walking away too. "Leave her alone. She loves Eden."

"I do," said Rafe sadly. "I do love her."

Abby shook her head and rolled her eyes because she didn't think Rafe was taking her advice seriously as she and Jude ogled another woman walking by their table.

Letty finally got a moment to take a break, went over to the table, and sat down. "I'm glad to see you're out," she said, noting they were all finished eating, and the waitress hadn't come to clear their plates yet. She let that issue go to focus on a more important matter. "I was surprised Eden left Bronte with us last night. Is she still trying to make up for what she said in the damn article?" she asked hotly. "That baby deserves to be with the people who love her."

Rafe looked at Letty, and her temper flared. She slammed her fist on the table disrupting dishes and cutlery. "Stop it!" she roared. "Eden loves her baby. I don't want you saying things like that anymore," she said as she looked at her sternly.

"She's the one who said it," said Letty defensively.

"No, she didn't say it!" she said angrily as she looked Letty in the eyes. "You're wrong, Letty! It doesn't matter how she felt about the insemination. Bronte is her baby, and she loves her," she said resolutely. She looked at everyone around the table gravely. "I don't want to hear anyone saying Eden said she doesn't love Bronte. She loves her, *capito*?" She flicked her hand angrily with her Italian gesture. "Understand?" she repeated in English. It was clear Rafe's temper had been let loose, and they all should beware. It did not happen often with their friends, but they knew when it happened, Rafe took no prisoners.

"Of course she does," said Jude as she winced. "It's okay, Rafe," she said trying to calm her.

"We know she does," Abby assured her as she cringed under Rafe's gaze.

"I'm sorry, Rafe," said Letty regretfully. "Don't be angry. You're right. I was wrong to say that. Do..." she hesitated, wanting to calm her anger, "do you want me to call Ephraim and have him bring Bronte to you?"

"No, Eden has made arrangements to pick up her baby," Rafe said curtly. As Abby looked from Rafe to Jude with concern, Rafe's phone rang. "Excuse me," she said and took the call. "Hello. Yes, this is Rafe Salvaggio. I see. Yes, Friday morning should be fine. Thank you, goodbye," she said and hung up. "Hey, you guys want to go shopping with me?" she said, changing the subject to the relief of her friends.

"Sure," said Abby knowing it might not be a good idea to let Rafe go out alone with a head injury, a credit card, and a temper. She looked at Jude to see if she was going.

"Can't," she said with a shrug. "I have some appointments later."

As Eden walked up to the table, she heard Rafe ask about shopping. She stood beside Rafe's chair holding Bronte. "We'd like to go shopping too," she said and smiled when Rafe looked up. "I need a new dress for Friday night."

"Hi," said Rafe as she got up and kissed Bronte. She looked at Letty daring her to say something. "Bye, Letty. Let's go if we're going," she said and walked out not really caring if anyone followed.

"Is she okay?" Eden asked Abby.

"Depends on what you mean by okay," said Abby mysteriously then headed after Rafe.

"Thanks for taking care of Bronte last night, Letty," said Eden anxiously dreading another confrontation.

"No problem," said Letty as she stood. "I'm sorry about what I said. Rafe pointed out to me how wrong I was. I really am sorry," she said regretfully. She would apologize a million times if it meant keeping Eden from leaving, causing them to lose Bronte again.

"She did?" asked Eden surprised by the apology Rafe made happen. Regret filled her again for ever leaving her as she remembered how Rafe had always stood up for her. "Well," Eden said softly and smiled, "thank you again." She hesitated for a moment then followed Abby and Rafe outside.

34

AFTER RETRIEVING THE car seat and stroller from Eden's car, everyone loaded into Rafe Salvaggio's car. The trip to the shopping district was mostly made in silence. Rafe kept looking over at Eden with a frown and could see she was tired and worried. She couldn't help wondering if her worry was over the fact that her plan was backfiring and she was being attacked because of the article too. Rafe wasn't sure if she really felt sorry for her or not. She couldn't remember anything from last night. All she knew was the recording on her phone had been deleted, and Eden made it quite clear—Bronte was her baby and no one else's.

Rafe parked and got Bronte's stroller out of the trunk then Eden loaded Bronte into it and secured her. Finally, they were ready to go.

Abby looked around at the shops. "Where to first?" she asked.

"I'd like to look in some boutiques," said Eden as she looked into Rafe's eyes then gave her a small kiss. "I want to find something special for you." She started pushing Bronte forward.

"Okay." Rafe sighed and followed Eden and Abby. She snatched Abby's arm and held her back. "I think you better tell me exactly what happened last night."

"You were so fucking funny." Abby laughed as she enjoyed having Rafe's attention.

35

ABBY VAN FALKOV HAPPILY filled in Rafe about the events from last night between shops and fittings. She put a positive spin on the whole thing, but Rafe wasn't smiling. As they were sitting in a waiting area, watching Bronte and waiting for Eden as she tried on a few dresses, Abby chronicled the night and the fact Rafe had tried to get them to listen to the recording on her phone.

Rafe put her head in her hands. "I wish I had just said no," she groaned. Now everyone knew about the recording. She decided to just leave it saved in the cloud in case she needed it later. Abby didn't mention the recording being deleted so Rafe was certain Eden must have found it last night and deleted it. If Eden deleted it, she may not have realized her phone backed up automatically. For now, since the recording was safe, she just wanted to figure out what had happened last night and see what she could salvage.

"Rafe, it's cool," Abby assured her smoothly. "I mean, she knew you were high when you said all that, and it was funny."

"Rafe," Eden called from the dressing room, "can you come help me?"

Rafe looked at Abby with uncertainty. "Coming," she called back to Eden as she handed Bronte to Abby. She walked back to the dressing room area and stood outside Eden's room. "What do you need?"

"Come in," she said. "I need some help with this dress." Rafe opened the door and saw Eden was in a dress that needed to be zipped up the back. "Can you zip me?"

"Sure," said Rafe and zipped up the dress trying not to touch her soft skin.

When the dress was zipped, Eden turned and kissed Rafe. "Thank you," she said and stepped back. "What do you think?"

"I think you look beautiful," said Rafe surprised by the kiss.

"You've said the same thing about every dress," she said as she ran her hand down Rafe's arm. "Is there one you like best?"

"This one is fine," said Rafe. "Really," she said fretfully. "You shouldn't go to too much trouble. It's just one night." She wished she could remember what had happened last night after everyone left. Eden was acting as if nothing had happened, and it made Rafe nervous.

"What, just one night?" asked Eden with a soft throaty laugh. "It's a very important night." She touched Rafe's face gently. "And you're the reason for the celebration." She smiled sweetly. "I want to look good when I stand next to you."

The shopping trip, to Rafe, had become themed. Eden would try on dresses and need her help buttoning or zipping things, and every effort was rewarded with a touch, a kiss, or a seductive smile. Rafe was becoming confused because, according to Abby, she had been cruel to Eden. Then there was the problem with the deleted file. But Eden was acting as if nothing happened... or something else happened. Abby was no help at all when Rafe questioned her about what was happening because she thought the whole thing was very funny. Finally, they found just about everything they needed and loaded back into the car.

"I just have one more stop to make," said Rafe then drove to the nearest computer store. "Okay, we're here."

"A computer store? You're kidding, right?" scoffed Abby.

"No." Rafe smirked. "I need a new computer."

36

AFTER A LIGHT dinner, Rafe Salvaggio dropped Abby and Eden off at their cars. Eden followed Rafe and Bronte, along with all of their purchases, home, and Bronte fell asleep on the drive. Eden was putting the little girl in her room while Rafe brought in all of the purchases from the day. She put Eden's things in her room and took the boxes with her new computer into the living room and started opening the boxes and pulling things out.

Eden found Rafe in the living room. "You're not going to do all of that setup tonight are you?"

"No," she said as she looked over things. "I just want to make sure everything's here. The FBI will be here Friday to pick up my other computers, so I want to make sure I can transfer some files before then."

"Oh," said Eden surprised, "the FBI. Friday?"

"Yes." Rafe looked up at her. "You seem surprised."

"Katheryn told me they may be involved," said Eden nervously, "but I didn't know they would be here Friday. I guess I should get my old one out of storage for them." She didn't want to tell her that Flynn had the computer and possibly open herself up to questions. She had her own meeting that Katheryn had scheduled with the FBI coming up, and she was very anxious about where it might lead.

"You should," Rafe agreed. "They said they wanted all of them checked. But don't worry. Those people are after me, not you." She looked at Eden wondering if she was the real reason the group who filed the lawsuit got her information. She had no idea how they would have been able to get into her computer if they even had, but Eden could have helped them. She frowned and pushed away that troubling thought.

Eden wanted to change the subject from the FBI. It made her nervous they would be talking to her so soon. "I can't believe you spent so much money on a computer," she said to change the subject.

"You don't need to worry about how much I spend," Rafe said through clenched teeth, annoyed Eden was complaining about her spending money again.

"I'm not worried," Eden said cautiously. "I just... It's an expensive computer."

"I need it," said Rafe as she looked up at her with a frown. "It'll help me with my photography, and the sales girl said it was top of the line."

"I think she was a little too helpful," said Eden as she sat next to Rafe.

Rafe continued to look over her computer stuff ignoring Eden's unfounded jealousy.

"I think it's great you're so into your photography," said Eden wanting to ease the tension. "Maybe you can take some pictures of me again," she offered. Rafe looked at her, and Eden smiled and touched Rafe's hair. "Would you like to take pictures of me modeling the clothes I bought," she asked and bit her lower lip, "or maybe without clothes?" She leaned in and kissed her.

"Eden," said Rafe as she pushed her back, "Abby told me some of the things I said and did last night. I'm sorry."

"It's okay," said Eden shrugging it away. "You were really stoned. You did say and do those things, but you were also very sweet after they left."

"I was?" asked Rafe wondering just how sweet she could have been while stoned and having a head injury.

"Yes," Eden said and kissed her. "I love you."

"How sweet was I?" Rafe asked cautiously.

C. L. CATTANO

"Come on," purred Eden as she took Rafe's hand and started to pull her up.

"I think we should stay here," Rafe said and pulled her back.

"No," Eden said softly then kissed Rafe deeply. "Come into my room." She smiled suggestively then got up and walked into her room.

37

PACING IN FRONT of Eden's doorway, Rafe Salvaggio was trying to decide what to do. After seeing and touching Eden while she helped with her fittings today, and Eden's assault on her senses driving her crazy, Rafe's body was telling her it wanted Eden. But on the other hand, her mind was telling her not to go because she was still angry over everything in the article and the fact Eden made it clear Bronte was her child and no one else's. Then there was her heart—it knew she loved Eden and wanted to be near her, wanted and needed the comfort of her.

Rafe walked to the door and touched the knob then walked away again tormented. If she went inside, would it just be for self-gratification like the article accused? If she didn't go inside, was she being emotionally abusive or disregarding Eden's needs? Then there was whatever happened last night. How was the recording deleted from her phone? Did Eden listen to it? What did she hear? Question built in Rafe's mind. She could not remember what she said to Eden or what she did. Abby said she was cruel, but Eden said she was sweet. How cruel? How sweet? The uncertainty of what to do frustrated her as she paced the floor.

Eden had changed into a negligee she bought, and she hoped Rafe would like. She watched the bedroom door and saw Rafe's shadow as it passed over the small opening. Eden could tell Rafe was pacing in the hallway. All night last night and all day today, she thought about what Rafe had said to her. What Jude had talked to her about last night was on her mind too. Jude told her maybe Rafe needed something more, and Rafe had confessed she was in pain and out of control. Did it have something to do with whatever was on her phone? It filled her with dread that Jake might be leaving Rafe messages. Then there was Rafe's confession about loving Greer, which felt like a stab in her heart. Tonight Eden wanted to reassure Rafe again of how much she loved her and how she wouldn't leave her. She didn't want Rafe to worry about Jake or think about Greer.

Eden looked at the door again wondering what Rafe was doing. Finally, her patience wore out, and she got up and went to open the bedroom door. She saw Rafe with her back to the door running her hands through her hair. "Rafe?" she said softly. Rafe turned, and Eden looked into her eyes. Eden could see the pain and torment filling them.

"Eden," said Rafe surprised, "I..." she started.

"What's wrong?" asked Eden as Rafe just looked at her. "It's okay," she said as she saw her hesitation. She took her hand and led her into the bedroom, and they sat on the bed.

"Eden, I can't stand *not* knowing what happened last night," Rafe confessed. "What did I say, what did I do?"

"You really don't remember anything?" asked Eden surprised.

"No," Rafe shook her head, "sorry. Well, I remember Jude and Abby showing up uninvited, and Jude bringing her little box over. I remember ordering food. Then..." She shook her head. "Will you tell me what happened?"

"Don't worry, babe." Eden smiled and brushed a lock of hair from Rafe's face. "You were in pain," Eden hesitated, "from your fall in the shower. We didn't have sex if that's what you're worried about."

"No, it wasn't," Rafe stammered, "I mean," she pointed to the mark on Eden's neck, "you have a mark on your neck. I just wish I could remember."

"You put the mark there," Eden affirmed with a nod, "you wanted to do an experiment."

"I did?" asked Rafe confused.

"Yes, and I think I figured out what you wanted," she said and smiled invitingly.

"Really?" asked Rafe getting her meaning. "Do you think I still want it now, or do we need to get stoned for it?"

"I'd like you to remember it," Eden flirted, "so I don't think we should get stoned."

"Will you tell me what I said?" Rafe asked as she frowned.

Eden took Rafe's face into her hands and spoke between her kisses. "You told me what you loved about me."

"I love everything about you," Rafe whispered as she closed her eyes and melted under Eden's kisses.

"That I should stay with you," Eden said softly and kissed her.

"You should," agreed Rafe.

"And you feel connected to me," Eden said and kissed her deeply.

Rafe closed her eyes and returned Eden's kisses. "I do," she whispered, "is that all?"

"Maybe," Eden said as she smiled and kept kissing Rafe. "I just want to let you know," she whispered, "I'm in control tonight."

"Really?" asked Rafe as she opened her eyes with a cautious grin. "What makes you think you should be in control?"

"Some other things you said last night," she said as she moved her kisses to Rafe's neck.

"I was stoned last night," Rafe reminded her. Her mind tried to go into alert mode in case Eden was talking about the recording.

"True," said Eden as she pulled back and looked at Rafe, "But I think you tend to speak truthfully when you're drunk or stoned, so I'm pretty sure I should be in control tonight."

"What did I say?" Rafe asked with her head against Eden's. She wanted Eden to tell her everything, but on the other hand, she didn't want Eden to stop kissing her.

"No, I'm not going to tell you," Eden said playfully. "I'm in control. I'm what you like to call Alpha E tonight."

"Alpha E?" asked Rafe as she fell back onto the bed chuckling. She realized Eden was on a mission, and she would get nowhere with her on the subject of last night. "I was joking," she teased deciding to play her game.

"It's better than Wildling Rafe," Eden said as she followed Rafe and laid over her.

"Oh, you think so?" Rafe scoffed.

"Yes, I do." Eden smiled and kissed her again.

"Okay," said Rafe grinning, "let's see if you can control me."

"I did okay the other night," Eden bragged as she kissed her.

"Oh, I see," said Rafe between Eden's kisses. "You think that was being in control." She chuckled. "Just so you know," she said teasingly, "it wasn't. It was me giving you," she kissed her, "what you wanted."

"Well, if it was, then thank you," Eden conceded. "You can do it again tonight," she said as she pushed away from her. "Stand up and take off your shirt," ordered Eden.

Rafe just looked at her, and Eden motioned to her with her chin to do as she said. "Your first command?" Rafe asked as she looked at Eden slyly. She stood and began taking her shirt off very slowly. She kept eye contact with Eden, running her hand down her arm, unbuttoning her cuff, and then did the same to the other cuff. She ran her hand over her chest and over the buttons lining down her shirt.

Instead of starting from the top, she started at the bottom, exposing a sliver of her stomach first and opening the shirt slowly, then running her hands under it and over herself, taking it down over her shoulders, revealing herself inches at a time before finally dropping it to the floor. She stood with her hands on her hips and waited for Eden's next command.

Fighting her impatience, Eden couldn't believe Rafe was still in control. She knew she was because watching Rafe strip had made her very wet. She looked up at Rafe's tawny well-etched body and cleared her throat.

"Take off your bra."

Rafe smiled and took off her bra slowly, reaching behind her back to unhook it, then letting it slide down her arms until it fell to the floor. She didn't try to cover herself or hide how erect her nipples had become.

"So, do you want to kiss me now?" she asked with a wink.

Eden did want to kiss her, but Rafe was not in charge. She fought the urge to touch her.

"Take off your pants," she commanded softly but firmly.

Rafe looked down at her pants and then at Eden and smiled. She moved very close, so she was standing between Eden's legs with her waist near Eden's face.

"I'm sorry, I couldn't hear you," Rafe said sensually. "Did you say take off my pants?"

Eden leaned back on her elbows, looked up at her, and smiled as she nodded determined not to let her take control.

"Okay," said Rafe. She put her hand flat against her stomach and ran it down herself until her thumb was under the waist of her pants and her fingers lingered over her crotch. With her other hand, she unbuttoned and held the waist of her pants, and then ran her fingers from her crotch slowly up the zipper until she reached the zipper pull. She held onto it for a moment then slowly took it down as Eden watched her hand. "Do you want to help?"

Rafe's voice broke through, and Eden fought her desire to yank the pants off her. She had to stay in control tonight. "No," she swallowed. "Take them off. You," she cleared her throat, "you can go slower."

Rafe grinned and bit her lip, realizing Eden was trying a little reverse psychology, so she continued to go slow. "Slower?" asked Rafe and smiled. She put her hands on her waist and slid them into her pants and under the edge of her panties, running them from her butt to her crotch and inching her pants down slowly. When they had lowered past her hips, they glided down her legs. She stepped out of her pants then leaned over and slid her hands up Eden's legs to her hips. "Do you want me to take your clothes off now?"

Eden tried not to smile because Rafe was doing what she wanted to do and not what she was told. "You're supposed to be standing up."

"Well, I'm already here." Rafe smiled then kissed her stomach through her negligee. "So maybe you should let me stay."

Eden closed her eyes so she wouldn't lose herself in Rafe's smile. "Stand up," she repeated and swallowed.

"Okay," Rafe whispered. She got up slowly brushing herself against Eden, standing in front and very close to her. "Now what, Alpha E?" she asked as she stood naked in front of her.

With her eyes still closed, Eden took a deep breath then sat up. She could smell Rafe in front of her. "Kneel down," she said. She felt the air move and knew Rafe was kneeling. She opened her eyes, and they met Rafe's. "Touch me gently," she whispered.

"Where? Show me," Rafe whispered and held up her hand for Eden.

"No," Eden shook her head. "Touch my breasts." She watched as Rafe moved her hand to her breast and touched it so lightly Eden could barely feel it through her negligee. "More," she whispered.

Rafe could see and feel Eden's nipple trying to burst its way through the material, but she kept her touch very light. She smiled impishly up at her. "You said gently," she said softly. "Tell me to take off your clothes."

Eden could feel the heat from Rafe's hand as she teased her with her light touch.

"No," she said fighting herself from giving in. "I'm in control."

Rafe just smiled at her.

"Kiss me," said Eden.

Rafe leaned in, putting her mouth very close to Eden's, and held the kiss back. "Where?" she breathed over her lips. "You have to tell me exactly what you want."

Eden felt Rafe's breath on her mouth, and she started to fall into the kiss as Rafe's words broke through to her, and she realized Rafe was now telling her what to do.

"Stop," she said and smiled. Rafe stopped touching her. "Stay still," said Eden. "I'll kiss you," she whispered. "I'll touch you." She held Rafe's face in her hands and kissed her, Rafe returning her kisses. Eden pulled away and moved her kisses to Rafe's neck as she ran her hands over her breasts. She kissed her shoulders then took her breast into her mouth.

"That feels so good," Rafe whispered as Eden kissed her body. "Eden, what do you want me to do to you? Tell me," she whispered. "Show me."

"Touch me," Eden whispered. "Touch me here." She took Rafe's hand and put it between her legs.

"Oh, you're so wet," Rafe whispered into her ear. "Will you let me take off your clothes now?"

Very frustrated, Eden fought the sensation of Rafe's breath on her ear. "Fuck!" she moaned and heard Rafe laugh softly. She stripped off her top, yanking her panties down, and Rafe pulled them the rest of the way off. Eden pulled Rafe up from her knees and plunged herself back into her kisses. She pulled Rafe back on the bed, taking her hand and forcing it back between her legs. "Rafe," she begged.

Holding her hand where Eden put it, Rafe did not move it. "Tell me," she said smiling at her.

"Rafe," Eden said kissing Rafe hungrily, "I need you inside me, please," she moaned.

"Okay, Alpha E." Rafe smiled as she ran her fingers through Eden and covered her with hot kisses then sweet whispers in her ear. "Eden, do you want to know something?"

Eden pressed her body and lips against Rafe, trying to touch every part of her, breathless for her kisses. "Tell me," Eden said softly. "Oh, god, Rafe," she moaned. "That feels so good. What, what do you want to tell me?"

Rafe stopped what she was doing and looked into Eden's eyes and smiled. "I don't think that was you being in control," she said trying not to laugh. "I think that was you," she kissed her, "being bossy."

"What?" said Eden miffed.

"That was Bossy Ede," said Rafe with a soft laugh.

"No, I was in control," said Eden sitting up annoyed.

"You call telling me what to do being in control?" asked Rafe grinning. "Eden, I was planning to take my shirt and pants off, and touching you. You just gave me a reason to be defiantly in control. You were just being," she kissed her softly, "bossy."

"Defiantly in control?" asked Eden doubtfully.

"Yes," said Rafe. "You told me what to do, but I decided how to do it." She grinned and kissed her. "And you got very wet."

"Are you trying to get out of having sex with me?" Eden pouted.

"No," Rafe assured her, "but I just didn't want you to think being bossy was the same as being in control."

"I didn't know there was a difference," said Eden as she leaned into Rafe. "You were telling me what to tell you, so you were bossy too."

"Well, I just thought if you were going to be bossy, I could make some suggestions," Rafe explained with a grin.

"I was not being bossy," insisted Eden.

"Eden, have I ever told you what to do?" Rafe tried not to laugh.

"Honestly," said Eden as she looked at Rafe thinking, "I don't know."

"You don't know? Ede..." She chuckled.

"Well, you just," Eden stammered, "sometimes you just. You do this thing," she tried to explain, "and I..."

"What?" Rafe smiled at Eden's lack of words.

Eden lifted up and grasped Rafe, straddling her and showing her frustration. "You make it so I can't think, and half the time, I probably couldn't even remember my own name," she growled playfully.

Rafe smiled at the feeling of Eden's wetness against her. "Well, you do the same thing to me," she said and winked. "You do know you've been in control before, don't you?"

"I have?" Eden asked suspiciously.

"Yes, and I liked it," Rafe admitted. "But you didn't tell me what to do or tell me to strip for you," she said softly. "You weren't bossy. Though Bossy Ede was kind of sexy." Rafe laughed softly.

"When was I in control?" Eden asked doubtfully.

"You were in control a lot, not just once or twice," Rafe said and then pulled Eden down and kissed her as she ran her hands over her naked body. "Sometimes, I need you to be in control," she whispered in her ear.

"Well, I want to be in control tonight," Eden whispered back and kissed Rafe.

"You can be in control anytime you want," said Rafe smiling. "You just have to take it." She kissed her. "I love you."

Eden brushed Rafe's dark hair back from her face. "I love you too," she whispered and leaned down to kiss Rafe's face and neck. She moved her hands through Rafe's hair and down to her breasts as she moved her body against Rafe. "Rafe," she said as she poured her kisses over Rafe, "kiss me everywhere," she moaned, "touch me everywhere. I think I'm out of control. We should both just be out of control."

Rafe lifted herself, twisting her body, taking Eden over and down as she kissed her, and then she smiled. "Stop being so bossy," she purred then ran her warm hands down Eden's body, touching her everywhere and kissing her everywhere.

38

THE DAY OF the big celebration for the Jackson-Goyer Grant Award party had finally arrived. Rafe Salvaggio had a busy day planned to get ready for the party, including an appointment with the FBI. Eden had left to take Bronte to day school before going into work. Rafe had just finished cleaning up the breakfast mess and made herself a cappuccino to enjoy while she read the news on her tablet.

Eden's night of 'control' a couple of nights ago took a little edge off the tension Rafe had been feeling. Abby and Jude had cooled off a bit because Rafe had been showing signs of improvement. By keeping Abby and the others at arms distance, it seemed the tension between them and Eden had eased, to the relief of Rafe. She knew it was only a matter of time before Abby let what she knew slip, and Rafe didn't want to give Eden any reason to leave her.

She was still worried and unsure about what was going to happen Tuesday at the court hearing. She had again asked Eden to tell her whatever it was she was keeping from her, and again, Eden had requested more time. No one had said a thing about deleting the recording on her phone, so she decided to leave it in the cloud and pretend like she hadn't noticed it was gone. Because of the worry and stress that she was feeling about Jake and about Eden's secrets, Rafe continued being cautious with her heart, but she was starting to think maybe things were going to work out.

To help confirm her feelings, she decided to look over the list she had made a while ago of things that compared proof that Eden would stay or if she would go. She hoped the 'She's Staying' side would finally be the winner. She looked it over and added more things she remembered to the lists including the article. As she worked, it became much too depressing to look at because of the amount of things Jake had said that were true, and the things Eden might be hiding, weighed down the 'She's Leaving' side. It dwarfed anything positive Eden had done or tried to reassure her about.

To take her mind off those problems, Rafe got out her new computer and experimented with some of the new programs she bought to manipulate her photographs. The program recommended by the surfer kid named Mason she had helped out was amazing. She asked Flynn to help her yesterday. He transferred some files, installed the programs she needed, set up the wireless internet connection and got everything working perfectly. As she was working, the doorbell rang, and she went to answer the door, opening it to find two people in dark suits.

"Rafaella Salvaggio?" the first person asked formally.

"That's right," said Rafe worried something else bad was about to happen.

"Special Agent Foster, FBI," the agent said as she showed her credentials and badge. Motioning to the man behind her.

"This is Special Agent Brewster." He showed his credentials and badge too.

Rafe took the ID's and looked them over. "Are you here for the computers?"

"Yes, ma'am," said Agent Foster. "This was in your door," she said and handed her an envelope.

"Thank you," said Rafe relieved as she took the envelope. "Come in. You can call me Rafe," she said and took them to the living room, setting the envelope on the table. "The computers are there in the dining room," she directed, and Agent Foster went to look at the computers.

"Nice place," said Agent Brewster as he looked around at the art on the walls. "We saw you do building restorations and checked out some of your work here locally. You're very good."

"Thanks." Rafe smiled at hearing her work was still appreciated. "That was when I owned my old company, Eroina Conservazione e Design. What made you check out my work?"

"We had to research you for the case," Agent Brewster revealed with a smile.

Rafe returned his smile. "Well, I'm glad you liked what you saw."

"I liked some of it," admitted Brewster. "Agent Foster was disappointed you sold the business. I think she needs help on her old place. We've been really busy lately on detail, watching some foreign diplomats from Barcelona, so she hasn't been able to get much done," he explained.

"Oh, I think I have a card for the new owner with his personal number. He worked with me for a long time and is very good. He's gearing the business to residential so he may be a good fit. I can get it if you'd like," Rafe offered.

"Really? That would be nice," Brewster said appreciatively. "I can surprise Agent Foster with it later." He gave Rafe a wink.

Rafe led him to her office where she looked for the business card in her files. "So, how does this work?" she asked. "Will you give me some sort of receipt for the computers?"

"Actually, Agent Foster has a few questions to ask and a form to fill out on each computer. Another agent will be in contact with you to do an interview, if necessary," Brewster explained.

"Okay," Rafe said and handed him the business card. "I hope this helps her," she said. "Would you like something to drink?" she asked as they made their way to the dining room where Agent Foster was looking over the computers.

"Agent Brewster, why don't you do the questions while I get the information from the computers and fill out this paperwork," said Agent Foster as she started writing things down on a form.

"Fine," agreed Brewster. "I don't need anything to drink, thank you. Why don't we sit?" he suggested and motioned to the living room. "It's just a few simple questions at this time," he said while he got a form and a clipboard from Agent Foster's case. "Like I said, the hard ones will come during the interview if they do one."

"Okay," said Rafe as they entered the living room and sat on the couch. "Ask away."

Brewster sat down with the clipboard and took out his pen. "Did you have exclusive access to all of the computers?"

"Yes, to two of them, the larger laptop and the desktop," Rafe acknowledged. "The other belongs to my roommate Eden Kingsley."

"Kingsley," said Brewster under his breath as he took a small notebook from his coat pocket and flipped back a few pages in the book. "Yes, I see she's listed here as someone else who may be interviewed," he said and made a checkmark on the clipboard. "Next question. Did you buy the computers new or used?"

"New," said Rafe.

"Good, we don't have to track down previous owners." Brewster smiled and made another checkmark. "Did you ever take the computers out of the state or out of the country?"

"Yes, I've taken my laptop to several places in Europe and to several states when I traveled for work. Most recently, I went to New York. I don't think Eden took hers anywhere out of state or out of the country, at least in the last two years, unless she took it to Canada last year. You'll have to ask her. I used mine more for work and hers was more for personal use."

"Okay," he said, "we'll make a note for the investigator to ask her more detailed information. Have you had any repairs made by anyone other than the manufacturer?"

"I did have more memory put in my laptop. That was done by the store I bought it from. I think that's all the repairs. The rest I just called tech support, my assistant did them, or I made them myself. I'm not sure about Eden, but I don't think she had any problems. Oh, her ex, Jake Thompson, may have used it."

Brewster looked up at Rafe surprised she knew that name. "We'll look in to him," he said and made a note. "Having repairs done at the store makes things easier," he continued still looking at his notes. "So you had an assistant that had access to your computer?"

"Oh, yes." Rafe laughed lightly at her gaffe. "I had an assistant when I owned Eroina Conservazione e Design, Ashton Miller. But the only time he had access was when I had an issue or needed help. He didn't use it regularly or have access to it when I wasn't around."

"Okay," said Brewster as he made notes on the clipboard. "Next question. Did you host or subscribe to any pornographic sites or terrorist sites known or unknown?"

"Is that a trick question?" asked Rafe confused. "How would I know if they were unknown?

"Yes, that is a poorly written question." Brewster concealing his annoyance with the bureaucracy it was taking to get field questions corrected on forms. "It's supposed to be asking about terrorists unknown to us, the government, at this time. You, of course, would know if they were terrorists," Brewster explained.

"Definitely not then," said Rafe perturbed.

"Sorry, we have to ask it," explained Brewster with a shrug. "You would be surprised at what people do on their computers. Criminal masterminds are everywhere." He sighed at the truth of his statement.

After a few more relevant questions, Brewster closed his notebook and had Rafe sign the questionnaire. "I think that's it for us," he said and turned to speak to the other agent. "Agent

Foster, do you have the paperwork on the computers ready?" he called out.

"Yes," Foster said as she walked into the living room to join them. "I've recorded all of the serial numbers, model numbers, and I've taken pictures of everything. If you'll just look over this paperwork and make sure you agree with everything, you can sign at the bottom of each page, and we'll be finished."

"If everything looks correct, we'll load the computers and be on our way," added Brewster.

Rafe looked over the paperwork. "It looks correct." After signing each page, she handed the papers back to Agent Foster. "Is that it?" she asked, surprised it went so fast.

"That's it," Brewster confirmed with a chuckle. "Painless."

"Here's your copy of the paperwork and the receipt," said Foster as she handed Rafe the papers. "Keep those for your records."

"I hope this helps stop those people from doing this to someone else's life," said Rafe as they walked into the dining room to pick up the computers.

"It may seem strange," said Foster, "but if those people did hack into your computers, you're lucky, because otherwise, it would be very hard to prove they're committing a crime. Anyone can file a lawsuit for any reason. I just wish we had been able to get to this sooner. The only thing you'll be able to do is to let the judge know there's a federal investigation pending. Unfortunately, it may not be enough unless your lawyer can get an extension," she explained.

"Our court date is Tuesday," said Rafe. "I've been waiting almost two years for this because the date keeps getting changed. I don't think I can take waiting any longer."

"Two years? Wow." Brewster whistled. "Sorry to hear that. Well, let's go," he said as he took the desktop, and Agent Foster took the laptop.

"Don't you need the monitor and keyboard and stuff?" asked Rafe.

"No, we just need the part with the hard drive," said Foster. They went to the front door, Rafe held the door open for them, and they walked out.

"Thanks, bye," said Rafe as she shut the door. She then took the papers to her office, placing the receipt for the computers on her desk to give to Katheryn later.

Rafe went back into the living room and saw the envelope on the coffee table. She picked it up and sat down on the couch. It was an unaddressed 8x10 manila envelope marked *Photographs Do Not Bend.* Rafe smiled. She was sure it must be something one of her students left for her to look and comment on, or it could be something of hers she left at the office, and they dropped it off. She opened the clasp, lifted the flap, and pulled out the photograph.

In that instant, her dreams came to an end.

Her heart hammered in her ears, her breath caught in her lungs, as a rogue tear ran down her cheek. She could only whisper to herself, "It's over."

39

AFTER JUST SITTING and holding the photograph for over an hour, the image had burned into Rafe Salvaggio's mind. She thought she should be crying like she had when Eden left her for the second time with Jake. Or become sick like she did when Jake told her Eden was still sleeping with him. Only one tear escaped. The rest were burned out of her as the heat of anger and grief scourged her body. She couldn't believe it at first. She didn't want to believe it. But as she looked at the photo, it became very clear she had no choice.

The photograph was of the four of them, Jake, his son Hunter, Bronte, and Eden in the park. Jake and Eden were sharing a kiss, and the two children were smiling and happy. She knew this was the kiss Jake told her about, and she chose to ignore. Hunter was holding a yellow ball. It was the same one from the pictures Eden had shown her of Bronte on their 'lazy day' in the park. On the back of the photo, in black marker, the date written along with a message that didn't have to be written—*Our Happy Family*. Rafe wasn't sure if the photograph was meant for her or not, but if it wasn't, Eden would have it soon anyway.

She walked to her room and opened her closet. She moved some boxes aside, punched in the code on the safe, and opened it. She reached in and pulled out a small box that used to hold some of her old letterhead. She took it to the bed and opened it then took out the envelope on top of another stack of papers. The envelope held the list she had made to compare what Jake told her and what Eden confirmed, and included a few other pieces of damning evidence. She added the photograph. Looking over the contents Rafe felt a dizzy sensation at the thought of just how far Eden was going to execute her plan.

40

IN A KIND of daze, Rafe Salvaggio made her way through the rest of the day and her errands to get ready for the event happening later in the evening. She never really considered how she would feel if she found out Eden was really leaving and taking Bronte and that Jake was right all along. She supposed it was the arrogance in her that Eden was using against her so well, just like Jake had pointed out.

It was strange how she felt a kind of relief that everything was really over and knew for sure what was going to happen. But then there was the anger burning in her. The anger that had been burning all this time and now was just an even flame not flaring anymore. Now it was a slow burn that just never left. There was also a profound grief for the loss of the dream she had been clinging to so desperately for so long. She had to figure out how to handle the situation. For her she knew it had to be quick and clean because she couldn't take any more of Eden's plan.

In the back of her mind, she knew Katheryn was still fighting the injunction. If by some miracle she won it, what should she do? Did she want to force the second-parent adoption and be the person Eden so aptly described in the article as controlling and domineering? What would that do to her relationship with Bronte?

She decided she would rather have no relationship than cause any emotional pain to Bronte by fighting over her and subjecting her to more exposure in public by dragging her through court. It just became devastatingly clear there was no connection between Bronte and her, other than a piece of paper—and how she felt in her heart. It looked like it wouldn't be enough.

She wondered if Gabri would ever be able to look at her again after betraying his trust that she would be the mother of the children he helped them have. Facing him after this was going to be one of the hardest things she would ever have to do—losing him would mean she had lost everything and everyone in her life she loved.

Then there was her heart. She thought she was holding it back from Eden, but it was clear to her now she had been careless. For months, she had been in turmoil, and it looked like her nightmares had held the truth she didn't want to face. The feeling of something boring into her chest and into her temple had been growing worse. At times, she even found it difficult to swallow. Now those feelings had intensified seeming to penetrate painfully into her. The pain flooding through her at the moment was crushing her, immobilizing her at times. It wasn't like the love sickness Greer said she had experienced before. It was more like a vital organ had been ripped out, yet she stayed animated like the walking dead.

Eden.

There was no fever or sickness for her this time. Even if her heart wasn't prepared, the rest of her body was at least partially prepared. She saw now she should have saved herself and gone with Greer instead of putting herself through this torture. Her own plan underestimated how much Eden must really despise her and overestimated how much her efforts mattered.

There was no longer a need for the recording she made to catch Eden talking with Jake, so she deleted it from the cloud so it would no longer be there to torment her. She thought she could ignore Jake and make Eden love her, but she had thought wrong.

Rafe went over her plan again and realized she had done this to herself. She gave herself false hope Eden would change her mind and she was being sincere. It was hard to take in how all the times Eden said she loved her were lies.

Several times throughout the day, someone had stopped her to ask if she was okay, so she knew the effect of learning this truth was written on her face. She had to pull herself together. She had to make it through the party tonight and then make a clean break. She left her hair and nails appointment, her last appointment of the day, and made her way to the bank for her passport and other things she knew she would need, and then made her way home.

When she finally arrived home, she went straight to her room with her laptop and locked the door. She had a few hours before Eden would be home, so she decided meditation was what she needed. She did breathing exercises to calm herself and to help herself cope, and then she opened and turned on her new laptop. She had some work to do.

41

RIGHT AT FIVE-THIRTY, Eden Kingsley got home from work and walked into the house. She had plenty of time to get ready before Lydia brought Bronte home. Lydia would arrive just before they left so they could kiss Bronte goodnight then would stay until they got back home later. Eden made her way to the kitchen, got a drink, and took it with her to look through the mail on Rafe's desk in the office. She saw the receipt for the computers and knew the FBI had picked them up. She lingered over it nervously wishing she had been here when they came so she would know what questions the FBI had asked Rafe. If she knew, maybe her meeting with them in a couple of days would be easier. She looked around for Rafe and found that her bedroom door was locked.

"Rafe? Rafe, I'm home," she called through the door. There was no answer, so she spoke louder. "Rafe, I'm home! Do you want to have a snack before we get ready to go?"

"No, you go ahead," called Rafe through the door. "I'm not hungry. I'm getting ready right now."

"Okay," Eden called back. "I should be ready by six-thirty. Will that be okay? Do you need to be there earlier than seven?"

"Six-thirty is fine," Rafe answered shortly.

"I love you," Eden called. When there was no answer, she thought maybe she didn't hear her, so she went and grabbed a snack before she headed to her room to get ready.

She got out the new dress she bought for the occasion. She was excited to dress up and go out with Rafe tonight. It would be the first event they had gone to as a couple since they got back together, and Eden wanted it to be perfect.

After freshening up, putting on some light makeup, and putting her hair up, she was ready to put on her dress. She slipped into it easily and looked at herself in the mirror. She was happy with what she saw and hoped Rafe would be too. She put on her jewelry, slipped on her shoes, and was ready.

Eden went to the kitchen to make sure there were plenty of ready-made options for Bronte to eat while they were gone and saw Rafe had already taken care of everything. She smiled remembering Rafe's worries about staying home. It looked to Eden like Rafe shouldn't worry about anything.

The doorbell rang, and she went to answer the door. "Hey, baby," she cooed to Bronte as she reached for her. "Was she good today?" she asked Lydia.

"She was great," said Lydia. "I think she's getting a new tooth, and she got to dance with the big girls today."

"Oh, my!" exclaimed Eden excitedly to Bronte and kissed her. She sat down with her and gently rubbed her gums feeling for new teeth. "I think Lydia is right. I feel a new tooth! You're getting quite a collection," she said and tickled Bronte. "If she needs them, there are cold chews in the freezer and teething biscuits in the cabinet." Bronte wiggled down off Eden's lap and toddled over to her toys.

"You look great tonight," said Lydia as she watched Bronte from the corner of her eye. "Where's Rafe?"

"Thanks." She beamed. "She's still getting ready. It's going to be a great night."

Eden had been ready for fifteen minutes and was waiting on Rafe while Lydia and Bronte were playing in the living room. Eden wasn't sure what was taking Rafe so long to get ready, but she was cutting it close.

"Rafe, it's six-thirty," Eden called as she knocked on Rafe's door. "You have to hurry, or you won't have time to say goodnight to Bronte."

Rafe opened the door and walked out. "I'm ready," she announced as Eden stood in her path.

"Rafe," Eden said, stunned by Rafe's appearance. "You look beautiful." She smiled warmly and reached out to kiss her.

Rafe gave a small smile and avoided her kiss. "Thank you, so do you," she politely returned the compliment. She walked around Eden and went to see Bronte. She picked her up, kissed her, and hugged her tight. "Goodnight, my B Girl," she cooed softly then handed her to Lydia. "We shouldn't be too late."

"No problem, this is your night, have a great time," said Lydia. "You look great."

"Thank you." Rafe smiled appreciatively.

"She does, and she's all mine," bragged Eden and smiled as she took Rafe's hand.

"Tonight, I belong to CCAD," Rafe said and pulled her hand away. "Let's go."

42

THE OFFICIAL CCAD-sponsored celebration of the Jackson-Goyer Foundation Grant Award was underway at The Kiki Bistro. Rafe Salvaggio and Eden Kingsley had found parking a block away and were walking up the sidewalk on their way to the party. Eden tried to take Rafe's hand, and Rafe made a pretense of straightening herself, so she didn't have to hold her hand just yet. Images of the photograph flashed before Rafe's eyes as she looked at Eden. She realized this would be the last thing she ever did with her. The last moments she would spend with the woman she had wanted to spend the rest of her life with. She realized this might be the last time she could keep her close.

Rafe stopped and faced Eden. "Eden, I need to ask you something," she said as she stopped her.

Eden looked at Rafe and could see she was troubled. "Ask away," she said trying to be nonchalant.

"This may be the last time I get to do something like this with you," Rafe told her as she forced a smile.

"I don't think this will be the last party we ever go to," said Eden with a puzzled laugh. "The Conservatory won't let you go."

The sound of Eden's laugh raked over Rafe's nerves painfully. She wondered if she laughed the same way when she talked with Jake about what she was doing to her. The image of them kissing in the photograph appeared in front of her eyes and Jake's words about her laughing and going down on him as they made their plan rang in her ears. She struggled with the wave of sickness threatening to overcome her. She wanted to scream and tell her she knew exactly what she was doing so she could stop pretending. She fought the urge remembering she had made a plan herself. She would let Eden put on her play for one more night.

Rafe could feel the bleak darkness at the edge of her world and knew this was the last party. This was the last anything with Eden because she now knew the truth and there was no need for another act after tonight. She would play her part as best as she could through the pain she was feeling, and then she would close the curtains and turn out the lights.

She looked up at the crowd in front of the bistro then back at Eden and tried to smile. "There will be a lot of people here tonight, and not everyone knows we're living together again," Rafe said as she fought to hide her despair and remain calm, "so I just wanted to ask you if you would mind staying close to me." She knew it would hurt, but she wanted one last good moment with Eden even if it was a game to her. "You know, so people will see us together," she said making what she thought would be a reasonable excuse for her request.

"I'd love to stay close to you." Eden chuckled as she beamed warmly. "I love how you want people to see us together. I really love that you're proud to be with me again."

"Okay, take my hand now," said Rafe as she looked longingly at her knowing she was going to miss who she thought Eden was all this time. She already missed the woman who she believed used to love her and was sad she couldn't get her back. "Let's go in."

43

INSIDE THE CROWDED bistro, everyone from CCAD suits to art students and everyone in between were enjoying the night. Rafe Salvaggio led Eden to their table by clearing their way through a lot of handshakes and congratulations. Rafe kept a firm hold of Eden's hand as they watched the stage. At the podium, President Biggalow gave a speech acknowledging Rafe but mostly touting the Conservatory. She invited everyone to meet and congratulate Rafe and the staff who had worked so hard to obtain the Jackson-Goyer Foundation Grant.

Rafe lined up with her staff in the congratulation line still holding Eden's hand. As the people passed by, Rafe steeled herself so she could remain in a place of calm, remaining polite and untouchable, so the emotions tearing through her didn't betray her as she introduced Eden to everyone.

The air around Rafe filled with comments about the article and rumors about why she hadn't been seen at the Conservatory. The most popular, and just one of the many rumors, was that Rafe had parted ways with Eden and was available to work her wildling powers on someone. It annoyed Rafe at first because she knew Abby was probably behind it somehow, but then she realized she didn't care anymore. Eden was feeling uncomfortable because of the rumors and because many women were showing up at the public part of the event just to see if they had a chance with Rafe.

Rafe had been determined to keep Eden close tonight but found she was fighting to keep the desire to have her near. The need was ebbing away as her despair started to resurface under her mask of calm. Yet another woman approached Rafe with a come-hither look.

"Hello, I'm Amanda," she said as she shook Rafe's hand and held it. "What you've done for the Conservatory is fantastic," she gushed and looked Rafe over openly.

"Thank you. You're very kind," Rafe replied, and then she motioned to Eden. "This is Eden. She's the woman I live with right now."

Eden missed the inviting look the woman gave Rafe. "Hi, good to meet you," she said cordially.

"I'm sure you're very proud," Amanda muttered absently to Eden then turned to Rafe. "It was very nice to meet you." She squeezed Rafe's hand, leaving her card behind, and then mouthed 'call me.'

"Nice to meet you too," said Rafe and gently pulled her hand free. She dropped the card as the woman walked away and took Eden's hand again as she squeezed it gently.

"Congratulations, Rafe," offered Dr. Jones as he approached. "This is quite a triumph. And who is this you're holding on to?"

"Dr. Jones, this is my good friend Ms. Kingsley." Rafe smiled, but her eyes did not. "She will be giving a lecture at the school soon."

"Ms. Kingsley, it is a pleasure," Dr. Jones said charmingly as he held out his hand.

"Thank you." Eden smiled as she accepted his hand. "It's nice to meet you."

Abby nudged Jude. "Did she just introduce Eden as her 'good friend' Ms. Kingsley?"

"Yeah, she did," confirmed Jude.

"Why would she do that?" asked Abby confused. "It's the second time she's done it, you know."

"I don't know. Maybe that guy's a 'phobe or something." Jude shrugged then took a step toward Rafe. "Hey, congratulations."

"Yeah, congrats," Abby added with a smile.

Rafe smiled weakly and shook their hands. "Thank you."

"Hey, Eden," said Abby as she shook her hand and hugged her in her own little way of apology.

"Hey, Abby, I'm glad you're here." Eden smiled when she realized what Abby was doing. It was a relief to have her friend back.

"Hi, Rafe," drawled Jillian as she kissed Rafe on both cheeks. "It's really great to see you again. This is a great party. I'm available if you want to get together tonight." The redhead laughed invitingly. "I even think Leslie is here."

"I think I'll have to pass tonight," replied Rafe with a wink as she gripped Eden's hand tighter. "Eden, you remember Jillian. Jillian, you two were never properly introduced. This is my roommate Eden."

"Roommate?" Jillian asked surprised. "So, Rafe," she said as she looked Eden over, "you took her back?"

"Yeah, she did," Eden assured her firmly and stood closer to Rafe. "It's nice to meet you."

"Well, she'd make a great fourth." Jillian winked at Rafe.

"I don't think that is going to happen," growled Eden glaring at Jillian.

"You know my number, Rafe. Bye," she whispered as she touched Rafe's arm with familiarity.

"Bye, Jillian." She put her arm around Eden's waist and pulled her close. "Sorry about that," Rafe apologized to Eden. Though, at the moment, thinking about the photograph of Eden kissing Jake, she was having a hard time really feeling sorry about anything. "That's why I need you with me."

"Rafe," greeted Gretchen as she shook Rafe's hand vigorously and spoke loudly. "I just want you to know I think the article was horrible, and I don't blame you one bit for drop kicking that bitch to the curb."

"I haven't done that yet, Gretchen." Rafe said stoically then motioned to Eden. "Gretchen, this is Eden. Eden, this is Gretchen, Economics Professor at CCAD."

"Nice to meet you," said Eden apprehensively.

"Rafe, you're a better woman than I am." She looked at Eden and gave her a smirk then spoke to Rafe. "Congratulations on that," she grunted with a faltering smile, "and the grant."

"Thank you, Gretchen," said Rafe appreciatively.

After Gretchen moved on, Eden looked at Rafe. "They teach Economics at an art school?"

"Of course," said Rafe as she shook hands with more people. "All the students get a core education in Math, Science, Languages, History, Literature, Writing, and all that. They have a wide variety of courses. Conservatory arts students work as hard, some harder, than students who go for other degrees.

They not only have to study all the core subjects, but at the same time, they have to create original art." Rafe found talking about work helped take her mind off her despair. "One of my projects was putting together a master program since they don't offer one now. Hopefully, someone will make that happen for the students."

"Oh, exalted Dean Salvaggio, your shoes have been a challenge to fill," extolled Dalia as she hugged Rafe.

"Well, Dalia, it's why I recommended you," Rafe admitted with a laugh, hiding the depth of how much she was missing her work even though it had only been a week. "I knew you were up to the challenge."

"I hope the board gets its act together and makes you come back soon," she said then looked at Eden. "It's good to see you again, Eden."

"It's good to see you again too," replied Eden. "I know she'll be back soon."

"We all hope so," said Dalia generously. "Her presence and compelling force are missed."

A dark-haired woman wearing a revealing outfit that showed off her sculpted body slipped her arms around Rafe and kissed her cheek with familiarity. "Rafe, I can't stop thinking about you," she purred with a sexy voice into Rafe's ear. "Congratulations." She winked as she released Rafe

"Thank you, Leslie," said Rafe with a sexy smile of her own as she looked over Leslie's body, thinking of the promises she knew it could keep. "I can't stop the things I'm thinking right now," she chuckled softly. She looked over at Eden who wasn't smiling. "Eden, you remember Leslie," she said still holding

Leslie's hand. "Leslie, this is Eden," she started, but Leslie interrupted.

"The ex," she said with disdain and sniffed looking down her nose. "I saw the article. What's next, a viral Facebook attack on Rafe?" she asked with disdain. She looked at Rafe and put her hand on her arm. "You deserve better. When you figure that out, make sure you call me first."

"She won't be calling," said Eden evenly. "Get your hands off her," she seethed and pushed Leslie's hand off Rafe. "She's mine and the article was full of lies!" Eden was doing her best not to cry, but this, on top of what the economics professor had said, had brought her anxiety level up and her anger out.

"That's right," Rafe confirmed with a nod and a small shrug. "Thank you for your concern, but I think everything is already all figured out." She took Eden's hand and kissed it for what may be the last time.

Leslie gave a short laugh. "You really are amazing, Rafe. I probably wouldn't want to share you again, either." She looked at Eden and leaned close to her ear. "You should be much more careful. If you ever touch me like that again, you'll have another regret in your life."

At that threat, Eden looked at the dark-haired woman in shock. She looked at Rafe, but she hadn't heard Leslie. Eden looked back at the dark-haired woman who flashed a smile full of arrogance. "I think you should move on," warned Eden as her face flushed red with anger, "from here and from Rafe. She doesn't want or need you, or anyone else, except me. If you touch her again, you'll be the one with regrets."

"We'll see," said Leslie with a smile and walked away.

Eden watched as Leslie joined a group of people and began talking and laughing as she looked back at her a few times. "Rafe, I really need to get a drink and go to the restroom," said Eden flushed with anger and embarrassed because now people were pointing and whispering about her. "Will you be okay without me for a while?"

"Are you okay?" Rafe asked and watched Eden nod. "Sure, go ahead. I'll be fine."

Rafe continued to shake hands with people, and very few comments were about the Jackson-Goyer Grant. It seemed everyone had come out to see what happened to her and what her latest availability status was. Several women made blatant passes at Rafe and others were more subtle. But now that Eden wasn't standing next to her, she had run out of rebuffs and motivation to think of anymore. She had a hand full of cards and a couple of gifts from women who were all out after her.

44

SIPPING THEIR DRINKS as they sat around the table, Abby Van Falkov and Julia Hawthorn were watching the crowd looking for new faces. They had both agreed attending Rafe's party would be a great way of expanding their horizons and meeting new women, which was actually the same thing in their minds. Abby was sipping her drink extra slow tonight, wanting to make it last.

"Well, Letty has cut me off again until I pay my tab." Abby sighed as she took a sip of her drink. "This may be my last drink for a while."

"You really need to take a budgeting class or something," said Julia earnestly.

"I have no money to budget," complained Abby. "How do people live on a budget?"

"They aren't you," Julia quipped sarcastically, and then they both laughed.

"Lucky them." Abby sneered then took a sip of her drink. "Did you know Rafe introduced Eden as Ms. Kingsley to some guy?"

"So? It's who she is." Julia shrugged determined not to be surprised by anything Rafe did lately.

"So? She's never done it before," said Abby emphatically. "Then I heard her introduce Eden as the mother of the baby she is adopting, not the mother of my daughter. Then as her roommate or the woman she sleeps with sometimes. Come on," she said animatedly. "Oh, then as her very good friend, not her partner. She hasn't called Eden 'babe' or 'baby' or even whatever the Italian name she used to call her since they got back together."

"*Mia dolce*," Julia said remembering the endearment Rafe used to use for Eden.

"Yeah," nodded Abby, "she hasn't called her that or anything else lately, except maybe that night she was stoned. Just Eden or maybe Ede."

"Well, what are they exactly?" asked Julia unworried. "Maybe neither one of them knows yet. Was Eden upset?"

"I don't think she even realizes what Rafe's doing," said Abby as she looked toward Rafe and noticed she was practically surrounded by women. "Julia, I think you should go stand next to Rafe. Look at her. She's surrounded. Some people just don't know when to leave people alone. Where is Eden?"

"Abby, you're not doing it again, are you?" asked Julia skeptically.

"This is serious. Just look." Abby pointed toward Rafe. She was working hard to keep the secret and promise she made to Rafe not to tell what she knew, but it was getting frustratingly difficult.

"You know," offered Erica knowingly, "there's a fragile time period when people get together that's critical. It's when someone can come in and mess things up."

"Right." Abby nodded in agreement with her favorite baby butch and protégé. "Rafe has it worse because of all the shit that's going on and the," she paused checking herself because she almost spilled her secret, "the sacrifices she's making for Eden."

"Sacrifices? What are you—" Julia started to ask as she looked up at Rafe. "Oh, my god. She is surrounded. That girl's going to get her in trouble. It looks like Rafe isn't working very hard to discourage any of them, either. Okay, I'll go. You go find Eden."

"I'll save the table," said Erica as she continued to video the action around her.

Abby forced her way through the crowd heading toward the restroom. She made it inside and looked for Eden but found Stacey and Jude, instead. "Have you seen Eden?" Abby asked them.

"No, we just came in," said Jude as she washed her hands. "I think she went to get a drink. Why?"

Abby frowned at Jude. She wasn't sure why Jude was washing her hands if she just walked into the restroom, but she had her suspicions and would investigate thoroughly later. She shook her head to get back on point. "Guys, it's obvious Eden doesn't know what's going on with Rafe," whined Abby unhappily. "You guys were right about her, and it's why she's been acting so weird."

"Oh, Abby, not again," said Jude annoyed as she dried her hands.

"Why's she doing it?" Stacey laughed and bounced from foot to foot.

"I'm not sure," said Abby in frustration. "I mean she keeps asking Eden what she wants." She paused. "Maybe she's asking Eden to want her and just her. You know, like, just the canvas and the artist and nothing else. I think her passion is all bottled up or something. But Eden doesn't understand. I think she really still believes Eden will leave her again for a man, and this is her way of letting Eden choose what she wants. It's so twisted, but I can see it. I mean, I knew Rafe before she met Eden. I don't think Eden knows any of this stuff about her."

"You have no proof," said Jude as she shook her head.

"Proof? You want proof?" exclaimed Abby. "Just go out and look at what she's doing. I mean she introduced Eden as Ms. Kingsley, for god sake!"

"That's not the Rafe I know," said Jude. "I mean, your theory is Rafe is giving Eden what she wants, or what Rafe thinks she wants, and the core of the whole thing is she is..." She paused. "Is..." She shook her head disbelief. "That's fucked up, Abby."

Abby hesitated, but then decided it was time to spill her secret. "For your information," she started determinedly, "I talked to her Saturday and confirmed the whole twisted thing. Julia is out there right now fending off the pack. You know the wildling vibe she gives off, and the rumor she's available is bringing out the sharks. I think every girl in the place is on the hunt, and she may be looking for some..." she paused, "release."

"Abby, Rafe always has this problem with women." Stacey frowned doubtfully.

"Not like this," Abby insisted. "The article has brought out every woman in town. I think there are even a few committed married couples after her."

"Okay, okay, Abby, stop!" Jude laughed at Abby's exaggeration. "We'll help you find Eden. I still think you're overreacting." Abby followed Jude and Stacey out to find Eden and rescue Rafe.

Inside one of the restroom stalls, Eden had overheard Abby. She wasn't exactly sure what Abby was talking about and quietly laughed to herself. It seemed like Abby always saw problems where there were none.

"Such a worrier," mumbled Eden then chuckled as she wiped the tears she was in the restroom hiding. "If she only knew the real problems." She sighed sadly and wiped away another tear. She left the stall and washed her hands. She then looked at herself in the mirror and tried her best to fix her makeup.

Dealing with the fallout from the article was hard tonight because she had to watch all the women who approached Rafe. Most of them wanted to come to Rafe's defense and blame Eden. The hardest thing to deal with was knowing they were right. It was all her fault. If she hadn't left Rafe and got involved with Jake, then none of this would be happening. She did her best to push all the thoughts of Jake and the Stewards out of her mind. Tonight, she wanted to focus on having a good night with Rafe no matter what.

45

JULIA HAWTHORN HAD rescued Rafe Salvaggio from the mobs of women surrounding her. She swept her away to sit down at their table, but a few people still approached to congratulate or hit on her. Both Julia and Erica worked to fend some of the women off. They each had promising conversions with a few of the women for themselves, so they didn't mind the job at all. Rafe just displayed a tolerant smile and didn't discourage anyone since Eden wasn't around. The table was full of cards and drinks women had sent to her.

Abby, Jude, and Stacey had worked their way through the crowd and finally made it to the table.

"Rafe, are you okay," Abby asked as she sat down, worried about how she looked. Rafe was her usual hot self, but there was darkness around her eyes and a kind of hollowness to her face making her look haunted. Abby was worried she was sick.

"Of course, I am," said Rafe waving Abby off. "I've ordered dinner for the table. Have you seen Eden?"

"No. Are you sure you're okay?" Stacey asked curiously. "No one has slipped you a drugged drink or anything?" she asked, seriously thinking someone had drugged her because of the way she looked.

"What is wrong with you guys?" asked Rafe as she looked at Stacey as if she were crazy.

"Nothing," said Jude as she laughed nervously and kicked Stacey under the table making her squeak. "I'll go look for Eden."

"I'm here," announced Eden as she walked up to the table before Jude got up.

"Thank god!" Erica exhaled in relief as she looked around at the women poised to make their way over. It was overwhelming for her to have so many women approach the table in a night. She wasn't sure how Rafe and Jude handled things but knew if she wanted to be like them, she needed to hang out with them more to learn their secrets.

"Now maybe they'll start leaving some more cards for me." Julia chuckled and winked at Erica who was several shades of red from some of the things suggested.

"You were gone a long time," Rafe said to Eden. She wondered if maybe she had met Jake somewhere in this crowd. "Did you run into someone you knew?"

"Eden, you need to stay here and claim your woman before those vultures make their way in," Abby cautioned her and wondered why Eden hadn't noticed the way Rafe looked. She looked at Stacey and Jude, and they just shrugged and shook their heads.

"Not to worry," said Julia as she smiled confidently. "I'll handle the vultures personally." She loved the opportunity to meet so many women.

"Hey, I think I can lend a hand." Erica smiled as she showed Julia the numbers she had collected. Julia gave her an approving nod, which made Erica's head swell.

"No, it was just hard to get through all the people," Eden answered Rafe as she sat down. She smiled at Abby thinking about what she had heard in the restroom. "Abby, Rafe loves me. Those vultures can flap all they want," she said with a laugh, confident in her words.

"You're pretty sure of yourself, aren't you?" asked Rafe. Pain shot through her head from hearing her laugh again, but she was doing her best to smile.

"No, I'm sure of you." Eden smiled back at her. "I love you," she affirmed reassuringly.

"Here's our dinner," Rafe announced ignoring what she now knew as Eden's false declaration. "Can you take away some of these drinks and paper," she asked the waiter as he served them. The girls grabbed what they wanted before it was all whisked away.

46

KEEPING UP HER game face was wearing on Rafe Salvaggio. She had barely taken three bites of food as she pushed it around on her plate. It didn't help that everyone was so happy while she was suffering and holding on to the last threads of her dream. She had become quiet over the last hour, letting the others fill the evening with laughter and conversation. She looked around the bistro and saw a flash of someone she thought was familiar. She rubbed her eyes and looked again. The dark-haired, dark-skinned girl looked right at her with her dark eyes. Rafe closed her eyes again. *Impossible*, she thought. She opened her eyes, and the girl was gone. She rubbed her temples and wondered if what she had seen was real or a vision. Finally, she decided she needed a break from everyone.

"Eden, would you like to dance with me?" Rafe asked as she took Eden's hand and stood.

"Of course." Eden smiled up at her. "I thought you'd never ask."

They made their way to the dance floor, and Rafe took Eden into her arms, holding her close as they moved to the slow beat of the music. "I love dancing with you," Rafe whispered into Eden's ear.

Eden closed her eyes feeling the sensation of Rafe's breath on her ear and the feel of her body against her. "I love how you hold me," she said softly and let Rafe lead her to the slow rhythm of the music.

As the slow song ended, and another faster song began, Rafe ran her hand up Eden's back, pulled her close, and kissed her deeply. She buried her face in Eden's neck and could feel the tears about to pour out of her. She took a jagged breath controlling her emotions as she always had. "Excuse me," she said close to her ear then gave her a small smile. "I'll meet you back at the table." She walked quickly through the crowd toward the restroom.

In the empty restroom, Rafe blotted the tears as they threatened to spring from her eyes, forcing herself to stop more from forming. She looked at herself in the mirror and couldn't look at the pain in her own eyes, so she closed them. She would not lose control again. She heard the door open and began to wash her hands. She knew her refuge would not last long, but she would take what she could get.

"Rafe, are you okay?" Abby asked as she saw something was wrong and was worried.

"Abby." Rafe swallowed back her pain. "I can't do it anymore," Rafe revealed as she looked at her sadly.

"You mean," Abby hesitated, "with Eden." She watched as Rafe nodded. "Does she know what she's doing to you? Have you told her?"

"Of course, I haven't told her." Rafe laughed bitterly. "Do you think things would have gone this far and she would still be here if I had?"

"What are you going to do?" Abby asked dismayed as she tried to comfort her. "I thought you said you'd be fine."

Rafe went pale as the vision of the photograph she saw this morning made it into her mind again. "I don't know what I'm going to do yet. I'm working on it," Rafe claimed with a raspy voice. She didn't want her to know she already knew exactly what she was doing because Abby had a hard time keeping things to herself. "Just don't say anything. I'll figure it out." She was actually surprised Abby had kept her mouth shut for this long. Rafe felt a sharp pressure in her chest.

Abby watched Rafe as the color drained out of her face, and she held her hand to her chest. "Rafe, you don't look so good, are you getting sick?"

"No, my head just hurts," Rafe said moving her hand to her head. "It's just becoming too much." She felt like her mind and body were being physically crushed by the reality of everything happening.

"Maybe you should call it a night and go home," Abby said, very concerned.

"No, no," said Rafe as she took a deep breath and let it out slowly. She had to take back control of herself. "Let's go back now."

Abby and Rafe made it back to the table, and Abby stared at Eden, barely holding back her temper. Rafe nudged Abby to stop her from glaring.

"Rafe, you look like you aren't feeling well," observed Julia as she looked at Rafe's paleness and noticed the dark circles around her eyes that Stacey and Jude had been telling her about. She had been so busy looking at the scenery that she hadn't noticed Rafe's pallor.

"I'm fine. I just have a slight headache," said Rafe with a forced a smile.

"Maybe you should go home and take something for your headache," offered Abby knowing it was more than just a headache. "It looks like it's more than slight, and you're getting very pale. That bump on your head may still be working on your brain," she said trying to give Rafe an excuse to leave.

"No, I want to stay and have a nice time tonight with Eden," Rafe insisted as she looked at Abby with a frown. "It's been a while since we've done this with you guys."

"I don't want to stay if you're not feeling well," said Eden as she looked at Rafe with worry. She thought she was just nervous about tonight, but now she wondered if Abby was right and Rafe was sick.

"We can hang out anytime," said Jude with concern. "You should go if you're not feeling well."

"That's right, and you've met everyone in the place and done your duty for the school," added Abby. "Plus, Erica is running around recording everything. You should go."

Rafe looked at her friends broodingly and then at Eden, her head now throbbing with pain. "Okay, let's go." She sighed and got up from the table.

47

AS THEY DROVE home in silence, Eden Kingsley became more worried as time went on, and Rafe seemed to become more withdrawn. Eden was driving them home because Rafe didn't feel up to it, which was unusual for her. Abby followed them home, and when they got out of their cars, she walked with them toward the house.

"I'll be fine now. You didn't have to follow us home," Rafe told Abby annoyed. "You're probably right about the bump on the head." She gave a forced a laugh. "I'm going to take some aspirin and go to bed."

"Okay, well, I'll see you later," Abby promised, giving up easier than she normally would as she watched Rafe head inside. She pulled Eden to the side as soon as Rafe was out of earshot. "Eden, can we have breakfast tomorrow?" Abby asked her. "It's important. I want to talk to you about an article I may write."

"Sure," Eden said wondering what she was going to write about and if it would help Rafe. "I'll see you in the morning at The Kiki Bistro," she called as she followed Rafe inside.

"Is she okay?" asked Lydia when Eden walked in the house. "She barely said anything and went to her room."

"She says she has a headache," Eden explained. "Thanks for watching Bronte tonight."

"No problem." Lydia smiled at the appreciation she was being shown. It was one of the many reasons she valued her position as Bronte's nanny. "I love my job," she said and walked outside to head home.

"See you later, Lydia," said Eden and closed the door behind her.

Eden made her way through the house toward Rafe's room. She knocked on Rafe's door, but there was no answer. She left reluctantly and went to check on Bronte who was sleeping. Finally, she made her way to her bedroom unsure of what she could do since Rafe had locked her out again.

She left her door open in case Rafe decided she wanted to come in and sleep with her. She changed into her pajamas then crawled into bed and started reading one of the scripts on her nightstand. After a while, she put the script away and lay back on the bed but couldn't sleep. It was late when she heard Rafe come out of her room and make her nightly rounds through the house. She heard Rafe approach her door and saw her shadow.

"Eden?" Rafe called softly.

"Yeah, babe," Eden answered and sat up in bed.

"I can't come in tonight," Rafe told her softly. "I'm sorry," she said then closed Eden's door and walked away.

"Rafe," Eden whispered sadly wishing she had come in. She was worried about Rafe's headache and hoped she would feel better in the morning after getting some sleep.

48

EARLY SATURDAY MORNING, Eden Kingsley was up and out of the house with Bronte to meet Abby for breakfast. Rafe was still in her room when they were ready to go, so Eden left her a note to meet them when she woke up. When she got to The Kiki Bistro, it had been transformed back into its familiar arrangement for normal service. She ordered breakfast for herself and Bronte, and they took the tray with the drinks to the table where Abby was sitting.

"Hey, Eden. Thanks for coming," said Abby gravely as they sat down, and Eden put Bronte in a highchair. "Hi there, Bronte." She smiled at the baby who was in a happy mood and babbling with a lot of actual words she had learned. Abby was impressed with how many words the kid knew and couldn't wait until she could actually talk.

"What kind of article are you working on?" asked Eden as she poured almond milk into a sippy cup she brought with her and gave Bronte her drink.

"Listen, I really just need to talk to you about Rafe," admitted Abby. "I'm worried about her."

"I know," said Eden as the waiter brought their breakfast and placed the food on the table.

"You know?" asked Abby in surprise. "What do you know?" she asked suspiciously.

"I overheard you in the restroom last night," Eden revealed with a small smile as she cut up a strawberry for Bronte. "I think you better tell me what you think she's doing."

"I'm sorry you had to find out like that," said Abby a little embarrassed. "I was very worried last night, and I'm sure I sounded like a ranting mad woman."

"It was a bit confusing," said Eden as she gave some more strawberry to Bronte and ate a small piece herself, "but I guess the bottom line is," she paused and swallowed, "you think Rafe wants me to choose her over men or something. I have chosen her," she assured her emphatically. "I'm not with Jake or any other man or any other person. I'm with her, and I don't want to be with anyone else."

"That's part of it. I don't know how to say this delicately," Abby said apprehensively.

"Just tell me, please," implored Eden impatiently as she wiped off Bronte's hands then put some scrambled egg in front of her.

"Okay," said Abby determined to get through this conversation. "How's your sex life?"

Eden looked over at Abby in surprise at the question. Abby wasn't laughing, so it didn't seem to Eden like she was joking around. "Well," she said hesitantly, "Rafe tells me she's using her technique on me." Eden blushed at the memory of the things Rafe did to her.

"Her technique?" Abby asked, worried. "Eden, I'm not sure her telling you that is a good thing."

"Honestly, Abby, it's been fantastic." Eden smiled as she gave Bronte more food.

"So," Abby dragged out the word. "How does it compare to," she paused, "other things. Uh, sex with other people you've, you know, been with."

Eden looked around then back at Abby. She wasn't sure why she wanted to know such a personal thing. She wished they were not in the middle of a crowded restaurant. She leaned closer to Abby so she could speak softly. "Sometimes it's been very different from anything I've experienced with Rafe," she admitted softly, "or with anyone else before." She bit her lip and took a breath. "Who am I kidding?" She chuckled and could feel herself turning red. "No one has ever done the things Rafe does for me, and I probably would never let anyone else do what she does to me."

"So you're more," she fidgeted nervously, "satisfied with Rafe?"

"Abby, where is this going?" asked Eden feeling uncomfortable. "Really, it's been fantastic being with her."

"Okay, that's great," said Abby twitchily. She hesitated and looked at Eden as she gave Bronte more food. "So, how is it for Rafe?"

"She's there, so I guess it's the same for her." Eden smiled shyly as she flushed from embarrassment.

"So, you do the things to her that she does for you?" pressed Abby.

"Abby!" Eden burst with surprise by the question. "We do," she paused embarrassed, "different things for each other. Not always the same thing." She shrugged and looked away uncomfortably. She gave Bronte more egg then looked at Abby demurely. "Is this what Rafe calls your 'lesbian need to know' or something? Why are you asking about this?"

"Eden, I'm going to tell you why," said Abby ignoring the remark Eden said Rafe told her. "After I do, you have to make

248

some hard decisions, and considering the state Rafe is in, you need to make them fast."

"What state?" Eden asked perplexed.

"Okay, I'm just going to come out with it," said Abby as she looked intensely at Eden.

"Good," said Eden as she gave Bronte more fruit.

"I know what she's doing..." Abby paused, "giving you what you want."

"Giving me what I want?" repeated Eden smiling in confusion.

"Yes," Abby nodded in frustration, "that you're comparing her to Jake or men."

"Comparing?" repeated Eden very confused. "Comparing what? Abby, I have no idea what you're talking about."

"I'm talking about," Abby paused and looked around then leaned close to her, "the strap-on!" she hissed quietly.

"The what?" asked Eden not sure if she had heard right.

"Oh, don't play dumb," warned Abby as she sat back in her chair and crossed her arms. "I talked to Rafe, and I know you're forcing her to use one."

"Oh, my god!" Eden laughed at the ridiculousness of the accusation. "You think..." she tried to catch her breath, "you think," she shook with laughter. "Abby," she breathed, "we never," she shook her head, "she never! She must be teasing you again!"

"Then why's she acting so weird?" asked Abby as she frowned angrily. "I saw it," she nodded confirmation. "You can't lie to me. You're making her miserable. She can't release her passion, or whatever, and that's why!"

"I'm not lying." Eden laughed with tears in her eyes. "Anyway," she started and controlled herself, "I would never make her do anything she doesn't want to do," she explained, "and she wouldn't make me do anything I didn't want to do."

"If she's teasing me, she's a very good actor because I still think something's wrong," said Abby feeling disgruntled and crossing her arms.

"Abby, a lot is going on in her life right now," explained Eden trying to make Abby feel better. "I agree with you she hasn't been herself, but can you blame her? I think your constant worrying is giving her fuel to tease you. I'm sure she set you up and is teasing you just like that night at the dinner party."

"I..." Abby started embarrassed, "I'm sorry then. The next time I see her, I'm going to get her back for this." She sighed and pouted. "I am so fucking gullible! I can't believe it!" She crossed her arms again disgruntled.

Eden teased Abby about her mistake while they had breakfast and waited at the bistro for Rafe. They ended up having a very nice morning together, but it got to a point where Bronte was ready to go. So Eden and Bronte made their way home happily. Eden was laughing about Abby and her worrying and couldn't wait to tell Rafe about her.

She was sure Rafe would tease Abby about this for the rest of her life. She even considered going to the toyshop to pick up a few things to tempt and tease Rafe with tonight. She thought about the things Rafe had been doing to her, and she wanted to do more for Rafe.

Since Bronte was getting fussy, and needed to get out of her stroller and car seat for a while and play, she decided to save the toy idea for later. *Besides*, Eden thought, *I don't know if I can take what Rafe could probably do with one of those toys.*

Thoughts of the last time they made love ran through her mind. That was supposed to be her night in control, but it turned into her night out of control. She felt herself become wet at the memory of Rafe taking her from behind, then after making her come, flipping her over to climb between her legs. She loved feeling Rafe's warm body moving on top of her, kissing her, whispering in her ear, and pressing her clit against hers over and over until they both came again. That was another entire night of sex. Her body gave an involuntary shiver breaking her out of that rabbit hole but leaving her aching. The sex was great, but as she told Abby, she would be happy to just be able to see her face and just touch her every day.

As she parked the car on the street, Eden looked in the rearview mirror back at Bronte who was holding her toy car keys. "There's no doubt about it, Bronte," she cooed to the baby, "your mommy is hopelessly in love with your mama."

Eden walked happily into the house with Bronte hoping Rafe was feeling better this morning. "Rafe?" Eden called out and laughed as she put Bronte down to play with her toys. "Rafe, I have something very funny to tell you! Where are you?"

Rafe walked out of her room with a bag over her shoulder and took in the scene of Eden smiling with Bronte at her feet, and her heart broke again. "I'm right here," she said then bent down and gave Bronte a hug and a kiss.

"Are you going somewhere?" asked Eden as she looked at her then at her bag in confusion because Rafe didn't travel last second for work anymore.

"Yes," Rafe answered as she stood and turned to Eden. "I have something for you," she said and handed her a large envelope. "I love you, Eden."

"I love you too," she said in confusion as she looked at the envelope then at Rafe. "Where are you going?"

Rafe looked at her and gave her a wary smile. "It's okay, just say goodbye," she requested firmly.

"Goodbye?" she said confused.

Rafe looked at Eden for a moment feeling conflicted. Leaving her was much harder than she thought it would be, even when she knew Eden didn't love her. She gave into the need for her one last time then leaned in and kissed her deeply. "You win," she whispered. "I'll leave this time. Goodbye." Rafe looked at Eden for a moment, taking in the image of the woman it seemed like only yesterday she had painted, and then turned and walked out the door.

"Rafe?" Eden called out in a panic not understanding what was happening and followed her onto the porch. "Where are you going? What are you talking about?" She looked at the envelope again in confusion. "What's going on?"

Rafe looked back sadly and nodded to the envelope then turned away and started putting her bag into the car parked at the end of the driveway. Eden didn't think anything about it when she pulled up and had to park on the street. She looked at the envelope Rafe had handed her and opened it. She pulled out the photograph on top, and when she saw it, she looked up in shock at Rafe and began to shake.

"No!" Eden choked as she rushed down the steps toward Rafe's car as it pulled out and sped away. "No!" Eden screamed. "Rafe! Stop! Rafe, please, stop! Rafe!" she screamed over and over again, as Rafe's car disappeared around the corner. Eden let out a long and mournful scream. "No!" She fell in anguish to her knees as her legs gave way under her, and she sobbed and screamed. "Rafe! Rafe! No!"

"Eden!" yelled Flynn as he ran out of his house after hearing Eden's screams. "What's wrong? What happened?"

"Rafe," she cried and gripped the envelope tight. "Rafe!"

"What about Rafe?" Flynn asked in worry as he tried to lift her off the ground.

"She..." Eden sobbed. "She..." she stammered.

Flynn saw the photograph in Eden's hand and took her by the shoulders. "Did she see this?" he asked firmly. "Did she leave?"

"She's gone!" Eden nodded as she shook and sobbed. "We have to find her, Flynn! We have to find her and tell her everything!"

"Come on," encouraged Flynn as he helped Eden to her feet. "Let's get inside."

Flynn brought a distraught and sobbing Eden into the house and sat her on the couch. He poured out the contents of the envelope out on the coffee table as Bronte played on the floor with her toys.

Inside the envelope, along with the picture of Jake and Eden kissing and holding the children in the park, were printouts of the pictures Eden had sent Rafe of Bronte with her yellow ball. The yellow ball was circled on both photos. Under those were the small photos from Eden's wallet of Jake and Hunter that Rafe had taken from the trash, a copy of the article, and a list that compared what Jake had told Rafe and then confirmed true by Eden. There was also a page titled 'Eden's Plan' with an outline of what Jake told Rafe that Eden was doing, and a list comparing proof Eden would stay against proof she would leave. The proof she would leave was the clear winner.

Also, there was a letter dissolving the cohabitation agreement, giving Eden thirty days to move out, with a cashier's check for seven-thousand five hundred dollars, a copy of an email sent to Katheryn stating her services were no longer required for the injunction or the second-parent adoption. There was an attachment of a letter to the court stating Rafe's intention of withdrawing her adoption application and a copy the cohabitation dissolution letter. Finally, there was a letter to Eden letting her know her plan was a success and now she could go live her life with Jake and wishing her happiness always.

Flynn looked at Eden in horror. "He's been talking to her all this time," he said anxiously. "You must have been right about him calling her and leaving messages. He's been telling her more lies."

"We have to call Katheryn," sobbed Eden still crying and looking in disbelief at the evidence against her. "We have to find her." She dug her phone out of her bag and dialed Katheryn.

"It looks like he's been telling Rafe that you're behind all of this to punish her and take Bronte away," Flynn deduced as he looked through the items on the table, "and that you instigated the injunction procedures and all the other things just to postpone the adoption. He's provided Rafe with all of this evidence against you."

"And I've been proving him right!" cried Eden as she went pale with realization.

49

FLYNN OGDEN LET himself inside Rafe's house and saw Eden Kingsley still on the phone pacing and crying as she talked with Katheryn. Flynn had made a fast trip to his house next door so he could use his computer. Not long ago, he had helped Eden with setting up her computer and had taken the opportunity to upload a tracking app to Eden's phone. After learning the possibility Jake was leaving messages for Rafe Flynn decided to put the app on Rafe's phone too. He installed the app on her phone the day after Rafe had been stoned with Jude and Abby, then she slipped in the shower injuring herself.

He knew it was an invasion of privacy, but after his ordeal with Jake, and all the promises and secrets he had been keeping, he felt like the app was a small insurance policy. Plus he only planned to look at it in cases just like this. Eden had desperately called Rafe dozens of times with no answer and had become more upset with each unanswered call, so Flynn knew he had to do more. He had hoped he would be able to find Rafe quickly and help Eden. For a moment, he thought he had found her when an address popped up, but it was Rafe's house. This meant Rafe had left her phone behind somewhere in the house. Flynn sat down at the dining room table frustrated and disappointed he couldn't help more.

Eden saw Flynn had come back inside but kept her focus on talking with Katheryn. She told her about everything that had happened with Rafe and about the contents of the envelope. Of course, some of the things Katheryn already knew about because of the information Eden had given her. Finally, she hung up the phone and wiped her tears. She looked at Flynn who was at the dining room table where the contents of the envelope were placed.

"She hasn't called me back or answered my calls," said Eden with tears in her eyes. "Katheryn said the emails were sent early this morning," reported Eden as she paced the kitchen and dining room trying to stop her tears and keep her anxiety in check. "I told her to ignore them and not to stop work on the injunction. I told her I want to fight it on Rafe's behalf. She said it was pushing the legal boundaries since Rafe wrote a letter to the court for Katheryn to file as her last act on her behalf in the case. She said she'll have something figured out by Monday, but she wants to see me later today." Eden stopped and looked at Flynn in desperation. "We have to find Rafe. I'm not sure where to start."

"Eden, we need help," said Flynn distraught. "Maybe we should report her missing. There are just too many places she could be."

"She's not missing, Flynn." Eden started crying again. "She left." She looked up at the painting of the Blue Woman and whispered, "Greer." She swallowed back her tears. "Oh, no, no, Flynn. She... she may be going to Greer." She cried and put her face in her hands. "Flynn," she said and looked up at him, tears falling freely now, "she's going to her. She told me Greer would help her if I left her," she sobbed, "and she thinks I was going to leave her. Greer said if Rafe went to her again..." She swallowed painfully as fear ran through her.

"What? What did she say?" asked Flynn worried.

A new wave of tears fell from Eden's eyes. She swallowed again and could barely speak. "She said..." she croaked out, "I would never get her back." She stood up quickly. "We have to go to the airport!" She rushed and picked up Bronte and her bag, then headed out of the house with Flynn following her closely.

They made it to the airport and drove around the parking lots looking for Rafe's car while Bronte napped in her car seat. Eden went inside the airport carrying Bronte and closely followed by Flynn to see if Rafe was still at a departure terminal. They split up so they could check all the terminals with flights going to New York and Baltimore but couldn't find her anywhere. Eden tried to get an airline employee to help her, but they were unable to provide any helpful information because of security issues. She met Flynn in front of one of the terminals feeling defeated. She kept calling Rafe's phone, and

Flynn didn't have the heart to tell her calling was futile. They drove through the parking lots again, and since they couldn't find Rafe's car, they decided they needed to talk with Letty.

They made it to The Kiki Bistro, and Eden, carrying a sleepy Bronte, found Letty. "Letty," Eden called to get her attention.

"You're back already?" Letty asked, surprised to see them again so soon.

"Have you seen Rafe?" Eden asked anxiously.

Letty could see Eden was upset. "What's wrong?"

"Can we go to your office?" asked Eden as she looked around anxiously.

Letty gave a worried nod and motioned to her office. "Come on. What happened? Is Rafe hurt again?"

Eden followed her and turned to Flynn. "Flynn, you should see if Abby and Jude will help us look for her." Eden turned and went inside Letty's office. She sat down with Bronte and looked at Letty with despair. "Letty," she hesitated, "she left." She looked up desperately, "She's gone."

"What?" Letty asked thinking she didn't hear correctly.

"She left," Eden whispered trying to stay calm. "I came home," she burst into tears, "she was packed. She kissed us and said goodbye, and left." She looked up at her and wiped away her tears. "Letty, we have to find her."

"So, she finally had enough of you," Letty looked at Eden without sympathy. "I knew she was holding back how she was feeling. It's all because of you, Eden," she accused, becoming angry. "You and that damn article!"

"I'm sorry," Eden sobbed in misery.

"I'm calling her," fumed Letty. She dialed Rafe and got her voice mail. "Rafe, it's Letty," she said heatedly. "Eden just told me you left her. Please call me if you need anything, Cugina. I'm here for you."

"Tell her Bronte is with you!" Eden begged desperately through her tears. "Tell her I'll leave her with you and Ephraim so she can see her." She sobbed hoping Rafe would see she didn't want to take Bronte from her. "Tell her she has to be there for the court date on Tuesday." She wept. "Please, Letty!"

Letty looked at Eden shocked she was willing to leave Bronte with her. She spoke into the phone again. "Rafe, I'll be at the courthouse to support you on Tuesday. You need to be there. Eden is letting me and Ephraim keep Bronte for a while. Come and see her anytime. Call me, Rafe," she said and hung up the phone.

"Thank you," said Eden in misery. "I...," she sniffed, "I need to go look for her," she said as she shifted Bronte.

"Eden, you come and make sure you spend time with Bronte too," she said as her anger turned to sorrow as she took Bronte from Eden's arms. "She doesn't need to lose both her mothers."

50

FLYNN OGDEN HAD called the girls and told them to meet them at the bistro while Eden was in Letty's office. It wasn't long before they had all arrived wondering what the emergency call was all about. Flynn was informing them about the situation with Rafe as they stood together outside the bistro.

"I knew something was wrong!" Abby fumed. Her emotions were flaring in a negative direction about Eden because she had just sat in front of her saying everything was fine and dandy. Well, it wasn't, and she wanted answers. "Rafe told me last night she couldn't stay with Eden anymore," she revealed wishing she would have listened to her instincts and offered to help Rafe more. She knew Rafe hadn't been messing with her.

"If she doesn't want to be found, it'll be hard," said Jude in dismay.

"We checked the airport, but Eden doesn't know where else to look for her," said Flynn anxiously.

"Maybe we shouldn't look for her," suggested Stacey. "If she left Eden," she shrugged, "then it's Eden's fault for using her to figure out her feelings."

"She wasn't using her!" yelled Flynn angrily. "She loves her!"

"Rafe always has things organized," said Abby as she paced trying to figure out where Rafe might have gone. "Wherever she's going, she's probably halfway there by now. Running around won't find her faster. We need to think this through. If we were Rafe, where would we go?"

Eden walked out the door trying to control her sobs and saw Flynn and the girls. "Flynn, I need to go," she croaked, "I have to find her. Abby, Jude," she said holding back tears, "will you help us?"

"I'll look for her, Eden," conceded Abby, torn between anger and sympathy, "but just to make sure she's okay. Did she leave because of the article or did you smack her in the head again last night?"

"Abby, stop," said Jude, chastising her.

"Eden, we should tell them," said Flynn as he looked at her pleadingly.

"Tell us what?" asked Abby suspiciously. "What else could you have possibly done to her?"

"Please, Eden," Flynn implored her with a tinge of desperation in his voice. "They have to understand what's happening so they can help us find Rafe."

Eden closed her eyes and knew Flynn was right. "Okay," she relented softly and looked up at him. "Have everyone meet at Katheryn's in an hour. I have an appointment with her then. I'm sorry," she whispered and walked quickly away from the café.

"What the hell is going on?" Abby demanded as she watched Eden walk away.

51

ONE HOUR LATER, in Katheryn Hardam's home office, the group of Rafe's friends and family had gathered. The only people missing were Flynn and Julia. Flynn was driving around town looking for Rafe's car and any evidence of where she might have gone. Abby was miffed with Julia because she was missing too. They left several messages for Julia hoping maybe she was with Rafe, but so far, she hadn't returned her calls.

Katheryn looked over all the faces of the people gathered in her office and waited patiently until they had settled. Eden Kingsley was sitting in a chair away from the others feeling raked over from her anxiety. Abby, Jude, and Stacey were on the couch. Letty was in a chair with Bronte, and Ephraim was sitting next to her.

"Well," started Katheryn as she stood in front of them with a large file folder, "Eden has informed me you all know Rafe has left, and we don't know where she is at the moment. You all may be a bit confused and angry. It is understandable because you don't know the facts. Just like Rafe doesn't know the facts."

"What the hell facts are you talking about?" demanded Abby. "Rafe left because of Eden and the things she's doing and the things she said in that article."

Katheryn looked over at Eden and pursed her lips. She had kept her word to Eden and said nothing to Rafe about her involvement with Jake and the Stewards. Unfortunately, Eden didn't take her advice and tell Rafe what had been happening. Now Eden was paying the price for her hesitation. Now it was up to her to deliver the news Eden couldn't. "Things she thinks Eden is doing," Katheryn said firmly as she laid out the contents of the envelope on the table in front of the couch.

Abby snatched up the picture of Eden kissing Jake. "What the fuck, Eden! I was right! You were comparing her to Jake!"

"No," Eden began then started to cry and couldn't speak.

"Calm down," commanded Katheryn. "Let me start from the beginning. The group who is responsible for filing the injunction against Rafe's adoption petition is called the Stewards to the Protection of the Innocence and Morals of Youths. They are a group that, by almost any means, try to take children out of situations they believe are immoral according to their beliefs. One of which is situations like Eden and Rafe's. Some information came to our attention that confirmed Jake was part of this group. Rafe and Eden were targeted through a chatroom where this group hacked into one of their computers and got their information." Katheryn looked at Eden then back at the group. "They used this information to get close to them and to begin gathering information to use for the injunction." She opened the legal file. "They've used everything they can against Rafe to help uphold the injunction from her sexuality, to the photographs of her at the beach, to the presentation she gave at the Conservatory, and now they have published the article in the L. A. Light."

"You've been keeping this from her?" Abby asked as she looked at Eden in confusion.

Katheryn took a breath and looked sternly at Abby. "Rafe knows about the group and what they're doing, but now we know Jake has been speaking with Rafe directly and telling her that Eden is behind the injunction."

"I don't understand," said Jude. "If Rafe knows about them, why does she think Eden is behind it all?"

"She doesn't know Jake is part of the group," explained Katheryn. "Eden received information about him anonymously, and it's how we know he's part of the group. He's been feeding Rafe information that's true but spun in a way to make Eden look guilty and like she is behind the injunction."

"You were sleeping with one of the people responsible for the injunction?" asked Abby shocked as realization set in.

"When were you going to tell her about this, Eden?" asked Jude upset.

"I was going to tell her," swore Eden as she cried, "after the court date."

"What if you lose?" asked Abby in disbelief. "Then you'd never tell her?"

"I don't know," Eden cried. "I don't know. I didn't know Jake was talking to her and telling her these things. If I knew, I swear I would have told her he was part of everything."

"So you just thought he was only following her around and getting information on her?" asked Abby maddened. "Jesus, Eden! That's just as bad!"

Stacey looked over the items on the table and frowned. "I'm sorry, but," she paused and pointed at the items, "all of this stuff is true, whether it's spun or not. You really do hate her." She shook her head. "She was right when she said she thought you did, back when you didn't tell her about being pregnant. You've been punishing her for over two years! You should just fucking let her go!" She laughed nervously and pushed her thick glasses up.

"Screw off, Stacey!" screamed Eden. "I don't hate her! I didn't know this was happening to her! I'm not punishing her! I'm not taking Bronte away from her! I love her!"

"Give me a break!" scoffed Stacey defensively. "Everyone knows what you were doing to her. You said all of this stuff." She picked up the photo. "This is a picture of you and Jake. Maybe it's about time Rafe left you and got away from someone who puts her through this hell," she said disdainfully. "Do you now say that none of this stuff is true? How do we know you're not playing us too?"

"I'm not playing anyone!" Eden cried in frustration.

"Stacey, stop," said Jude before Stacey could say more, then looked at Katheryn. "I think we need to know exactly what we're dealing with," she said reflectively. "She's out there now, and we don't know where, but these people might. What exactly are they capable of doing?"

"There were never any incidents that caused physical harm to Rafe," said Katheryn decisively. "Everything they used was public information and available to anyone."

"Physical harm? What about mental harm?" Abby screeched. "He was fucking with her mind, and her emotions, Eden, and so were you!" she spat with disgust.

"I don't understand Eden," said Letty trying to comprehend. "Why didn't you tell her any of this?"

"Because," Eden said anxiously, "because it's all my fault. I thought I could fix it and protect her from my mistake," she tried to explain without crying.

"What do you mean it's all your fault?" asked Letty confused and trying to stay calm as she held Bronte.

"It was me," she confessed as she looked at her hands, "my computer." She looked up at Letty. "I was the one," she swallowed, "the one in the chatroom."

"Well, why couldn't you just tell her?" asked Letty perplexed. "What's wrong with being in a chatroom?"

Eden took a deep breath and looked at Katheryn then at the group. "It was," she hesitated, dreading having to make the confession she was about to make. "It was when I started having feelings for men. I talked to a man online and," she paused, "and we—"

"Oh, my god!" Stacey laughed maniacally before Eden could finish. "You got a cyber fuck from him, didn't you?" she asked as she looked at the printout with the dates for the online chat. "You were cheating on Rafe even before you got pregnant, and before Jake! You really did just hate her!"

"No, I—" Eden started and knew she had no real defense. She felt her guilt and anxiety grow and then paled at the thoughts of what she had done and what it had led to now.

"Oh, Eden," Abby groaned as she saw Eden pale. "You?" she asked in disbelief that she had cheated on Rafe. "This is so fucked up."

"I just couldn't tell her all this started while I was—" Eden stopped unable to say what she did. "She was so mad at me, I couldn't. Then when we got back together, things just suddenly started to happen very fast. I was so happy she wanted to be with me again." She looked at them pleadingly. "Things were going so good, and I didn't want to mess things up."

"Well, it's a hell of a mess now!" exclaimed Abby.

"Eden, my cousin loves you, and she loves this baby. Don't you love her? Couldn't you find one good thing to say about her after you left her? If you could have, maybe none of this would be happening."

"Letty, please," Eden said in misery. "I do love her. I said good things about her, I did," she assured her earnestly.

"You don't act like you love her or trust her," said Letty feeling like Rafe had been betrayed. "You couldn't trust her enough to tell her what was going on. Don't you believe she would have been there for you and you two could have fought this together?"

"I really do love her and trust her," said Eden in tears. "I thought I was protecting her. I wanted to show her I could take care of her."

"What a bunch of shit!" said Stacey not convinced at all. "Eden, just admit it, you were being selfish. You were looking out for yourself and what you wanted, even if it hurt Rafe."

"No!" Eden denied the accusation as she shook her head. "I wanted us to be together. I wanted us to be a family." She looked around the room. "It was what she wanted too. I know it was. I was trying to give that to her. I love her!"

"Eden, look at all this," demanded Stacey as she indicated the items on the table. "Do you even know what the truth is anymore? You're kissing Jake in this picture. How did that happen if you're telling us the truth?"

"We were in the park, and his son wanted a hug," Eden explained. "Jake tricked me and," she stammered, "and I didn't know someone was taking pictures."

Letty picked up the photo from the table. She saw the date on the photo and the clothes Eden was wearing. "That was the day you came in looking for her." Letty looked up at her in surprise. "Why didn't you tell her what happened?"

"I was going to at first," she confessed, "but then I changed my mind after I calmed down because I didn't think it would help anything. Then she said I could move in with her, and I..." she shrugged sadly, "I wanted to live with her again. I didn't want to tell her anything that would make her change her mind."

"This is just blowing my mind," muttered Abby as she put her hands on the sides of her head and shook it in bewilderment.

"You left her because she cheated on you, but you're the one who cheated first. I'll bet she doesn't know that, either," said Stacey with disgust. "How can you say you love her?"

"We can argue about whether or not Eden loves Rafe later," interjected Katheryn ready to get on with the rest of the meeting. "Right now, Eden needs you to know some things for certain. She has asked me to make assurances to you because she knew this possibility of discord would happen. Here are the assurances." She looked at all of their confused and confounded faces and then began to pace as she talked. "One, she plans to go ahead and fight the injunction. I believe we have enough to win and with luck, we may not even have to go into the courtroom because Eden is allowing me to expose her as a source so we can use the information she received on Jake."

"Wait a minute," said Jude concerned. Katheryn stopped to look at her. "Expose her? Does that mean she's in some sort of danger?"

"Like you mentioned, we really don't know what these people are capable of," Katheryn acknowledged, "so they could go after her either with litigation or other means."

"Other means," repeated Abby troubled. "What does that mean?"

"Are you telling us that by knowing this information, Eden has been in some sort of danger?" asked Letty disturbed.

"They don't know she has this information," explained Katheryn, "yet. But Tuesday, when we have to reveal the information we have, they will know, and it could be a problem. We've involved the FBI, and Rafe knows about them." She looked at Eden. "Eden has met with them as well and has officially turned over evidence and testimony to them. Hopefully, because of the FBI involvement, the cult will have other things to worry about besides Eden and the injunction."

"Eden," Jude said softly as she looked at her with worry.

"Assurance number two," Katheryn continued and began pacing again. "Eden plans to go through with the adoption. Rafe wrote a letter withdrawing the petition but, since she wasn't made aware of certain facts, her decision is uninformed. As her lawyer working in what I believe is her best interests, I'm not going to submit her letter at this time."

"I know she wants the adoption, she loves this baby," insisted Letty. She looked at Eden knowing if she was going through with the adoption there must be some truth to her story. "I'm glad you're still doing this, Eden. It means so much to her and to all of us."

"Assurance number three," Katheryn continued as she nodded. "Rafe will be informed immediately about all of this as soon as she's found. I'd like you all to agree I will be the one to tell this information to her, so she gets the facts without additional opinion. There are certain facts you're not aware of that I feel Rafe should know about first. If Rafe wants to, she can tell you about them later. Also, we may not know everything Jake has told her, and it may take some time to sort everything out with her."

Abby looked around at everyone and saw they were speechless. She wasn't sure how she felt about how Eden handled things, but she did know she would do whatever it took to help Rafe. "I guess this means we better start looking for her," she said determinedly. "Any ideas?"

Eden looked up and saw them all looking back at her, their faces filled with questions and accusations. "I'll do anything," she professed desperately. "Please, help me find her."

52

DESPITE ALL THE help from her friends, it had been three days, and Eden Kingsley still had not found Rafe. The memory of Rafe leaving, and the damning evidence she had collected against her, still brought Eden to tears. She wanted to blame it all on Jake and the Stewards but knew she was at fault too. The guilt stirred her anxiety to the point of physical illness at times.

She held herself together for Bronte, and because she had to find Rafe to explain everything to her.

It was nine in the morning, and Eden was waiting with Letty and Bronte in circuit court conference room number one. The last two and a half days had been very hard on Eden, and it showed in her drawn and haggard appearance. She had barely slept or eaten because she had been spending every possible moment looking for Rafe. She even took the week off work to dedicate time to finding her if she didn't show up to the injunction court date.

Monday, Eden had called everyone they knew. She even called Rafe's assistant at the Conservatory to see if anyone there had news or had spoken to her, but no one had seen or heard from her. She attempted to call Greer but couldn't do it. She couldn't give Greer a reason to call Rafe if she somehow decided not to go to her. The thought of Rafe being there when she called Greer was unbearable. Instead, she checked the airport for Rafe's car twice on Sunday and three times Monday, just in case Rafe booked a flight on those days. She checked it again this morning but still hadn't found her or her car.

Flynn and the girls helped by driving everywhere they could think of looking for Rafe's car or for any signs of her. Eden even pulled out the photographs Rafe had taken and found the places in them thinking she may go back to them. They checked train stations, bus stations, and even all the museums thinking maybe she would visit one or more of them.

Abby and Jude checked all the hotels, bars, hangouts, and Abby put out a phone tree alert, but still, there had been no sight of Rafe by anyone. It was becoming clear to Eden, wherever Rafe was, she wasn't going out in public, and her car must be parked in a garage somewhere. Or even worse, she was driving cross-country to be with Greer.

While Eden paced the conference room and worried, Letty held Bronte and talked to the baby softly. Finally, Katheryn entered the room.

"I've just met with the other lawyers and gave them the opportunity to withdraw the injunction," Katheryn informed them. "They're talking with their clients. All we have to do now is wait to see what they'll do. Their choice is to drop the suit and go away quietly or walk into court where they will do their best to paint Rafe in the worst possible light with hearsay and peeping tom photos. I think a few of the photos they have are ones taken by Jake and altered like the ones in the package you gave me, Eden."

"Of the girls?" asked Eden not knowing what she was talking about.

"Yes," said Katheryn as she shook her head in disgust. "It looks like he put Rafe and Bronte and some drug paraphernalia into the shots of the girls. It makes it look like Rafe exposed her to sex parties with drugs and alcohol. Since I know she wouldn't do anything like that, I knew the photo had to be altered."

"What if they decide not to drop the injunction?" asked Eden frantically.

"If they do that," said Katheryn with a smug smile, "I get to go in and reveal everything we know about them, what they do and stand for, in open court. The cherry on top is that the FBI is investigating them. And, because of you, Eden, the FBI may be able to find enough on the group and its members to put most of them and their leaders behind bars. As a matter of fact, I may help them do just that after we win this case for a little legal exercise."

"So how long do they have to make their decision?" Eden asked nervously.

"Well," said Katheryn as she looked at her watch, "it's just after nine now, so they have a little less than an hour left. The judge will expect us to be in the courtroom at ten o'clock. We have to hope they drop the suit." Katheryn sighed wishing all this drama had waited until after the court date. "It won't look good if my client doesn't show up for the hearing. But technically, she doesn't have to be here."

"Did you," Eden faltered and looked at her anxiously, "did you have to tell them about what I know?"

"I held off as long as I could," Katheryn said frankly, "but yes, I let them know what we have, and how it came into your possession. I think that information and the research I did is what will decide their case. They won't want the exposure or the attention the information will bring to their group."

"I hope it's enough. I hope it works." Eden said, worried, as she shivered, suddenly cold.

"It will be," said Letty as she put her hand on Eden to comfort her. "They won't take that kind of risk."

"Confidentially, whatever their decision, the FBI got warrants on Monday and have been listening and watching their offices to get information for their case," Katheryn informed Eden quietly while Letty cared for Bronte. "You just sit tight, and I'll be back shortly." She walked out of the room and into the hallway.

"Letty, what am I going to do if it goes to court and they win?" asked Eden as she paced anxiously.

"Katheryn knows what she's doing," Letty assured her, and she held Bronte's head to herself. "Rafe says Katheryn is the best, so it'll be okay."

"I need you to be right, but what if you're not?" asked Eden as tears ran down her cheeks. "What if we never find Rafe?"

"It won't matter," said Letty boldly. "We both know she's Bronte's parent, and she'll always grow up knowing it. She'll turn up, I know she will eventually."

Abby walked into the room and saw Eden crying. "Hi, oh, I'm sorry," Abby apologized with a cringe, not sure what she had just walked in on.

"It's okay," Eden wiped her tears. "Come in."

"We just got here," said Abby quietly. "Jude and everyone is out in the hall, and I left another message for Julia. So what's happening?"

"We're just waiting," said Eden fretfully. "Katheryn has given them an ultimatum to drop the suit."

53

THE LAWYERS FOR the Stewards were gathered in circuit court conference room number eight with Rev. Cazzak, Mason Essex, Jake Thompson, and Daniel Fuller. They sat at the conference table discussing the injunction and the new information handed to them by the lawyer retained by the defendant, Rafaella Salvaggio.

Attorney Jack Cavanaugh laid out the information given to him by Counselor Hardam in front of his clients. "If we go to court, they will enter this as evidence, and it will become public record," he informed his clients. "Because of the article Jake had published, there's a lot of interest in this case by the press, and things could get complicated."

"We recommend you drop the case and negotiate on the countersuit," advised Larry Weaver the second attorney on the legal team. "It's only one child, and if this information gets out, it could compromise all of our other cases," he said pragmatically. "We have assurances the Kingsley woman will not give the information to the press if the case is dropped."

"This is unacceptable!" bellowed Rev. Cazzak as he pounded his fist on the table. "Unacceptable, Jake!" He thumbed through the evidence against Jake and the group. "How did this information get into the Kingsley woman's hands?" he asked Jake pointedly.

"I have no idea," said Jake nervously. "None."

It took everything inside Mason Essex to hide the pleasure he was feeling at Jake's situation. All this time, Eden and the lawyer knew he was part of the Stewards. He wondered if that meant Rafe knew too, and she had been fucking with Jake. Mason shook his head because if Rafe knew, she probably wouldn't have let things go as far as allowing Jake to crucify her in the paper. She would probably have had a restraining order issued, and her lawyer would have kept her from negative exposure. Eden must have just given the information to the lawyer recently. Jake must have really had her terrified if she was afraid to reveal she had the information until now. In any event, they were probably both laughing their asses off at Jake just as he was at the moment—but on the inside.

Watching the reverend confer with the attorneys, Mason decided this was an opportune moment for him to implement another part of his plan. He got up from his chair and walked over to the reverend and his cronies.

"Excuse me, Reverend," said Mason quietly.

The reverend looked up at him with a frown because of the interruption. "What is it, my boy?" he asked impatiently.

"Sir, with this new information revealed, I have a serious concern," said Mason just loud enough for the attorneys and the reverend to hear. "One I think you need to know about before you make a decision here. Can we talk privately?"

The Reverend Cazzak glared at the two attorneys with a questioning look. "Is there another place where Mason and I can go talk or should we clear the room?"

"Whichever we do, we'll want to make it look innocuous because it concerns someone in the room," said Mason who looked at Jake quickly then back at the reverend. "I suggest you ask for private prayer time and send us all out. Then I'll slip back inside. One of you can watch the door while the other watches the others while the reverend and I talk," he said to the cronies. "Just give me a bit to get back to my seat."

The Reverend Cazzak nodded. "Very good."

Mason went back to his seat, and the reverend continued to speak to the two attorneys for a few minutes. Daniel watched the reverend and Jake watched Mason. Jake was nervous and trying to hide it behind the stern look on his face. Mason knew that just because they lost a case, it wasn't always a reason to punish a Soldier. Losing or winning the case was the attorney's job. But there was no precedent for when information about the Soldier and the Stewards like this came out on the day of court.

"Gentlemen," said Cazzak abruptly. "I need a moment alone for reflection and prayer. Take a few minutes and go get coffee or take a walk. Be back in fifteen minutes." Everyone stood then headed for the door. The attorneys ushered them all out, and the reverend bowed his head as if to pray.

Mason took his time and let everyone go ahead of him and out of the building. When they all turned to walk toward a café, Mason went the opposite way saying he needed to get something from his van. Mason re-entered the courthouse through a side entrance and made his way back to the conference room where the second attorney was waiting. Mason gave him a nod and walked into the room, quickly closing the door behind him.

Cazzak looked up as Mason entered. "Tell me, what's so important, my boy?"

Mason sat down next to the reverend, pulled his laptop out of his messenger bag, and turned it on. "Sir, when that lawyer presented the information they had about Jake and the Stewards, I had a bad feeling. I thought it through and knew I had to show you some things. I didn't say anything before because," he paused, "well, because I knew Jake was one of our best, and I didn't want to believe it." Mason opened a program and clicked on a video. "I had an issue with some missing items," he revealed, "so I decided to use some of our surveillance cameras in my building. I thought someone might be breaking in." The video played showing Jake entering the building, picking locks, and looking through file cabinets. "I never in a million years thought this is who I would see."

"Is that Jake?" asked Cazzak in surprise. "What's he doing?"

"It looks like he's searching for something," said Mason. "The thing is, I don't know how many times he's broken in or what he's done. I did a full inventory, and here is a list of things I found missing." He pulled up a document with the list for the reverend.

Looking over the list, Cazzak read it aloud, "A gun, video cameras, surveillance bugs, USB drives." He read the rest of the list to himself then looked at Mason. "This is serious."

"I thought so," said Mason with a sigh. "The most troubling thing is what he took that I can't see." He saw the reverend frown and knew he hadn't followed. "Information, sir. I don't know if he got into my computer and took information. The missing USB drives tell me he took something. I just don't know what else he took."

"What else could he have taken?

"Well, we have hacking software on my computer," Mason reminded him. "With simple, easily obtainable instructions, he could have found anywhere on how to use the hacking software, he could have stolen all kinds of information. Even information from our database." Mason stopped talking and showed another video of Jake picking the lock on a file cabinet and rifling through it. His back was to the camera, so it was unclear if he took anything or not.

The reverend looked over at Mason with concern. He felt lucky he had someone like Mason on his side. He had told Mason many times, the more young people they could recruit and indoctrinate in the faith, the better. The unrighteous seem to be getting younger, and they can't infiltrate them if they don't have young people in the faith. Ten years ago, it was hard to find young homosexuals starting families, but now they start in their twenties or even younger in some instances. The evil in the world has been infecting the minds of people faster, and it was getting harder to keep up. He knew if he were to do the Lord's work revealed in his vision, he would need young men like Mason. They would be the ones who carried on his work on earth when he went to his position as Leader of God's Army in heaven. The reverend thought Mason may even turn out to be the next in line to hold his position as God's Great Leader on Earth in the Stewards.

"Don't be hard on yourself," the revered sympathized and gave Mason a pat on his shoulder. "You're young and naïve, but now you've learned even those who we hold in high regard can be corrupted." He looked at the list again. "What are your thoughts," Reverend Cazzak asked Mason. He realized this might be a good time to start focusing on mentoring and grooming the boy for his next exalted position in the church.

"I think you're right," said Mason as he looked at the reverend who he used to hold in high regard until recently. "I think Jake may be unhappy," revealed Mason solemnly. "I think he may have actually fallen for the Kingsley woman. He may even be the one who gave her the information. Who else would have all of those photos? They're all of him. No other Soldier was compromised. Maybe he thinks he can get her away from the Salvaggio woman after this and run off with her." Mason frowned and shook his head. "That's all conjecture," he said acting unsatisfied with his own assessment. "I actually thought he had feelings for the Salvaggio woman, the one we are here trying to prevent adopting the charge. Maybe he was overcompensating his focus on her to hide his feelings for the Kingsley woman."

"I just don't understand," said the reverend. "He was supposed to marry the woman and move them to one of our small parishes. He could have requested to stay and not go back into the field."

"It's possible he has an agreement with them," pondered Mason. "We know the Salvaggio woman has a lot of contacts and a lot of money."

"Hmph," Cazzak grunted. "So it's possible he's a burnout who wants to either go into a relationship outside our church or get paid off. And he's stealing information and who knows what else for leverage against us in case we come after him," he said musingly.

"Possibly," Mason nodded.

"So how do we handle him?"

"Well," Mason hesitated. He was excited the reverend was asking his advice, so he had a chance to steer the situation. "Until we know exactly what he's doing, I don't think we should show our cards. Probably, the best thing we can do is put him to a stress test and see what he does. Either way, he's headed to re-programming."

The reverend sighed heavily. He didn't like the idea of sending anyone to re-programming, but Mason was right. If Jake was working against their ultimate Mission, then they had no choice. "Very well," he agreed flatly.

"I'll leave this with you," said Mason as he took out a small recorder from his messenger bag. "Record what he says in case we need it later. I'll go put a tracker on his car and bug it too." He hesitated for a moment. "I didn't say anything because I can fight my own battles, but he's been very disrespectful to me." He watched as the reverend's frown deepened. "I know you talk to me about getting more youth involved, but if the Soldiers are allowed to treat us badly like he does, none will come or stay for long. How are those guys going to act if one of us outranks them someday? There has to be a better balance of respect. Just because we're young doesn't mean we're stupid. What was stupid was having no respect and breaking into the office of someone in charge of surveillance."

"I understand," said Reverend Cazzak sympathetically. He remembered being young and no one respecting him. Mason was more like him than he realized. To gain respect, he had to be ruthless when he was younger, and he knew Mason was telling him he needed to be ruthless to Jake.

The reverend waited while the attorneys gathered everyone and got them back into the room. He watched Jake as he sat at the table and felt the pain of betrayal in his heart. Jake had been one of his most enthusiastic Soldiers since they helped him get his ex-wife back on the right side of God. He could only hope they found some innocent explanation for Jake's break-in and as to how the Kingsley woman got the information about him.

"After reflection and prayer, God has revealed our path," Reverend Cazzak announced. "But first, there is another matter we must resolve. Jake?" he said and looked directly at him.

"Yes, sir," answered Jake as he sat up straight.

"I will ask you once more. How did the Kingsley woman get the information about you and the Stewards?"

"I really don't know, sir," he answered opening his hands to show he was telling the truth.

"Now you know why all of your efforts with her failed," said Cazzak as he looked sternly at Jake. "Because you failed! There will be a review immediately after I'm finished here. I've sent Mason to arrange everything. You will explain yourself and your actions."

Jake looked at the reverend, his emotions caught between anger and fear. The thought of Mason going to arrange another review shot his anger into high gear. He wondered if Mason had reported what happened in the last review and had shown the reverend his confession. "You put too much trust into Mason," he said acridly. "We caught him with a prostitute in his office," he tattled spitefully and looked at Daniel then back at the reverend.

Reverend Cazzak frowned at Jake. Mason was right. Jake was showing disrespect toward him. By engaging in petty tattling, Jake wasn't acting like a Soldier who could be trusted and depended upon. Soldiers were supposed to take care of each other and build trust in the ranks, not gather information to hurt other Soldiers. "I'm sure whatever Mason was doing, it was for the good of our cause," replied Cazzak. "Young Soldiers need to get sexual experience somehow, so if they are called upon, they can succeed in their Missions. Not all Soldiers start out after they have been married and have a child on the way." He looked at Jake sternly letting him know he would hear nothing more on the subject.

Jake's ire rose higher than he thought possible. Mason was getting away with it again. They all thought he could do no wrong because he was a favorite. "It wasn't that he was having sex," Jake tried to explain. "It was that he was keeping her there. He had her there for over a month."

"Enough!" Cazzak slapped is blue-veined hand onto the table. "This is about you, not Mason. I don't think you understand the ramifications of what you've caused. You exposed yourself and our Mission." He worked to control himself. Mason had encouraged him not to show his hand, but it was clear Jake's ego was giving him a false sense of confidence and safety. "Did you have feelings for the woman?" He watched as Jake's face turned red. Cazzak wasn't sure if it was embarrassment or anger.

Jake worked to control himself. Mason had lied about keeping the review to himself, and now the reverend believed Mason's lie that he had feelings for Rafe. "No," he said firmly. "Everything I did was for the good of the Mission. I took back what I lost and more!"

"But here we are," said Cazzak evenly, "about to lose this case and the charge you were sent to rescue. I think it is time for reassignment," he said grimly. He had kept the word re-programming out of the conversation purposely but was tempted to use it now. "After your review, you will be sent somewhere for," he hesitated, "re-training and to determine if your rank will be stripped away or if you will no longer be a Steward Soldier for our cause."

"Please," Jake said remorsefully. "Reverend, please forgive me."

"I forgive you, Jake." Cazzak sighed heavily. "But you've cost us too much due to your incompetence in somehow revealing information about us. You've also cost us financially. You're compromised, and from this moment forward, you'll be treated as the liability you've proven to be. Do you understand?"

"Please, don't do this to me," begged Jake fearfully equating the word re-training with re-programing. "I've been part of this for so long. I believe in what we're doing."

"I told you, Jake, we can't afford liabilities," said Cazzak sad he couldn't believe Jake anymore. "Liabilities have to be cut away before they infect the integrity of what we're trying to accomplish. Leave my presence now. I suggest you don't go far."

"But," Jake stammered in shock that he would be sent away and losing his position in the Stewards, "what about my son? I can't leave him."

"Your son will stay with his mother and her new husband," Cazzak informed him. "Get out," he demanded and pointed to the door. "Now," he growled and signaled Daniel to move him along. "Make sure to have our men keep him out of sight until everyone leaves and that he isn't seen leaving by anyone involved," he told Daniel. "You'll be contacted with further instructions." The powerful reverend looked at Jake. "Jake, I suggest, when you get home, you think well and hard while you pack about what you've done and prepare yourself for this inquiry."

"This wasn't my fault!" insisted Jake as Daniel was escorting him out the door of the conference room. "I can fix it! Please, don't do this!"

54

SITTING ON THE benches in the courthouse hallway, Abby Van Falkov and her friends Jude, Abby, Stacey, and Flynn were waiting anxiously to go into the courtroom with Eden. They were still reeling from what Abby told them about Katheryn having to reveal the information Eden had about the Stewards. They worried about how it might affect Rafe and Eden if this group felt threatened.

Abby was beside herself over the fact she couldn't find Rafe anywhere and that she hadn't returned any of her calls. Rafe always answered her phone or returned calls if she missed them. She even returned the calls Abby made when they broke up, and Abby had her meltdown. She even returned them, eventually, when she would leave town suddenly for weeks or months with some girl. This just wasn't like Rafe. She had never just been 'unavailable' before, and it made Abby even angrier with Eden. Eden may have thought she was doing the right thing, but it was very clear to Abby she was wrong. She was almost tempted to be on the same side with Stacey, but she could never bring herself down to her level.

Abby knew Rafe loved Eden because of the things she told her. So she knew, if Rafe just knew the truth, maybe things would be okay—if they ever found her to tell her. Abby just hoped everything went well today in court or things might go from bad to worse. She didn't know how much more 'worse' she could take.

"How much longer?" complained Abby. "I can't stand it!"

"It's only nine fifty, they have ten more minutes," said Flynn looking at his phone. He avoided looking at Abby because she kept trying to call Rafe. He didn't know if he should tell her that Rafe didn't have her phone anymore. It may cause her to be even more out of control than she had been the last few days. "They have to be in the courtroom at ten o'clock."

"Look, there's Julia," Jude pointed down the hall. "Julia, over here!"

"Is this the right courtroom?" Julia asked as she approached and pointed to the double doors.

"Don't you listen to your messages?" asked Abby perturbed. "Where have you been?"

"I haven't checked them all weekend, and yesterday, I was tied up in meetings," explained Julia.

"You didn't check your messages all weekend?" asked Stacey suspicious. "What were you doing?" She laughed and raised her red brow suggestively.

"None of your business," said Julia frowning at Stacey.

"Who is she?" asked Abby smiling. "Was it that Selina woman?"

"No, it was no one," Julia said sharply as she shook her head.

"A lot happened over the weekend, Julia, and no one can find Rafe," said Jude trying to change the subject.

"Yeah, the lawyers are having a meeting, and court is at ten if they don't compromise," Abby informed her.

"Compromise?" asked Julia confused. "The last I heard they just had to show up to file the motion to dismiss."

As Julia sat down, they all started informing her of the basics about what was going on.

55

UNABLE TO SIT, Eden paced conference room number one and kept looking at her watch. They had to win. They had to find Rafe. *Rafe*, she thought as she paced. She looked over at Letty, who was straightening Bronte's dress getting ready to go into the courtroom, when Katheryn walked in smiling.

"I know it seems like the impossible just happened, but they've dropped the injunction," Katheryn told them happily. "We spoke with the judge, and he signed off on the dismissal and the countersuit," she revealed as she showed Eden the papers. "It was the information you gave, Eden, that made it possible," she said soberly.

"Thank you, Katheryn," said Eden as she sat down in relief. "Thank you."

"Thank God!" praised Letty and kissed Bronte. "You'll have your two mamas soon, baby!"

"So is the adoption still on the docket in two weeks?" asked Eden wanting confirmation.

"Yes, I confirmed it with the court and everything should go smoothly," said Katheryn proudly.

"I hope we can find Rafe by then," said Eden fretfully. "I'm running out of places to look."

"Come on," said Letty as she stood and patted Eden's shoulder. "Let's go tell everyone and get out of here."

56

OUTSIDE THE COURTHOUSE, Jake Thompson and Daniel Fuller were talking and making their way to their cars after waiting for Reverend Cazzak and everyone to leave. Jake was angry. He was more than angry. He was furious. He had paced and fumed the whole time he had been waiting to leave. He even humbled himself and begged the guard they left him with to tell the reverend he was sorry and that he would fix things. How he had to beg, and was then ignored, made him even angrier.

"What am I supposed to do now?" asked Jake agitated as he walked next to Daniel. "I have to leave town, quit my job, and leave behind my son. I've done more for the Stewards than almost anyone, and this is how I'm treated!"

"Jake, no one else has been compromised like you've been," Daniel pointed out calmly. "You cost us over a half a million dollars with this lawsuit settlement alone. You have to find out how she got that information on you. Did you have it in your apartment?"

"Of course, I didn't have it in my apartment!" spat Jake indignantly. "I told you I don't know how she got it! The bitch has ruined me! Ruined me!"

"It seemed like the reverend knew about the things Mason said too," Daniel speculated. "Mason has your confession. If he gives it to the reverend, you're finished."

"I don't have feelings for her!" Jake spat. "Look what I did! If I had feelings for her, would I have worked so hard to take her down?"

"See, that's the problem." Daniel sighed. "You've been so consumed with taking her down, you missed the fact Eden had information on you, and we failed an innocent charge. Those feelings you're denying," he paused and shook his head, "they're there. You feel something."

Jake looked angrily at Daniel because he was not helping. "If I feel anything, it's sorry for her," Jake growled. "Sorry she's going to have to deal with Eden again." Once the words were out, he wished he could take them back. He realized he sounded jealous. "Fucking Mason!" he yelled. "He's got all of you believing something that isn't true!"

"I guess you're not as untouchable as you think you are," said Daniel wryly. "Take it easy, Jake. You're lucky they're allowing you to go home and pack up on your own. They could make it worse. Just move back home for a while and lay low," he suggested. "All of this will blow over. Then you can see if the reverend will let you come back."

"Come back?" Jake laughed bleakly. "Come back and what, be a Deacon who just does the website and never gets to do any real work for the cause? I can't do that! My life is ruined, Daniel, and it's all Eden's fault!" He glowered at Daniel. "Mason and the reverend are wrong. If Eden hadn't had that information, we would have won the case!"

"But she had it, and we lost. I'll see you around, Jake," said Daniel as he got in his car. "Have patience and keep your eyes open. Opportunities always come up," he said then started his car and took off.

Jake walked the short distance to his black SUV seething with anger at Reverend Cazzak and Mason, but mostly at the reason he was in this position—Eden. He wished he had never been put on her case. He should have been on his guard when things went so easily and quickly with her, but he let his ego get the better of him. He fucked her within days of meeting her and barely had to try. It was too good to be true that, after only a couple of months on the Mission, Rafe was gone on a business trip, and Eden jumped into Rafe's bed with him. She practically ran to move out of Rafe's house and in with him. Then, when Rafe got back, there were a couple of minor blow-ups between them. After that, he didn't have to do much to convince Eden to keep herself and the baby away from Rafe. The blow-ups afterward just helped Jake steer Eden to where he needed her to go. It was easy to convince her the blow-ups had more meaning than they probably really did with all her crazy paranoias and anxieties.

How did she get that information?

His thoughts skipped to Rafe. *I don't have feelings for her*, he told himself. He remembered Mason in his chair getting a blowjob and Rafe's voice echoing through the speakers. He didn't want her fucking Eden, and he didn't want Mason fucking anyone to her voice. He remembered the first time he saw Rafe. He was watching Eden because she was his target. He wanted to get to know her schedule and more about her before he made contact. When Rafe walked up to the house, he had hoped to God she was just a friend visiting Eden. But he knew she was more when she didn't leave the house that night. Later he confirmed who she was by reading the files.

The next time he saw her, he had made contact with Eden. He remembered the thrill of taking Eden away from someone as beautiful and desirable as Rafe. He had wished the challenge had been to seduce Rafe instead of Eden. Dealing with Eden made him appreciate Rafe even more. Eden fucked up her relationship with Rafe just as she fucked up the one she had with him. Both he and Rafe deserved someone better than Eden.

He unlocked his SUV, and as he looked up, he saw Eden walking to her car and his fury built. She made a fool of him and Rafe. They both had lost their jobs because of her. He was certain Rafe had lost hers at the Conservatory, and he was losing his position in the Stewards. Because of her, he was also losing his home and his son—all because of Eden's fickle, overly emotional issues. Anger built inside as he realized the real reasons he had failed his Mission. Losing to Rafe was one thing because they were both up for the challenge and respected each other, but to know his failure came at the hands of Eden was too much. She was a fucking woman! A fucking worthless dyke woman! A weak-minded, waste of space woman! She should not be with Rafe or anyone!

He opened the back of the truck, pulled out the tire iron, and walked quickly to catch up with Eden. She would tell him where that information came from and he would at least get his position with the Stewards back.

"Eden!" Jake screamed and began running toward her to catch her. "Eden, stop!"

Startled at hearing her name screamed, Eden turned and saw Jake, and then she saw what he had in his hand. She began to run as her heart pounded with fear in her chest. "Oh, my god, no," she cried out in panic as she saw him catching up to her.

"Stop, you bitch, or I'll do more than beat the shit out of you!" Jake yelled as he brought the tire iron down on her and it glanced off her shoulder blade.

"Help!" Eden screamed in pain reaching for her shoulder. "Someone, help me!"

"Help you?" growled Jake. "You ruined my life, you bitch!" He grappled with her and pulled her to him, tearing her clothes. To stop her screaming, he backhanded her across the face and pushed her back against a car.

Eden slid down the side of the car, falling to her knees and could smell the asphalt. "No," she cried out reeling with pain and scrambling to get up. "Stop! Help! Jake, stop!" She lunged up and ran to her car. Her face and shoulder throbbed in pain as she tried to open the door. Her heart was beating so hard it felt like it was about to explode.

Jake shoved Eden from behind and into the side of the car. "I'll kill you!" Jake roared angrily.

Eden's body bounced off the car, her words muffled by her pain and tears. "No," she cried out weakly.

Jake flung open Eden's car door. "You want in your car?" he asked savagely as he grabbed Eden up and shoved her into the car brutally. "Fine, let's get in! Let's go someplace where no one can hear you scream!"

Eden fought him, scratching his face and arms, and kicking him as hard as she could, but he was too strong. He slammed his fist into her face and chest to make her stop fighting.

Flynn ran toward the sound as soon as he heard Eden's screams. "Stop!" he screamed in rage as he pulled Jake out of the car.

"Get away from me, you fag!" Jake yelled as he picked up the tire iron and swung it down viciously onto Flynn's arm then shoved him back. Flynn fell hard to the ground in pain.

Eden fought to breathe after Jake had punched her in the chest. She finally sucked in air painfully. "Run, Flynn!" she screamed. She got out of the car and tried to get away, but Jake was too fast for her in his rage.

Flynn forced himself up off the ground and ran to his truck, holding his arm in pain.

Jake snatched Eden's hair, pulled her back to him, and then struck her across her back with the tire iron. Before she could fall, Jake yanked her up, pushed her against a car, and then forced himself against her, spitting out his words in her face. "You will tell me where you got that information! Tell me now!"

"I don't know where it came from." Eden wheezed as she cried and shook in pain. "I swear!"

Flynn set off the panic alarm in his truck then grabbed his gun and ran back to Eden. "Get away from her, or I'll shoot!" Flynn screamed in a rage as he pointed the gun at Jake.

Jake looked at Flynn with disdain and spoke harshly. "You'll shoot?" mocked Jake with a laugh because, at the moment, he had nothing more to lose. He pulled Eden in front of himself choking her with the tire iron against her neck. "Go ahead!"

"Flynn!" Eden croaked, and she stomped on Jake's foot and clawed at him as she tried to twist away and under the tire iron. Jake's grip was too tight, and her clothes tore even more as the end of the tire iron caught them. Jake released her, but swung the tire iron again, hitting her hard across her ribs. Eden lost her breath and fell to her hands and knees crying and trying to breathe.

Flynn pointed his gun and tried to hold it steady as he screamed over the truck alarm. "Leave her alone, or I'll shoot! I will!"

"Fuck you!" spat Jake as he pulled Eden up and slammed her against a car and put the tire iron to her throat again. "Tell me! Don't lie to me!" he screamed into her face.

I'm telling you," Eden gagged from the pressure of the tire iron, "the truth."

"This is your last warning! Stop, or I'll shoot!" screamed Flynn and took aim.

"Go to hell!" Jake screamed back at him. He turned back to Eden, punching her in the jaw, causing the back of her head to bounce off the car. "Tell me, bitch!"

"Die!" Flynn screamed as he pulled the trigger and two shots rang out.

The echo of the shots faded, and Flynn watched as two bodies fell to the ground, falling for what seemed like an eternity. In reality, only seconds had passed since he first warned Jake to stop. Flynn dropped to his knees, dropped the gun on the ground beside him, and covered his face with his good hand as his other throbbed in pain at his side. "Oh, my god," cried Flynn as he shook with grief and pain. "What have I done?"

A crowd of people made their way to the scene attracted by the car alarm and the sound of gunshots. They saw two people lying motionless on the ground, blood pooling around them, and a third on their knees with a gun close by. The blood on the car and ground made some people scream. Several people dialed their cellular phones for help while others took video. Security guards rushed to the scene to secure it for the police.

In the air, the sound of police dispatch could be heard from the security radios.

"All units. Shots fired at L. A. County Courthouse. All available units, please respond to L. A. County Courthouse. Shots fired. Repeat, shots fired."

To be continued in Book Six — Fire of Wrath...

NOTES

Translations: For translations of Italian, French and Spanish use: www.Babblefish.com

The chapters in this book were arranged with the intent of saving paper. This chapter style saved 7 pages. Original Total Book Pages 314 — Final Pages 307.

Music mentioned in this book.

No financial incentive was given for the mention of the following artists in this work. The author is a fan and felt mentioning them worked in the story. For the use of their name, credit is given, and links to their work are below.

Enjoy!

Kristie Stremel

Website: http://www.kristiestremel.com/
Facebook: https://www.facebook.com/kristie.stremel
Twitter: https://twitter.com/kristiestremel
ReverbNation: https://www.reverbnation.com/kristiestremel
YouTube: https://www.youtube.com/user/Stremeltone

ABOUT THE AUTHOR

C.L. CATTANO LIVES in the Midwestern U.S. with her partner and their dog somewhere between the city and the forest. With a joy for traveling, she and her partner have visited many countries and have a love for meeting people and learning about the places they visit. When possible, she likes to include references in her work about the things she has learned, the places she has been and people she has met while on her travels and in her everyday life.

Cattano has a variety of creative interests including, but not limited to, creating fine art, writing, photography, and supporting women in the arts. She considers herself a 'Jack of All Trades' dabbling in what she terms the 'whimsies of her soul' that pull her toward happiness and fulfillment.

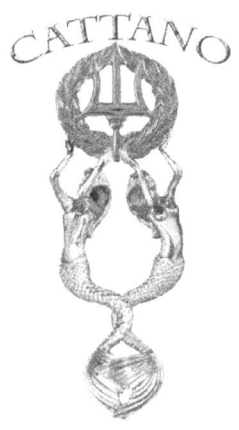

OTHER BOOKS

By C. L. Cattano

Cursed Hearts is a love story transcending time and gender. Separated from by a gift from a bored demon on All Hallows Eve two souls connected by the power of love have been searching through time for each other and incarnated as both men and women.

Over time, the gift became a curse and a game for the demons.

Now the souls have finally met again, and they must fight for a life together.

Will love prevail? Will they finally be able to live together again for a lifetime? They have one night to figure out the riddle and get it right to break the curse.

NOTE: 18+ Lesbian Romance. Some light erotic moments.

Available on Amazon Cursed Hearts

Salvaggio's Light Series
Available on Amazon
Shattered Paradise – Book One
Blue Inferno – Book Two
Secrets & Rivalry – Book Three
Wildling's Claim – Book Four
Sowers of Discord – Book Five

REQUEST FOR REVIEW

Thank you for reading **Salvaggio's Light** — *An Epic Contemporary Romance Serial.*

I hope you enjoyed book five, **Sowers of Discord**, and will consider leaving an honest review. It only takes a few minutes, so I encourage you to go now and leave a review!

Check out the Salvaggio's Light Facebook page to join in the discussions and fun!
www.facebook.com/pg/SalvaggiosLight

Join the CL Cattano Mailing List www.clcattano.com

I love getting fan mail, and you can contact me at
clc@clcattano.com

www.ingramcontent.com/pod-product-compliance
Lightning Source LLC
Chambersburg PA
CBHW070846280626
47161CB00017B/2690